AN ELUSIV

Other Titles by Diana Bachmann

BEYOND THE SUNSET
JANTHINA

A SOUND LIKE THUNDER*

available from Severn House

AN ELUSIVE FREEDOM

Diana Bachmann

This first world edition published in Great Britain 1997 by
SEVERN HOUSE PUBLISHERS LTD of
9–15 High Street, Sutton, Surrey SM1 1DF.
First published in the USA 1997 by
SEVERN HOUSE PUBLISHERS INC. of
595 Madison Avenue, New York, NY 10022.

British Library Cataloguing in Publication Data

Bachmann, Diana
    An elusive freedom
    1. English fiction – 20th century
    I. Title
    823.9'14 [F]

    ISBN 0-7278-4969-7

Typeset by Palimpsest Book Production Limited,
Polmont, Stirlingshire, Scotland.
Printed and bound in Great Britain by
Hartnolls Ltd, Bodmin, Cornwall.

These things shall be! A loftier race
Than e'er the world hath known shall rise,
With flame of freedom in their souls,
And light of triumph in their eyes.

HYMN   JOHN ADDINGTON SYMONDS

Contents

Chapter One

Land of Freedom

The wind tore the shed door out of her hand, slamming it wide against the wall with a crash. She hesitated a moment, listening, then grabbed her old bicycle and manoeuvred it out. Another crash. Still no sound from inside the bungalow. Perhaps they'd think it was the wind alone that had caused the noise. Hitching herself onto the saddle, she pedalled down the drive, praying that the gale would drown out the sound of scrunching gravel; the lawn would have been quieter but too slow. This had to be a quick getaway.

She had reached the gate when she heard Sarah's voice. "Suzanne? Is that you? You can't go out now, it's time for supper!"

You haven't heard that, girl. Or rather you wouldn't have but for the westerly gale. Keep going. Toby squeezed through the gate, passing her rear wheel a split second before it clicked behind her and they were away, the old James cycle which had accompanied her everywhere for the past three years, bouncing and clattering over the narrow, cobbled road with the dog panting along in pursuit. At least she had made her escape. By the time they left the road to follow a rough path through brambles and gorse to Fort Doyle, her heartbeat had returned to normal.

But the misery continued to claw at her stomach.

Leaving James propped against a large boulder, she clambered down over thick, springy tussocks to the rocks and out to the point where the gale carried salty spume over her head as each gigantic roller burst at the foot of the rockface below. They sat together on her usual granite shelf, Toby leaning against her, tongue lolling, both watching the breakers building higher and higher, waiting for the legendary seventh one, the biggest of all. Sue often held her breath, scarcely daring to believe the approaching mountain of water wouldn't surge right over them and drag them away. It was scary but terribly exciting. Turbulent. Passionate. Deeply emotional . . . or was it just her state of mind at present?

Toby scratched his ear before moving away to explore, leaving her sitting alone, arms wrapped round her long, bare legs, dark hair pulled away from her face by the salty wind.

Suzanne Gaudion's parents were both tall and she took after them, with her father's sea-green eyes and mother's dark brown hair. Though at fifteen she was still skinny, physically immature, mentally she was not. In years to come her type of maturity would be described as 'streetwise', developed the hard way. Born and raised an only child, up until the birth of her brother during the war, evacuation from the island of Guernsey just days before the Germans landed had cut her adrift from the love and

2

security of home and family, into a strange world where people were kind and polite, at least most of them were, but obviously indifferent to one's existence. The transition from being a loved only child to just a name on a list, one of X number of children to be counted, checked, taught and accommodated, had been bewildering. For five years she had belonged to no one, had had no one to confide in, to hug, to love or be loved by. It had been bewildering and painful, too painful for conscious thought, so she had deliberately 'switched off'.

In retrospect that might have been a bad mistake. She had felt guilty about it many times, wondering if that was why she had long ago forgotten what her parents looked like. It would have been interesting to know if other girls were the same, but the guilt made her too ashamed ever to ask. At school prayers every morning they had prayed for the war to end soon, and for their families to be safe and well. They sang patriotic hymns about winning battles, conquering evil and freeing the beloved homeland. Freedom was the key word: they prayed for it, extolled it, dreamed of it . . . the great moment when they would all be free to return home.

Like her love of Guernsey, love for her parents never wavered throughout the five years of separation. Love and loyalty had burned fiercely and continuously . . . or had it? Had she been idolising a mythical couple who bore no resemblance to reality? She hadn't recognised them in the crowd of parents waiting as the schoolgirls disembarked and walked down the quayside; it was a shock to realise the grey-haired couple who looked like someone's grandparents where actually her mother and father. And she had sensed a strained atmosphere, from that first reunion. Despite the smiles and anecdotes it was irritating to be constantly corrected on table manners, diction, clothes and 'respect'. Her parents seemed to expect to be revered like gods, correct in all things, wise and omnipotent, whilst in fact, cut off from the outside world for the past five years, they had retained the attitudes of the Victorian era.

And they treated her like a child. A ten-year-old child!

The shock at their reunion had been mutual. Greg and Sarah had stared in disbelief as the tall, self-possessed young woman in a tweed suit and high heels stopped in front of them and said "Halloo, luvs!" in an almost unintelligible Welsh accent. Suzanne? Was this the little girl to whom they had waved goodbye for a week or two . . . weeks which had stretched into five long years? The label on her suitcase said so, so it had to be. Hearts plummetting and swallowing hard, they had fixed smiles across their mouths and tried to remember all the things they had planned to say.

Matters hadn't eased since.

"We will have to give her more time to adjust, that's all." Greg held Sarah against his chest and planted a kiss on top of her grey hair. "Try to be patient, sweetheart."

Sarah sighed, pulling away. "For how much longer? She's been home more than a month, now, and shows no sign of settling down. She's rude, unco-operative, won't do a thing she's told."

"I'm sure she is trying . . ."

"You might be sure, but I'm not. Look at the way she

ignored me just now, when I called her for supper. I'm getting fed up with it. It's bad enough—"

"All right! I'll try having another word with her. You must remember, though, that we are like strangers to her."

"Strangers! We're her parents, for heaven's sake." Sarah's voice rose in exasperation. "She's the stranger, if anyone is. She went away a child and only five years later she thinks she's an adult. Comes back wearing grown-up clothes and high-heeled shoes . . ."

"One inch high."

"That's right, take her side!"

"I'm not taking sides. We're all in this together."

"First it was Ma and Aline coming back making trouble. Now this . . ." Sarah turned to stare, unseeing, across the kitchen sink and out over the garden, shaking with sobs.

Family! All those years dreaming of getting back to family, only to find there wasn't one. Years of living in billets where no one cared, of longing to be loved and part of family life, being comforted when one was sick or miserable . . .

Suzanne had felt dreadfully sick on the evacuation boat. And no one had cared so long as she didn't mess up her clothes, or anyone else's. She and Joan and Priscilla had sat on their shared bunk in semi-darkness, having a midnight feast on the sandwiches their mothers had made for the journey, which, with the excitement and emotional exhaustion, combined with the heat and smell of oil and paint, had had disastrous consequences. Even after being ashore for hours, floors and walls continued to pitch and roll with sickening effect. The Dutch cargo boat

Batavia III was never the most stable of vessels and, after the Channel crossing, the long wait outside Weymouth for a pilot boat to guide them through the minefields had completed the children's discomfort.

It was also unfortunate that their English hosts imagined they had all arrived carrying fleas and diseases, incarcerating the children in a cinema requisitioned as a clinic, where they waited their turn to be certified clean by a team of doctors and nurses. A nice WVS lady with the best of intentions, offered Suzanne a cup of tea and an iced bun, unaware that the ten-year-old had never drunk tea in her life and did not have a sweet tooth. Out of politeness Suzanne tried to drink the tea but it was so strong and bitter she began to retch again.

The train journey north was a novelty: Suzanne had never been on a train before. All the girls were exhausted and Suzanne's legs were nearly buckling.

Miss Watson, their form mistress, aware she would be required to play a dual role for the time being of both teacher and parent, smiled with unusual frequency and referred to her charges as 'my children'. Well past middle age her tall, bony frame draped in long, drab colours, she wore her iron-grey hair drawn tightly back into a thin bun in the nape of her neck, exaggerating a terrifying beak of a nose and thin lips stretched over huge, long yellow teeth.

Aching with weariness, Suzanne assimilated the unspoken message. "Are you going to be our mother until we get home?" she asked.

The yellow teeth flashed. "That is correct, dear."

All the girls in the carriage flinched: Old Watty had never called anyone 'dear' before.

The woman was no beauty, in fact compared with Mummy she was positively ugly, but her coat was furry and cosy. Suzanne desperately wanted to be cuddled and comforted: Watty would have to do. She shuffled along the seat until she could lean against the coat.

Touched by the move, Miss Watson put her arm round the child.

Suzanne snuggled up. "Can I call you 'Mummy'?" she asked sleepily.

The arm was swiftly removed. "No! I am not your mother. You must call me Miss Watson."

Suzanne wanted to cry but she was too tired. Moments later she fell asleep.

"Where on earth have you been, Sue?" Greg glared across the dining table, trying to look fierce to satisfy Sarah's sense of justice.

Suzanne glanced at her mother's stony face, the eyes glued to her plate. Oh hell! You could cut the atmosphere with a knife! "Out," she snapped, flouncing onto her chair.

"How dare you speak to your father in that tone!" Sarah almost shouted.

"Well, it's my business where I've been and nobody else's," the girl retorted in her heavy Welsh accent. "If he was that interested to know where I was, why didn't he ask nicely?"

Greg, as ever wanting to avoid a blazing row, shook his head sadly. "Sue, Sue. We are only concerned about you. You knew it was supper time before you went out. Didn't you? So why did you go?" His voice was soft and conciliatory.

Poor old Dad: he was always the one trying to keep the peace. He was much more understanding than Mum. "Because I wanted to get away from the house," she whispered.

"Why?"

She glanced briefly at her mother. "I was upset. I wanted to be by myself to think."

"About what?"

"Herself, of course," Sarah snapped. "That's all she ever thinks about. Self, self, self. To think we have spent five years grieving at not being with her, longing for us all to be together again, and all we get is tantrums and selfishness. She uses this place like an hotel, expecting to be waited on hand and foot—"

"Oh, for goodness sake, Mum, give over. I keep telling you, if you want me to do something, then ask. Surely the house is your responsibility. You're the one who plans what's to be done. What, where and when we eat. When the beds are to be changed and things like that. I've got plenty of things to occupy my mind without doubling up on your responsibilities. But I keep telling you, I'm always willing to help. But I'm not psychic, so don't expect me to read your mind all the time and know what you want done."

Sarah had sat wide-eyed and open-mouthed throughout Sue's outburst. As her daughter finished she gasped for breath and shouted "Ask! Are you incapable of seeing when a table needs laying? Don't you know what a tea towel is for? I cannot believe—"

Sue pushed back her chair. "I've heard all this before, several times. If you must repeat it yet again and ignore everything I say, then carry on. But don't expect me to

8

sit here and listen." And with a furious glare but head held high, she left the room, gently shutting the door behind her.

Sarah gasped, shaking her head in disbelief. "This is ridiculous. She cannot be allowed to get away with it!"

"And just what do you propose to do about it?" Greg pushed his half-finished meal aside and sat back. "You know, I did warn you before she came in. But you would go on nagging at her."

"I – what?" Now she was furious with him. "I was nagging? Rubbish! I was simply pointing out the truth . . ."

". . . As you see it. Not as she does."

"What has that got to do with it? This is our home!"

"And hers. But she has had a very different upbringing and background for the past five years from what it would have been if she'd been with us and you really must try to understand that."

"On the contrary. She's the one who has got to learn to obey the rules of this house and comply with the family."

Greg sighed. Sarah was becoming more like her mother than ever, he thought, remembering Marie's tight, Victorian attitudes even before the war. Why couldn't she see it and be warned? Unfortunately, it looked as though Sue was inheriting her grandmother's obstinacy, which was going to make the situation in the house totally unlivable. "Well? What do we do? Tie a rope round her neck and tether her down? Or let her have her head?"

"What about boarding school?"

Greg frowned. "You mean kick her out again when she's only just got back home?"

"Don't come the dramatic with me. Can we afford it?"

Greg's mind was spinning. If he said no, then Sarah would have to drop the idea. But it would be a lie and he had never lied to his wife, ever.

Sarah read the hesitation with perfect accuracy. "You don't have to lie to me. If you are dead against the idea, say so. But I do think we should talk about it. And even ask Sue how she feels. She might like the idea."

Richard was a cute little boy. Sue was sitting on a rug on the lawn with him, reading him a story while he watched her every dramatic facial expression, designed to suit each fictional character. Aready she was becoming very fond of him: well, he was the only one in the family she could trust not to misconstrue her words or turn on her for no reason she could fathom. Like dear old Toby, stretched on the rug beside them. Amazing how affectionate he was towards her. She was convinced the dog could remember her. Watching from a window, Sarah smiled. There were occasions when she felt confident that Greg was right, that given time Sue would eventually settle down. It was lovely to see their two children enjoying each other's company. She picked up her sunhat and went outside.

Richard looked up when he heard her steps on the gravel. "Come an' hear the story, Mummy," he commanded.

Sue smiled and moved up to make room for her. "We've got to the bit where Pooh knocks on Eeyore's door." She loved her mother's smile, and enjoyed the warmth that reached her through their thin cotton dresses.

When the story was finished Sue closed the book and stood up.

"Where you going? I want another story," Richard wailed.

"Perhaps Mummy'll read to you. I must hurry, now. I'm meeting the girls at four-thirty at the Gaumont."

Sarah's eyebrows shot up. "You're not going to the cinema, are you?"

"Yes."

"But . . . we're playing bridge at the Martel's tonight at seven-thirty and you're sitting in."

"Since when? You didn't tell me."

"Do I have to tell you every time we are going out?"

"Well . . . yes, if you want me to sit in with Richard. I told you on Wednesday that I'd arranged this with the others."

"No you didn't!"

"I did! Don't you remember? You were in the kitchen with Dad . . ."

"Will you stop arguing! We are going out tonight and you are to be home by seven."

"But the film doesn't end till seven-thirty!"

"Then you'll have to telephone one of your friends to say you can't come."

"I can't. They'll all have left home by now and if I don't turn up they'll be left standing around waiting. When did you arrange this bridge game, anyway?"

"This morning. But what has that to do with it?" Why did this child have to argue so persistently? Sarah ground her teeth.

"I told you before!" Sue's voice rose an octave. "I promised last Wednesday, and I told you. So you're the one who'll have to cancel." She ran across the lawn towards the house.

Richard burst into tears.

Sue stood in her bedroom, shaking with tears and anger. For a few precious minutes the atmosphere had seemed perfect, out there on the lawn. Then her bloody mother had to spoil everything. Damn her. Damn, damn, damn! She dragged a brush through her hair, rubbed a flannel over her face and grabbed her purse.

The cycle shed was locked. "Mum! Where's the shed key?"

"In my pocket." The reply came from the kitchen.

Sue ran to the back door. "Can I have it, please?"

"*May* I have it, you mean. And the answer is no, you may not."

"But I've got to get my bike out. I'm going to be late!"

"I've told you, you're not going."

Sue's temper snapped. She strode up to her mother and glared in her face. "Oh yes I am. Hand it over."

Sarah promptly yielded to the urge she had only suppressed with difficulty since her daughter's return. She raised her hand and slapped the girl across the face. "Don't you ever speak to me in that tone—"

The sentence was never finished, cut short by a resounding return smack from Sue.

"Aah!" Sarah shrieked. "That is definitely that! It's boarding school for you, my girl. Your father and I have discussed it. We don't want to send you away but you leave us no alternative. I'm not putting up with this a minute longer! Go to your room and stay there."

Suzanne stared at her, speechless. She realised she had overstepped the mark, hitting Mum back. But Mum had asked for it! Bloody hell! She had sat in for them three times in the past week, anyway. And she hadn't been offered a penny extra pocket money.

Sue lay on her back on the eiderdown, staring at the ceiling, deeply shocked, her breath coming in short gasps. Was this really the mother she had longed for, the home and family she had craved and cried for for years? Family members were supposed to love and support each other to be tolerant and understanding. Maybe it was necessary for parents to be strict with their children but not use them whenever they felt like it for their convenience. Anyway, I'm not a child. Haven't been since . . . the last time she had belonged to a family?

The train journey north to Oldham had ended at four in the morning, and through darkened streets the children were driven to a Baptist Chapel schoolroom where they slept on the floor on horsehair mattresses. Oldham was strangely dark and horrible with high buildings and no bathrooms so one had to walk to the public baths which were streets away, and most of the toilets at the chapel were outside in a smelly tent. Three weeks later, another bus journey took them into the Derbyshire hills which was much better, but despite all the girls and sharing rooms it was dreadfully lonely. Suzanne managed not to get weepy like some girls did, except when the staff discovered an outbreak of head lice, and her head had been bandaged up with paraffin for three weeks. The blisters it made on the back of her neck were so painful it was hard to sleep properly – and things always seemed more miserable at night in the dark.

The lice were gone and the scabs healed when yet

another bus trip took them to Denbigh in North Wales. The driver stopped at several places in the town before Miss Watson finally called "Suzanne Gaudion!" and the Billeting Officer helped her down with her suitcase and stood at a front door which actually opened onto the pavement!

An old lady opened it and said, "Hallo, love! Have you come to stay with us, then?" in a very strange, sing-song voice. And while the grown ups talked Sue was coaxed past them by a nice, smiling lady, through a tiny hallway into a cosy room. Even on this warm September evening the fire was lit in the black range alongside its two ovens above which, under the mantelshelf, was a brass rail hung with freshly ironed shirts. Keeping sentinel on top of the shelf sat two china dogs, one each side of a big ebony clock.

"I'm Mrs Ellis," the nice lady told her, "and this is my son, Bryn, and here's Myfanwy, my daughter." The boy was older, the girl younger than Suzanne. They said hello, shyly, but didn't attempt to shake hands. "Now this is Taid, my father," she said, leading her to the old man sitting in an ancient, plush-covered chair, "and it was Nain, my mother, who opened the door."

Suzanne smiled politely, struggling to understand the accent and remember what was told her. Much later they explained that Nain and Taid were Welsh for Grandma and Grandpa.

The front door slammed and Nain came in. "You must be tired after your journey, my love. We're just about to have our tea. Are you hungry?"

Suzanne nodded. "Yes, I am."

The table was large, occupying most of the room, which

was just as well, for more people appeared from upstairs, and Suzanne found herself wedged between two soldiers who Nain explained were also billeted in the house. Bread and butter, jam and Marmite, stewed fruit and custard were carried in from the kitchen.

"You take sugar 'n' milk?" Nain asked.

"No sugar, thank you," the newcomer replied, anticipating a nice big glass of cold milk . . . then her heart sank as a cup of tea was placed in front of her. The question had not been "sugar in milk" but "sugar and milk", in tea. She didn't like to say anything, she would have to force herself to drink it, unsweetened!

The meal was a very jolly affair. Everyone was nice to each other; they asked her questions, told her about themselves and soon a warm, family atmosphere wrapped itself round her.

That night she slept soundly in her comfy bed, in her own little room, the first time she'd slept alone since leaving Guernsey. There were drawers to put her things in, and a curtained corner to hang her uniform and overcoat. These people were so warm and friendly. Loving. Taid was head of the family, like Grandpa Ozanne had been, and everyone obeyed him. It was a proper household and felt like a home. Not *her* home, but a real home for all that. She felt safe and happy, belonging to a family again.

The loneliness quickly disappeared as she was adopted into her new surroundings. The first day Bryn and Myfanwy showed her the way to her school. It was a huge, splendid school where the Guernsey girls were accommodated in their own form rooms with their own teachers. The girls compared notes, some, like Suzanne, loving their billets, others near tears with disappointment.

During the light evenings, after school, her adopted siblings took her uptown, showed her the fish and chip shop in Back Street where you could get a bag of soft, vinegary chips for thre'pence. On Saturday mornings they went to the cinema to yell with excitement when the goodies chased the baddies out of town, and in the afternoon they explored Graig Woods. Saturday nights provided the weekly bathing novelty. A galvanised tub was set in the middle of the flagstone floor in the kitchen and filled with kettles of hot water in which the children took turns in 'first wash'. Naturally, Bryn was not allowed in when the girls were bathing.

Sunday mornings there was church parade in school uniform at St Mary's Anglican Church, and after lunch she went with Bryn and Myfanwy to Sunday School.

The only time she ever saw Taid angry was one Sunday afternoon just before tea when she had tried to catch up with her beastly stitching for needlework class next day.

"What is that, may I ask?" he had roared.

"My sewing!" she replied innocently.

"Sewing! Sewing on the Sabbath! What did the Lord say? Eh?"

She quailed.

"He said 'thou shalt do no manner of work on the Sabbath'!"

"Sorry," she whispered, and put it away. It was a good excuse to tell Miss Watson.

She had soon discovered that Sunday was the most important day of the week in that house. It was the one day that Nain took her curlers out and put her uncomfortable false teeth in, for the evening service which they all attended at Capel Mawr. Sue didn't understand a word

16

of the service, but sang lustily reading phonetically from the hymn book.

Sometimes, when extra family or friends came to stay, bed space was at a premium. Myfanwy would spend a night in Suzanne's bed, leading to much chattering and giggles and not much sleep, and on one occasion the evacuee was ousted from her single bed for a whole week by a visiting couple, whilst she shared the big bed in the front bedroom with Nain and her daughter, Taid having been sent upstairs to share with Great Uncle Dai and Bryn.

Christmas was approaching when Uncle Andrew, Daddy's brother, came to visit. Suzanne had never liked him very much, but she was pleased to see him and delighted to show off her new family, so much so that she failed to notice his grim disapproval. It was disappointing in a way that she couldn't share Christmas with the Ellises and Nain and Taid, but the thought of seeing Grandma and Grandpa Ozanne again was very exciting. She kissed and hugged her Welsh family and promised to see them again in three weeks, and Bryn helped carry her suitcase down the road to the station.

Auntie Aline met her at the other end, after a tedious journey with several changes of trains which were all full of soldiers. Grandma and Grandpa were waiting in the little flat they were renting and there were lots more hugs and kisses, but all three seemed cross and grumpy. Everything was wrong – the rationing, the flat, Hitler, the butcher, their landlord and the government. Only Mr Churchill had their approval.

Grandma contrived to create a Christmas cake from ingredients she had collected for months, and between them they enjoyed a sense of Christmas-in-miniature, so very different from the big family parties they were used to. The Christmas dinner Grandma declared a travesty, though it seemed perfectly all right to Suzanne, and after they had cleared away and listened to the King's Speech on the wireless, they exchanged presents.

"Ooh! Thank you Auntie." Suzanne was thrilled with the pony book. She said the same to her grandparents though she didn't feel quite so enthusiastic about the leather-bound Bible.

Several times during the holiday Suzanne was disturbed by questions asked about her billet: they were worded in a critical way, as though her grandmother wanted her to say something was wrong with the place or the people. Then the truth came out. They had had a letter from Uncle Andrew saying the billet was totally unsuitable.

Suzanne was furious. "It's not true!' she stormed, eyes flashing incredibly like her mother's when roused. "It's a lovely, cosy house and they are very nice, kind people. I don't want to leave there and go somewhere else. Some of the billets are awful: my friends say so."

However, Marie Ozanne had the bit between her teeth and ordered a taxi to drive them all the way to North Wales to ensure that the headmistress wasn't allowed to make the same mistake again.

That cosy home was the last in which she would enjoy family life for the next four and a half years.

Not that home and family in Guernsey was proving in any way comparable with her dreams and yearnings during those years. And now the threat of boarding school was hanging over her head.

Sue sat up, looked around the room and grinned. Draped over the mirror on her dressing table, the head and foot boards of her bed, and one corner of the pelmet were socks, a vest, a blouse and her face flannel, exactly where she had flung them in her fury half an hour earlier. Flinging clothes about always relieved tension and anger. Nearly five o'clock: Dad would be in soon to calm Mum down, thank goodness, but in the meantime she'd keep out of sight. Try not to think about boarding schools and babysitting. She slid off the bed and picked up a pencil from the desk to add a few more hairs to the forelock on the pony she'd drawn.

She thought about David Morgan's recent letter from Denbigh, the love and kisses at the bottom, remembered the real kisses they'd shared in Graig Woods and the back row of the cinema and she wondered how long they would have to wait for more. Then her mind switched back to ponies again.

Greg came home early in answer to Sarah's tearful summons, and listened to her alternating anguish and anger for nearly an hour. Then he stood outside Sue's bedroom door, forcing himself to knock and commence the dreaded interview. Nothing upset him more than discord and now he was stuck in the middle of the worst he'd ever known, understanding both sides but aware that both his wife and daughter expected him to support their respective arguments.

"Who is it?"

"Daddy."

Sue unlocked the door. "You're late today."

"Not really. I've been in the garden with your mother."

"Oh. So you've heard." She closed the door behind him

and crossed to the window, looking out so he couldn't see her misery.

"Honestly, Sue, you have gone too far this time."

"I know. I shouldn't have hit her back; it was just instinct. No one has ever hit me like that. Not ever." A sob caught in her throat.

He saw her shoulders heaving and hurried to put an arm round her, which opened the floodgates. Sue turned and buried her face in his shirt and cried.

Dammit it! he thought. It was Sarah's lack of understanding that was creating the trouble. The poor kid had had no one but the Welsh lad, David, to care about or care for her for years; she could not be expected to slot back immediately, emotionally and physically, into the obedient little daughter role of pre-war. He stroked her hair. "Calm down, old thing. We've got to talk this through."

"What is there to say? You and Mummy have already decided to send me away again." She shuddered, accepted his proffered handkerchief and blew noisily.

"We have done no such thing!"

"Mummy said . . ."

"I know what Mummy said in the heat of the moment, but I'm quite sure that if you were to tell her how sorry you are and that you promise to try much harder . . ."

"I don't know if I can!" she gasped. "I thought I was doing okay. Everything was so super this afternoon when we were sitting in the garden . . ." another noisy blow in the soggy hankie, ". . . and honestly, Dad, I had told her I was going out this evening."

"I'm sure you did, darling, but she had forgotten. The Martel's are going away on holiday tomorrow, you

20

see, and it was our last chance of a game for three weeks."

"Oh. I didn't know." Looking up at him she asked, "Do you think I might not have to go to boarding school?"

"Let's go down and talk to Mummy about it."

Sue grimaced, then smiled. "Okay."

Greg smiled back. "That's my girl. But one word of advice: try to remember not to say 'okay' in front of you mother. You know how she hates the word."

"Ok . . . er . . . all right."

Sarah hugged her daughter, who tried to respond with as much enthusiasm as possible. Over the supper table they drew up a sitting-in rota, and decided on the limited number of times she could go out in the evenings and till what time. Everyone was making an effort to be sweet and affectionate, but it was not easy for Sue to hide her aggravation at all the new restrictions that were suddenly being introduced into her life.

"Look at the time!" she exclaimed. "Aren't you going to be late for your bridge?"

"I cancelled," Sarah told her. "We felt it was important to get this all sorted out."

The subject was discussed again the following evening, when Greg and Sarah went out to St Saviour's to visit John, her brother, and Edna.

"Maybe she'll settle down better once school starts again," John suggested. They had all strolled up to the top fields where Sarah had loved to wander in her youth, before marriage took her away to live in the north of the island.

"We can only pray she does," Greg grimaced. "How

about you? How are things working out with your Ma and Aline?"

"Appalling! Ma won't speak to Edna, and because she and Pa had had a marriage contract, everything here belongs to her. So she, or rather Aline, has decided to sell the farm, lock, stock and barrel . . ."

"What!" Sarah, had been walking a few yards behind with Edna. She stopped, flabbergasted, mouth hanging open. "She can't! She wouldn't do it!"

Edna put a hand on Sarah's arm. "It's my fault, I'm afraid. John won't tell you but there was one hell of an argument with them, Aline shouting that if he took over the farm and anything happened to him after we'd married, then their family property would pass into the hands of 'that baggage who's no better than she should be'! There was no way your Ma would tolerate that!" Some time after John's sour wife, Mary, had been evacuated with their children, Edna had moved in with him, transforming the once solemn and unhappy man into a jolly, laughing one. But Marie Ozanne could not be expected to countenance an adulterous relationship, however tedious she had found her daughter-in-law.

Sarah shook with anger. "I thought it was bad enough when they came home and accused me of stealing their clothes: I think they would have preferred that we all died of pneumonia while the stuff all rotted in their wardrobes." She stared sadly out over the fields to the west coast, over a lively, September sea which melded into the sky on the blue horizon, a panorama that had provided her happy, contented childhood with an ever-changing, magnificently colourful backdrop. "John," she sighed, "what has happened to our family? Why has the reunion proved so disastrous?"

The four looked helplessly at each other, searching their minds for easy answers – but there were none.

"Where will you go? What will you do?" Greg asked.

John shrugged. "Edna and I haven't had much time to discuss it, yet. But there are one or two ideas knocking around."

Edna smiled affectionately at him. "We might as well tell them," and, when he nodded, went on, "I've been to see my advocate. I've got a bit of money of my own and some property my aunt left me which I could sell, and I've suggested that he might put in a bid for Val du Douit on my behalf."

"Really!" Sarah was immediately delighted at the idea, plus more than a little astounded that Edna Quevatre, sister of her late father's herdsman, was worth that sort of money. "Well, that would be wonderful. But would Ma consider selling to you?"

"I'm so glad you approve of the idea. The advocate said that if we set up a company to buy it, she needn't know until after the contracts were signed."

Greg laughed. "Brilliant! But, isn't the place going to be a bit big for you, or were you planning to start a large family?"

"Not on your life!" Edna exclaimed.

"No fear of that!" John added. "No. Edna's dead keen to start a guest house and maybe a tea garden in the summer months. We would have plenty rooms if we use The Wing, and maybe we could expand by turning the coach house and barn into an annexe. That is if things work out well."

"Well that would certainly sort out your problems," Sarah said enthusiastically.

"But it doesn't do much for yours! Any ideas how you are going to help Sue settle?" John asked.

Sarah told him about the boarding school idea and Sue's horror at the very thought of it. "We've all kissed and made up for the moment. Long may it last."

"What are her interests?"

"Some boy she's keen on in Wales. And horses. She longs to work with them."

"She's welcome to come and help out here with ours, if she wants. She could pick up a bit of pocket money that way. Do you pay her for sitting in?"

Sarah glanced at Greg. "No. Do you think we should? I mean, well, family and all that. Can you imagine Ethel ever getting anything from Ma and Pa?" The subject of Ethel, her adored older sister, remained a sore point. Having helped in the upbringing of her younger siblings, and much of the cooking and house chores for many years for a mere pittance, the older girl had allowed herself the luxury of a fling with the son of a neighbour, which resulted in pregnancy. The shamed couple had had a hasty wedding and, on the insistence of both mothers had been banished to New Zealand. Sarah never forgave her mother, despite the fact that Paul and Ethel adored each other and produce five healthy sons to help their father on his highly successful sheep farm.

"Ethel was Ma's slave!" John growled.

"A fairly willing one, though," Greg added. "She was always so calm and easy going. Super girl."

"I wonder if she'll ever come back for a visit?" Sarah mused. "I've written and asked them, you know."

"Good. And if they all come and we have Val du Douit we can put some or all of them up here," John raised a querying brow at Edna who nodded her approval.

The Michaelmas Term started very late in 1945.

Greg and Sarah were not pleased to learn that Sue was a year behind in her school work, but agreed to say nothing, for the time being. Also, they had decided to pay her one shilling and sixpence a time for sitting in.

It was great fun to be back amongst all the girls again, comparing notes on homecomings, but Sue was disturbed. Everyone gave glowing accounts of their reunions with their families, their homes and their happiness at being back in Guernsey. Of course, she said the same, guilty at the lie, and wondering if the others were telling the truth . . . or also lying. There was no way of knowing, and no way of finding out without revealing the shameful truth. The atmosphere at home had improved, slightly, to a state of unarmed truce. But no way could it be described as happy home life, with Mum constantly complaining about something – Gran and Auntie Aline mostly, but also about the Guernsey States (the island parliament) and their political decisions; also about the wartime black-marketeers and 'Jerrybags', those women who had capitalised on the German soldiers' loneliness; about the strain of looking after Richard who was indeed very lively, and, most of all, about Sue herself. Try as she may, she felt she could never be right, so inevitably there were many occasions when she made no attempt to co-operate at all.

In her end of term school report, the only good comments were on her drawing and cooking, the latter being extremely limited by the strict food rationing.

Greg laid the report on the supper table one night, having studied it with Sarah, and asked Sue what she wanted to do with her life. "What sort of a career do you want? There is nothing here to show any likelihood of a future in academics. Would you like to go to an Art College? Or follow up on cookery?"

"I'd like to work with horses," she replied.

"You mean, be a stable girl?"

"To begin with. But then I could become a children's riding instructor. Perhaps go on to have my own riding school."

"Do you think there is the call for it in the island?"

"I'm not thinking of the island. I was hoping to find an opening in North Wales."

Sarah pursed her lips. "You mean near that boy. I think we have enough problems to overcome already, without adding him to the equation."

Sue's eyes flashed.

But before she could work up a retort Greg cut in. "Well, not in the short term. Maybe when you reach eighteen or nineteen you will have had sufficient experience with horses over here to go off to the mainland. In Wales, if that is what you still want."

Sue shrugged.

So the unarmed truce continued.

Chapter Two

Family Ties

"No!" Richard pulled his hand away as Sue tried to grab it, and continued strolling along the edge of the water, saturating his shoes and completely ignoring her.

She ground her teeth, looked at her watch and lunged again. "Mummy said we had to be back by half-past-five and it's nearly six o'clock. It's almost pitch dark. You've got to come. NOW!" This time she held tightly to his wrist.

The five-year-old had never been a child to kick, scream or throw tantrums: he simply made up his mind what he wanted and refused to budge. Like now.

Sue tugged, but he had dug his heels in. If she tugged any harder he would fall into the freezing water and wet sand, soaking his coat and trousers. Anyway, she couldn't drag him all the way home on his backside by one arm, and he was far too heavy to carry that far. She resorted to bribery. "If you're very good and do as I ask, you can have some of my chocolate."

He smiled sweetly. "Where is it?"

"At home."

"I want it now. Then I'll come."

"I've told you, it's at home. So will you come?"

"No." The little beggar was still smiling.

It was nearly six-thirty when they walked into the kitchen at Les Mouettes.

"Where on earth have you been?" Sarah demanded. "I told you to be here by half-past-five at the latest." The day had been bad enough so far, what with the clothes line breaking and then the Ascot refusing to light. And they were due at the Schmits' at seven.

"Richard refused to leave the beach . . ." Sue began.

"Don't be ridiculous! Are you telling me you can't handle a five-year-old child?"

"Yes. What was I supposed to do? Pick him up and carry him all the way?" Sue was thoroughly peeved.

"Don't answer back! If I'd been there I'd have made sure he—"

"How? You can't control him."

Sarah banged her fist on the table. "I have warned you not to answer back! Once more and you'll be punished."

Sue turned on Richard who was watching the row develop with interest. "See what you've done. You wouldn't come when I told you, and now I'm expected to take the blame without being allowed to say one word to defend myself!"

Sarah was halfway down the hall. "Your suppers are in the oven. I'll have to leave you to see Richard eats his. Then you can bath him and put him to bed. I haven't got time now."

Later, much later, when her brother was finally asleep

28

looking quite angelic, Sue mooched around the house trying not to think, thinking made her feel so miserable. She turned on the wireless, and switched off again. She wasn't interested in gardening, and music only increased her depression. Dirty dishes were stacked on the drainboard, waiting. Was Mum right to expect her to 'play her part' by babysitting, washing dishes and changing beds when they were paying Daisy, the maid, to do it? Was this what being part of a family was all about? It was certainly nothing like the scenario she had dreamt of through the war. Home and family . . . like her first billet – not the second.

There was no denying that Clwyd Hall was splendid: way out in the country, it was vastly different from Nain and Taid's little home in the town. There were horses, a pony and dogs, stables and an old caravan they could use as a den in Beech Wood.

When Lady Matherson learned that Suzanne could ride, she gave permission for her to saddle the pony and join her granddaughter when the girl rode over on her skewbald in smart riding clothes. Unfortunately the saddle room was unlocked only for those rides – which failed to deter the evacuee who was perfectly happy to mount bareback, oblivious of her numerous tumbles but worrying Meggie to death.

Suzanne was so thankful that she and Meggie were billeted together. She had become very fond of her somewhat serious, bespectacled friend who, of necessity, frequently curbed some of their wilder escapades, and couldn't imagine how awful it would be at Clwyd Hall without her. She had overcome her anger at Grandma's journey of complaint which, as far as the old lady was concerned, had proved well worth the enormous taxi fare, satisfying her sense of snobbery despite Suzanne's refusal to complain to the Billeting Officer about the home she had been living in: the one with the lovely, affectionate family. Suzanne had been unable to withstand Marie Ozanne's determination to move her, but they couldn't stop her going back to visit Nain and Taid and Myfanwy and Bryn, except that it was a terribly long way from the Hall. She could only run down the hill in her lunch hour for a quick "hello" and a hug. Nain always looked so pleased to see her, unlike old Appleby.

"Appleby! See the girls have Scott's Emulsion," Lady Matherson's voice would boom instructions to her personal maid, "Appleby, see the girls have Wellington boots." And the girls were well aware of the old retainer's reaction. Long and bony, with a twisted neck and always draped in black, she was not unkind; it was just that she didn't really like having to look after children at her age, especially homeless refugees. They ate with her in the Servants' Hall, along with Mrs Sands the fat, jolly cook and her son who was very nice, and the starchy parlourmaid Ellen, who was not. Maisie the kitchenmaid was fun and giggly, but there was no family, no one to hug and praise you for good arithmetic marks or an essay like Mummy used to, like Nain had done. Only Appleby to scold if you got your feet wet, or forgot to wash your hands before tea.

One of the good things about Clwyd Hall was it's proximity to the river. The Clwyd was narrow and shallow but excellent for small fish and eels. Billy Sands showed them how to make a fishing line, and how to cut eels' heads off before they wriggled away back to the water . . . which made Meggie feel sick. Suzanne demonstrated how she caught cabous back home, sneaking up on them round the rocks and scooping them into her hands. Where the river meandered around shelves of shingle, forming tiny islets draped with silver birch saplings, they played at kingdoms going to war against each other. That game had had to be modified after a particularly good battle when they arrived home sopping wet and spattered with mud. Appleby had been very angry and made poor Maisie clean their clothes.

Sometimes, on dark nights, Meggie and Suzanne drew back the curtains and sat on the latter's bed to watch the bombardment of Liverpool docks. Not that they could see any detail, the docks being over twenty miles away, but the sky would be criss-crossed with searchlight beams and speckled with ack-ack fire, all the horizon bursting red and orange. Was this, they wondered, the way it had been in Guernsey? Had the Germans bombed and killed all the people? Suzanne was worried this might be the reason why she hadn't heard anything from Daddy and Mummy for more than six months. Auntie Aline had told her at Christmas that she knew of someone in England who had had a Red Cross message from a person in the island saying they were all well. But was it true?

There were many times when Suzanne had the urge to reach out for Meggie's hand, but she restrained herself. She was afraid her friend would think she was soppy.

*   *   *

Perhaps she was soppy-sentimental. Perhaps it was baby-ish of her to want the same demonstrative affection she had enjoyed before the war.

The Ascot still wasn't working so Sue filled the kettle to heat water for the dishes.

She was in bed when her parents got home but the next morning she hurried to join them at breakfast to receive acknowledgement of her effort. Unfortunately Daisy assumed her mistress had washed up for once, and Sarah assumed Daisy had done it; breakfast conversation was entirely dominated by a post-mortem of the previous night's bridge. No pat on the back from Dad, no appreci-ative smile from Mum.

Suzanne continued to make what she considered to be a huge effort to please her parents: worked on keeping her bedroom moderately tidy, tried to remember to set the meal table without being asked and even visited Grandma Gaudion, voluntarily. This was a very tedious chore as the old lady, not far short of ninety, was deaf as a post and got everything muddled.

Sue was always asked what she had done that day.

"I've been trying to teach Richard to count. He's not learning well at school," she replied one day.

Alice stared at her in horror. "How did you get him out?"

Sue frowned. "Out of where?" she yelled into the ear trumpet.

"It must have torn as he was pulled up. Who rescued him? He must have been frozen stiff." At that moment Greg walked in and Alice demanded, "Have you had the doctor for Richard?"

"What for?" Greg raised a querying eyebrow at Sue.

"Not Dr Whitmore! Dr Walker. He'd better give the boy something so he doesn't get pneumonia."

Sue wanted to giggle. "I have no idea what she's on about."

"And what's more, you'd better get the school authorities to close the blessed thing up! Fancy letting him fall down a well. Was it in the playground?"

"Richard! Down a well?" It was Greg's turn to look horrified.

Sue got up and walked to the window so the old lady wouldn't be offended by her uncontrolled laughter. "No, Dad. He isn't."

"Good grief! How the devil did you get us into this one?" Greg asked.

But at least visiting Grandma Gaudion was better than going to Grandma Ozanne, and Auntie Aline, who spent the whole time she was with them complaining about her parents stealing their things during the German Occupation. She remembered the pre-war hay-picnics and happy family Christmases; the beach picnics, and the way everyone gathered round to help if anyone was sick. What had happened? Why had everything had to change? Of course she realised that as a young child she wouldn't have been aware of the various undercurrents of ill-feeling – if there had been any, but now, in spite of all her efforts, the atmosphere didn't seem much better than in the Evanses house in Llewellyn's Lane . . .

After the 1941 Christmas holidays, Old Watty was waiting at Denbigh station for the girls to arrive on the train from Chester. "Come on. Come on!" she called. "Priscilla, where is your suitcase? Marjorie, put your hat on, please."

The bus headed straight up through town and much to Suzanne's surprise her's was only the third name to be called. "But this isn't where I'm billeted, Miss Watson! I'm going out to Clwyd Hall."

"Hasn't anyone told you? Clwyd Hall has been closed and taken over by the War Department." The elderly teacher examined the list in her hand. "You have been moved to a Mrs Evans, up here in Llewellyn's Lane. Let me see, yes, this is it. Number twenty-five. Hurry up now. Everyone wants to get settled into their billets."

Suzanne opened her mouth . . . and shut it again. She and Meggie had become used to the big, country mansion. For what it was worth it represented home. She peered out of the bus window at the pebble-dashed semi-detached house, wondering if they'd be a nice family like her first billet. Heaving her suitcase down the aisle after Miss Watson she asked, "Is Meggie here yet?"

"Mrs Evans has room for only one girl. Meggie has gone somewhere else." She thumped the door knocker.

Before the awful news had sunk in, Mrs Jones opened the door. A large, thin-lipped woman with a sharp nose, she gave a brief smile and a nod. "Come in then, love. Thank you, Miss. We'll look after her now. Goodbye."

The narrow hallway was dark, smelled of carbolic and led into a small, ill-lit room at the back, bursting with brown furniture, on brown lino, a brown rug by the hearth, and endless ornaments bearing place names. The front kitchen.

"This is Mr Evans," the woman said, and a tiny man with a bald head peered round the wing of his armchair. "Elwyn, this is Suzy."

The man held out his hand and Suzanne shook it,

wincing at the introduction. Suzy! That had been the name of Aunt Margery's awful cat.

"You can bring your suitcase upstairs right now and get it unpacked out of the way. Then come down as soon as you're done and have your tea." Mrs Jones marched up ahead and opened a door at the end of the narrow landing. "This will be your room."

Tiny, it was dominated by a very high brass bed with knobs that rattled; a bentwood chair was crammed between the foot of the bed and the window, and a small chest of drawers stood opposite it under a spotted mirror hanging from a nail. It was getting too dark to see much out of the window.

There was no space for a wardrobe so Suzanne hung her clothes from the two hooks behind the door. The books at the bottom of her case presented a problem: if she stacked them on the foot-square bedside table there would be room for nothing else, while standing them in a row on the chest of drawers would mean having to keep her hairbrush and comb in the top drawer with her stockings and knickers. Settling on the latter she pushed the empty case under the bed, trying not to think. Intent on keeping her mind numb.

"Here you are, then. You must have brought a lot of stuff in that suitcase, to take so long to unpack it. Sit down. That will be your chair while you're here. Rhiannon will be here in a minute." Mrs Evans left her sitting alone at the table, while she continued banging saucepans in the back kitchen.

Much to Suzanne's surprise, Rhiannon proved to be female. Tall, with a mass of frizzy red hair, she smiled, said, "Hallo," and proceeded to talk with her parents in

35

Welsh. From then on, apart from when someone was speaking directly to her, Suzanne never heard English spoken in that house again.

'Tea' consisted of watery soup with lumps in, bread and butter, cheese and pickles, and a piece of hard chocolate cake with a cup of strong tea. She sat silent, unable to understand the unceasing conversation between the two women, until Mrs Evans offered her another cup of tea, which she refused. She hadn't been able to finish the first one, so bitter with its meagre splash of milk.

The meal ended when Mrs Evans stood up and carried her dirty plates into the back kitchen. Rhiannon did the same, followed by her father. Suzanne wriggled out of her chair which was wedged into a corner and collected up her own dishes, which earned her a nod of approval. Without a word, Mrs Evans put a dish towel into her hands and proceeded to wash up while Rhiannon stood by, impatiently, waiting to put away. Mr Evans returned to his newspaper.

Later, when they were all seated in the front kitchen again, Rhiannon asked, "Who was you billeted with before comin' here?"

"With Lady Matherson at Clwyd Hall."

"Oh ho! All posh then! Well you won't find any servants waitin' on you hand and foot round here, will she, Mam?"

This caused her Mam's face to stretch into a rare smile.

"We weren't waited on at all," Suzanne corrected her, politely. "We had to clean our own shoes and make our own beds."

"I should think so too! Can't come here scroungin' off people and expectin' somethin' for nothin'."

"I thought you were paid billeting money." The child frowned, upset by the older girl's tone.

"Now you listen here, young lady," Mrs Evans cut in, "we'll have none of your back-answers, thank you very much. The billetin' money isn't a half what you cost in food alone. And any road, isn't it time you went up to your bed?"

Though it was only seven o'clock, Suzanne thought it a good excuse to get out of the room. She muttered "Yes. Goodnight."

No one responded as she groped her way upstairs alone in the dark. If only she could have had Meggie to talk to . . .

The room was freezing: it was necessary to spread her overcoat on the bed for extra warmth.

She cried herself to sleep.

But crying had always been taboo at home. A stiff upper lip meant you were tough, self-controlled, and earned praise from Mummy and Daddy. Tears, she had always been told, only proved you were weak, soft in the head. Gormless. Thereafter, Suzanne often chose to go to bed early, to read. "There's nothing else to do and no one to speak to," she told Meggie at school. "It's absolutely horrible."

"My billet isn't too bad but I wish you could have been with me instead of Marigold. All she ever wants to do is mess about with her stamp album."

"I wonder if she'd swap billets with me?"

"Would she want to? What will you tell her when she asks what your place is like?"

Suzanne laughed. "Lies, or she would never go. Anyway, we'd have to get permission." And she knew there'd be no chance of that. "It wouldn't really be so bad, I suppose, if only they'd speak English. I feel so . . . out of it. Oh well, let's hope things improve in the house as we get to know each other better."

Things didn't improve. Till the day she died, Suzanne would remember Friday the 30th of January 1942, as the worst day of her life. It was her twelfth birthday and for a start no cards had arrived the previous day, for her to open before leaving for school. It crossed her mind that Mrs Evans might have hidden them, meaning to put them on the breakfast table with their own card. Teeth and hair had minimal brushing; she raced downstairs, eyes darting to her place at table . . . but there was no post there. Unlikely as it seemed, she presumed Mrs Evans was having a leg-pull so she waited, straight-faced, eating the lumpy porridge and spreading margarine and jam on dry doorsteps of bread. She dawdled, but nothing happened.

"You'd better hurry up or you'll be late," her landlady called from the back kitchen. "And don't be late for dinner, I'm goin' out this afternoon."

School beret and coat on, and clutching the brown paper carrier bag of school books, Suzanne popped her head into the back kitchen. "I'll be off then. 'Bye." She waited.

"Ta-ra." Mrs Evans didn't look up from the sink.

Suzanne coughed. "Er . . . have you got anything for me?"

"Eh? You still here? What you talkin' about?" It was quite obvious she had no idea of the importance of the date.

The evacuee's heart sank. "Nothing. 'Bye." Never mind, there'd be plenty of post when she came back for lunch. Correction, dinner.

But there wasn't. Not one card or letter, let alone a parcel. And it was the same at school: Meggie might have remembered if she hadn't been absent with a cold, but no one else knew it was her birthday and one simply couldn't go round telling people, it would look as though she was asking for presents.

The house was empty when she got back to Llewellyn's Lane that evening. There were no cards or parcels waiting, but still she dared to hope that something would materialise when the Evanses returned.

They had had a successful visit to Elwyn's sister in St Asaph and tea was delayed while Rhiannon was told all about it when she came in from work. In Welsh.

It was the first time that Suzanne had received no card or present, no good wishes on her birthday. She had never felt so lonely, lost and unloved.

Sleep was impossible that night in her trough of misery and self-pity. Trying to distract her mind she immersed herself once more in *Exmoor Lass*, her favorite pony book. It was a lovely story with especially good pen and ink illustrations which she liked to copy. Twice she closed the book and turned out the light, but still sleep wouldn't come; so twice she sat up again, school cardigan on over her nightie to fend off the cold in the icy room.

Suddenly the door was flung open and Mrs Evans stormed in, furious. "Do you know what the time is? It's gone 'leven o'clock and here you are still readin' an' burnin' my electricity."

"You never told me I wasn't to . . ."

"Tell you! Haven' you got any sense? You should know better! Well, we'll make sure it doesn' happen again." She grabbed the chair, stood it under the light and using Suzanne's towel to avoid burning her fingers she twisted the bulb from its socket. "There. That'll remove temptation, won't it?"

Now, in retrospect, Suzanne reckoned that was the day she grew up. She had been too angry that night to cry, but lying in the darkness, boiling with rage, a vague realisation developed that she was totally alone: no one in her life gave any indication that they cared a jot about her, whether or not she was happy, healthy, or even existed. She was on her own.

Though she was not aware of it at the time, that day had marked the beginning of her independence – mentally, physically and emotionally; an independence she might have hoped, subconsciously, to be temporary, just to help her survive till she returned to her loving family. Till life regained its pre-war normality.

Unfortunately that 'normality' was a long time coming; she would have to extend her independence a little longer.

It was not too difficult.

Joseph Gallienne had run a taxi service in Guernsey until the Germans overran the island and commandeered all the cars and petrol supplies. However, having been born with the stubbornness of the traditional Guernsey Donkey, far from going out of business, he acquired a number of horses and ponies, and a weird collection of antique traps, gigs, broughams and landaus and carried on as near normal as possible. Unfortunately, apart from weddings and funerals, trade was not brisk and by the time the Germans were finally persuaded to depart the animals had eaten all his capital leaving nothing with which to buy new motorised taxis. Nor was he able to liquidate his antique assets. Undaunted, he put up a sign on his gate announcing *Gallienne's Riding Stables. Horses for hire. Lessons charged by the hour. Quiet ponies for beginners.*

Sue was thrilled when her father took her to the stables in the Axce Lanes, a short cycle ride from home, and introduced her to his old schoolfriend, Joe. The latter agreed he had far more work to do than he could handle and was pleased to offer her a job as part-time stable hand, on a month's trial. A month that stretched indefinitely. Joe and Mrs Joe liked Sue, she liked them and the job, and she loved all the horses and ponies. Sarah had no need to call her in the mornings: Sue was at the stables by six every morning, mucking out before changing for school. Likewise she worked in the evenings, and for much longer on Saturdays and Sundays. A happy and satisfying arrangement all round.

Meanwhile, there were lots of new girls at school, as well as those who had been evacuated or joined the school in Wales during the war. Sue maintained friendships with the latter and made some new friends amongst the former, but no one quite replaced Meggie. She missed her a lot . . .

She would never forget the day when, returning for the summer term in 1943 after a miserably boring Easter listening to Gran and Auntie's endless grumbles and criticisms of everyone with whom they came in contact, she met Meggie on the train from Chester to Denbigh.

"Had a good time?" Meggie asked, happily.

"Super!" Suzanne lied, valiantly. "How about you?"

"Lovely. Mummy and Daddy have moved to a nice big

house. There's a gazebo in the garden where we all played when it was raining."

All! "You mean you and your little sister?"

"And the boys next door. In fact there was a whole gang of us about the same age. I'll be leaving at the end of this term to go to their school with them."

Suzanne was dumbfounded. When she found her breath again she said, "Going! You won't be coming back?"

Meggie shook her head. "I'll miss you, but it will be nice to live with my parents again. And I'll be with a super crowd of friends."

Already depressed at the prospect of returning to Llewellyn's Lane, the news could have reduced the old Suzanne to tears. Not any more. Stiff upper lip, girl! She swallowed, smiled and said, "I'm so pleased for you, Meggie. Though I will miss you, too." A massive understatement.

However, she was met at the station by one good bit of news: "You are not going back to the Evanses, Suzanne. They found you didn't fit in very well," Miss Watson told her. "I don't know what you've been up to but you must try not to be difficult."

"The only trouble was I couldn't speak Welsh . . ."

"That's not the impression Mrs Evans gave the billeting officer. And we don't want to hear excuses, just an assurance that you'll try to behave better in future."

The unfairness of it! The girl boiled. There were so many angry answers waiting to erupt that in the end she was speechless. Emerging into Station Road she eventually asked, "Where am I to go now?"

"To the hostel, until another place can be found for you."

Anything had to be better than the Evanses, especially if there were other girls for company; the only pity was she had not had a chance to tell those Evanses how horrible, bad-mannered and unkind they were.

Suzanne had a quick, furious temper but she had never been able to maintain it for more than a few minutes, even when she felt it necessary to make a stand. Long before she reached the hostel her anger had evaporated.

And within a few days she was thoroughly enjoying herself. When Kathy Welbeck moved in a week later, the matron forgot to ask her for her ration book. So five of them pooled their pocket money and used the week's coupons to buy Spam, bread and other goodies for a midnight feast. Lacking plates and cutlery, they dug the Spam out of the tin with knitting-needles, making a dreadful, sticky mess, while smothering hysterical giggles in their pillows. All a great improvement on Llewellyn's Lane.

Ordinary friends, in general, were fun, but of course nothing quite made up for the loss of one's best friend, like Meggie.

Watching the demonstrative affection between her parents, Sue was reminded of David: dear, darling David. If only he was here, with her. If only she had someone to confide in, share secrets with, enjoy similar interests. Mummy and Daddy were keen for her to play tennis, which she had done with enthusiasm in Wales. But she saw the disappointment on their faces when she attempted to demonstate her skills! They made no effort to conceal their opinion that she'd never play a 'decent' game. Yet partnering David, had been such fun. They had won countless friendlies together.

The States of Guernsey, the island parliament, well aware that commerce and industry in the island had ground to a halt during the Occupation and that few islanders had the financial capital to re-start, decided that past and prospective businessmen should apply for States' grants: offices must be bought or rented, plus furniture and equipment, rolling stock for hauliers and buses for public transport. Many greenhouses had become derelict, or were destroyed during the war for firewood. Hotels had been commandeered by the Germans for administration offices.

Greg immediately applied for money to repair Les Marettes greenhouses, the heating boilers and piping, and cash would be needed for sterilising and feeding the soil before next season's tomato seedlings were planted. The application was granted shortly after Greg's brother, Andrew and his wife Maureen returned from Scotland where they had spent the war years. They stayed at Les Marettes with Alice, his mother, because their bungalow had been gutted by the Organisation Todt slave workers who had squatted there. Those poor devils who survived the starvation and ill-treatment had been returned to their own countries, France, Russia and Poland mostly, leaving the concrete shell without windows, doors or frames. Floorboards had been ripped up and ceilings torn down as firewood; who could blame them as they shivered in their rags? Except Andrew.

"Why the devil didn't you put padlocks on to keep them out?" he stormed at Greg, having been told several times that his brother had done so, and been obliged to replace them twice before finally giving up and rescuing and storing all the contents before the squatters moved in.

When Greg told him that the States had notified him that a grant had been made available to restart the business, Andrew breathed a sigh of relief and said, "Thank goodness. I'll get hold of Mr Rabey straight away to repair our bungalow."

"But . . . I thought I'd explained; the money is for the vinery. For repairing the greenhouses and starting us off next season."

"Fine," Andrew smiled. "We'll use what's left over when our place is finished."

"No! If you can't afford to fix the bungalow yourself, now, then you'll have to remain at Les Marettes with Ma till you can do it out of income." Greg was adamant.

So was Andrew. "Look here, young Gregory. I am the elder and if I say that my home needs are more important, then so be it. Where is the money? How do I get hold of it?"

Greg had lost several stones in weight during the Occupation, living on starvation rations, while his brother had become quite stout, but he still towered over Andrew by several inches. He had already regained some weight, though his face remained gaunt and lined. Gazing down with tired eyes at the older man, he shook his head. "This grant is purely for the business – to use it for anything else would be breaking the law."

"Rubbish. Anyway, at least half the money is mine by right."

Greg frowned. "I don't follow your reasoning. You had an excellent, well-paid job throughout the war, along with free housing. Surely you must have saved enough at least to make a start on your place?"

"What I may or may not have in the way of assets is none of your business. But I'm warning you—"

"And I'm warning you," Greg cut in. "If you attempt to use any of this grant for anything but our tomato business, I shall report you to the authorities," and he turned away to continue his list of necessary repairs.

Andrew's colour went from pink to purple, then he stamped out of the office slamming the door, viciously.

"What was all that about?" Sue had just cycled up the drive to visit her grandmother.

Greg thought a moment, then decided to confide in her as an adult.

Sue listened to yet another tale of family discord and was puzzled. What was the matter with everybody? It was never like this before the war . . . was it?

The following weekend, Aunt Aline and Grandma asked her out to Val du Douit for lunch; having invited her to spend some of the school holidays with them in England during the war, they wanted to maintain the affinity they felt they had established with her. After all, had they not played an important part in her upbringing, in the absence of her parents?

They would have been amazed to learn Sue's thoughts on that 'affinity'. True, the fact that members of her family were within reach had relieved the emotional isolation she had felt in Denbigh; to be able to talk about 'going to spend Christmas with family' at school, and receive post and pocket-money from them, helped. But the fact was that during those holidays her aunt and grandparents seemed almost too involved with their own problems to notice her. Grandpa was never very well and his health was a constant topic of conversation, punctuated by endless complaints about their landlords – who always seemed to Sue to be quite charming – the neighbours and other more distant family members. Listening to their grumbles was a source of constant irritation to the girl. And worst of all was when they were entertaining friends and Aunt Aline would put on a demonstration of cloying affection for her, silently demanding that Sue show the audience how much she loved her aunt. She had responded as required, for the sake of politeness and peace, but with her fingers crossed behind her back. Fortunately, her rapid maturing brought understanding and acceptance; it became easier to see how devastating their situation was at their age: the thought of the home they had spent their lives building being overrun by Nazis, and Grandpa's herd of pedigree Guernsey cows probably being slaughtered to feed them. So that gradually, over the five years, she had learned to excuse them, especially after Grandpa died. And now, not yet sixteen years old, she had a tolerant affection for them, and made the double bus journey out to St Saviour's quite happily.

Sue loved the old pink granite farmhouse and the rambling garden, remembering how it all used to be when she was a child: the horses nuzzling her hair with velvet noses, the smell of saddle-soap in the stables. She loved the walk from the bus which took her past the fields where, for generations, the Ozanne family had held hay picnics. The fact that the fields were full of weeds went unnoticed, but she grimaced at the monstrous concrete gun-emplacements and towers the Germans had had erected by their Todt slave-workers, to defend the prized, sole piece of British territory they had 'won'.

"Hallo, here you are. We expected you earlier." Marie Ozanne greeted her granddaughter in the kitchen.

"I just walked down past the top fields. It's lovely up there."

"Hmm. Don't tell me you've inherited your mother's habit of daydreaming," Aline remarked as she joined them. "It was her way of dodging the chores," she added with a forced laugh.

Sue gritted her teeth and changed the subject. "What's for lunch?"

"Freddie Batiste brought us some mackerel, luckily. The meat ration this week was such a pathetic little square. Bah! I could hardly be bothered to cook it." Marie opened an oven door and peered inside. "They're nearly done."

"I was saying to Grandma, we ought to change butchers. I don't think we're getting our proper share," Aline said.

A constant stream of criticism followed the baked mackerel and vegetable dishes into the dining room, and across the table Aline prompted her mother every time Marie appeared to run out of victims. Sue was convinced the pair of them were getting worse. Over coffee, they started on Uncle John and 'that baggage', then Uncle William and his family were slated.

Sue tried hard not to react but when, having demolished all other members of the family plus a few 'friends', they attempted to coerce her into agreeing that her parents had had no right to steal the clothes they left in the wardrobes at Val du Douit when they evacuated, her good resolutions snapped. "That's enough," she said sternly. "I love coming up to see you, but if you're going to spend the time accusing my parents, and all the family, of all sorts of wickedness, then I'm not coming any more."

"Well!" Marie huffed.

"Fancy speaking to your grandmother like that!" Aline looked pained. "We only feel you ought to know the truth of the matter."

"As you see it. Not as anyone else does!"

The inevitable argument finally ended with Aline saying "Well really. After all we did for you throughout the war," and Marie refusing to speak to her at all.

Sue was aware that she was the only person in the world that Aline cared a fig about, other than herself, and before leaving was able to wring out of her aunt a reluctant promise not to criticise any of the family, when and if she visited them again.

Wind tore across the top fields as Sue climbed the hill back to the bus stop, and clouds threatened a drenching, all matching her mood. Naturally gregarious, she enjoyed people and was quick to forgive and forget, as she had done with Auntie and Gran during the war. And would again. After all, they had been bricks when she became ill from living in that awful billet . . .

She shuddered at the memory.

There were not many people Suzanne avoided except Melanie. Not that she actively disliked her, but the tall, gangly girl had no go: she was limp and insipid, her only conversation a continuous attempt to make people laugh by telling dirty jokes learned from her older brother. So Suzanne was not amused to learn she was to be billeted with the girl. Mrs Hughes was very short, very fat and very proud of her little semi-detached. The front parlour, which was never used except to impress a teacher making a once-per-term inspection, was immaculate with its pristine three-piece suite, neat half-moon hearth rug and three china ducks flying across one wall in perfect formation. The lino shone in the hallway and stairs, leading to the three bedrooms and the gleaming bathroom . . . well, as Mrs Hughes proudly boasted to her neighbours, she only went on payin' the extra two shillings and sixpence on the rent for a bath after her husband died, for the evacuees to use. She couldn't fit into it herself.

However, the evacuees soon discovered that the rooms at the back of the house were not so clean. Anything but: the long-eared cocker spaniel with matted, flea-ridden coat saw to that. Daily he traipsed in from the back garden covered in mud which was mixed into a paste of long, black dog-hairs and grease from Mrs Hughes's frying pan. Children are not normally quick to notice such things, so it was not until the incident of the porridge oats that they realised just how disgusting the floor was. Reaching up one day to put her saucepan on a shelf, the lady's vast stomach dislodged a bag of oats from the drainboard, which burst as it hit the floor. The girls watched in disbelief as, having swept the oats up into her dustpan, Mrs Hughes tipped the lot into a used paper bag and put it away in the food cupboard.

Alone in their room, Suzanne and Melanie speculated on what possible use the woman could have for the oats. They discovered next morning at breakfast.

"Ugh!" Melanie exclaimed. "What's happened to the porridge?"

"Eh? What are you fussin' about?"

"It's full of grit and dog-hairs!"

"Pah! It won't hurt you."

"I'd rather have toast, please."

"Not until you finish that porridge!" Under a thatch of white hair the incongruous black eyebrows met in a terrifying frown. "There'll be no wastin' of food in this house."

She sounded so fierce and angry that both girls reluctantly stuck their spoons into the grey mush. The grit crunched in their teeth, and pulling the long hairs out of their throats made them retch. They left as much as they dared on their plates.

"Shall we tell Miss Watson?" Melanie asked on the way to school.

"I think we should," Suzanne said. "But . . . suppose she sends the billeting officer down to tell Fatty not to give us any more dirty food? She'll be flaming mad and take it out on us."

"Mmm. P'raps we'd better leave it, this time. I suppose it could have been worse: the dog might not have been house-trained." Melanie dissolved into giggles.

The bus to Town arrived at last and Sue climbed aboard, just as the rain was starting.

Fatty Hughes had decided to economise on laundry, Sue recalled, and when the girls had returned home from school one day they found they were to sleep in the best bedroom . . . sharing Fatty's double bed.

The two had an argument on the first night, hissing at each other in the bathroom against the dubious honour of sleeping in the middle. "I bagsy the outside," Melanie demanded.

"Not likely!" Suzanne retorted. "I'm not sleeping next to her."

But it was Fatty herself who made the decision. "I'm not havin' that Melanie next to me in bed," she confided, removing her teeth and dropping them into a glass of water on the dressing table, to sink through a sea of decaying food crumbs. "She's always complainin'. I don't like her. She's not nice like you."

Suzanne attempted a feeble smile at the unwanted accolade.

The chocolate cake incident brought Melanie's final downfall. One evening at the end of their meal, Fatty got out the rusty, round cake tin and cut three wedges of cake, conveying each to their respective plates with fat sticky fingers which she licked clean after each serving.

Suzanne took a large bite and nearly gagged – it tasted revolting.

Melanie, meanwhile, was fumbling with her portion over her plate, removing a layer from the base.

"What you doin', then?" Fatty glared at the girl.

"Er . . . nothing." Melanie picked up the cake and nibbled a little from the top.

Suzanne glanced up at the proud cook, at Melanie and then, for the first time, at the underneath of her piece . . . at the colourful blue, green and yellow whiskers growing there. Ugh!

"Yes you are. Why are you cuttin' it like that?"

Melanie, red in the face, was nearly in tears. "Because it's gone mouldy," she muttered.

"Mouldy!" The three chins which concealed the collar of Fatty's blouse, quivered. "Rubbish! My cakes don't go mouldy. That's good food, that, all made fresh last week before I went to Bodfari." Both girls knew she visited her cousin in Bodfari three weeks ago. Fatty planted her vast bosom into the remaining slices on the bread and butter plate as she leaned across to grab the cake from Melanie's plate and cram it, whole, into her own mouth.

In the instant that Fatty's attention was diverted, Suzanne grabbed her cake and held it in her hand inside her skirt pocket. "Will you excuse me, please? I need to go to the bathroom." And without waiting for an answer she dashed upstairs to flush the offending object down the lavatory, waiting to check that every crumb had disappeared before going back to the table.

Fatty Hughes was still ranting. "Why can't you eat up the good food I give you like Suzy does? Look, she's finished all of hers."

The price of popularity was to be kept at Fatty's house as 'favourite' while Melanie was removed to the hostel.

Arriving at the town terminus, Sue was relieved to see the Bordeaux bus had not yet left. Dashing through the rain she leapt up the steps as the engine rumbled into life, and took a rear seat where she could be alone with her thoughts.

A week or so after Melanie left, Fatty had gone to the doctor. She had been scratching a great deal, lately, particularly at the sores between her fingers. "Can't remember the name of the trouble what he says I got, but he gave me some ointment," the landlady told Suzanne over tea. "He says it has to be rubbed all over my body every night," adding, "O' course I can't do it all, I'm too big to reach. So you'll have to help me."

The thirteen-year-old choked into her teacup.

Fatty undressed in front of the fire while Suzanne cleared the table. Returning from the scullery she tried not to show any reaction to the vast acreage of mottled, pimply flesh; she had never seen a naked grown-up before and this was a pretty grotesque introduction.

"Here," the woman said, handing over a flat tin of pungent-smelling paste, "You do my back and I'll manage my front."

Thanking heaven for small mercies, the girl commenced pasting, her brain busy counting how many nights were left of the school term before she could escape to her grandparents for Christmas.

Suzanne knew she would be grateful for the rest of her life, for the way Auntie and Gran had cared for her. Looking back she could only guess at how horrified they must have been on her arrival.

Chapter Three

Escape Plans

Sue rubbed the condensation off the bus window and screwed up her eyes, trying to see the islands of Herm and Jethou across the Little Russel. They were just vague shadows through the thin blanket of rain. Even so, they were beautiful; the whole of Guernsey and its surrounding rocks and islets were beautiful, a glorious place to claim as home. A paradise, except . . . was it home any longer?

Surely the animosity, the misunderstandings between Gran and Auntie and her parents could soon be resolved: despite her threat this afternoon, it would be awful not to see her grandmother and aunt, simply to keep the peace with her parents.

"What in Heaven's name is the matter with you?" Auntie had demanded on the station platform when she sat heavily onto her suitcase to wait for the dizziness to wear off.

"Just that I've been sitting in the train for a long time, I suppose."

"You're very skinny," Gran remarked later at table. "Aren't you eating properly in Denbigh?"

"The food isn't very nice at Mrs Hughes's."

Marie Ozanne studied the blue circles round her granddaughter's eyes, the thin wrists protruding from dirty cuffs. "Aline, you'd better take her to Dr Phillips tomorrow. Look at her hair – it's a mess. Looks as though it's been chewed by mice."

"I think I've got nits, again. Mrs Williams says I haven't when she checks every week, but I'm sure they're there."

Marie was appalled. "And why are you scratching your hands all the time?"

"They keep itching."

Dr Phillips looked rather like a bloodhound with his long, droopy chin and perpetually sad expression. "There is a new and quite effective treatment for head-lice. You can buy it from your chemist," he commented after fastidiously parting Suzanne's hair with a wooden spatula which he hastily dropped into a sterile bin before pulling down her lower eyelids adding, "and she is very anaemic, too." Then he picked up her hands and held them under his desk lamp, peering at them through a magnifying glass. "Hm. This will be the worst problem."

"What is it?" Aline asked. "Surely not eczema?"

"No. Scabies."

Aline nearly fainted. She had heard of it before, a dreadful type of microscopic bug like a crab which burrowed in channels under the skin and was found only in the unwashed classes. "You must be mistaken," she shuddered. "That is impossible!"

The bloodhound raised his head, casting a watery eye over the woman who dared to question his diagnosis. He didn't utter a word; his expression silenced her. Sitting back in his chair he made notes on a pad, then smiled at Suzanne . . . which was not a particularly encouraging sight. "Well, young lady, you will have to take Parrish's Food three times a day for your anaemia. The scabies will be more difficult." He turned to Aline. "She must bath every day in permanganate of potash and then every inch of skin must be covered with sulphur ointment. And of course, her clothes and bedlinen must be changed and washed every day."

When Aline had got her breath back she asked in a strangled voice, "For how long?"

The heavy jowls shook despondently. "It varies. But in Suzanne's case it shouldn't take more than six weeks."

Six weeks of non-stop laundry! Aline's knees felt weak.

Six weeks! Suzanne's first thought was that she wouldn't be returning to school, or to Fatty, till well into the next term: the best bit of news she'd had in ages! However, at nearly fourteen she was well aware of the dreadful nuisance this must be to her aunt and grandmother. She felt guilty and embarrassed about it and said so when they got back to the flat.

Her grandmother's response had been immediate: she put both arms round the girl, who was already a head taller than herself, and said, "Don't you worry yourself about it. Your aunt and I are going to look after you and see you thoroughly fit before you go back. It's not just the scabies, either. You are completely run down and I intend to find out why."

The first clue came when Aline started applying the

ointment. That's funny," Suzanne remarked. "It's exactly the same stuff that Fatty Hughes has."

"Are you sure?" Aline exchanged glances with her mother.

"I should be!" and she went on to explain how she coated her billetor with it every night.

Aline was kneeling on the floor at the time. She rocked back on her heels, mouth hanging open, eyes wide in horror.

Marie gasped. "What did you say? Well!" Her face turned puce. "What in the devil is your headmistress playing at?"

"She doesn't know."

"Why not? Didn't you report it straight away?"

"No," Suzanne shook her head.

Marie opened and shut her mouth twice before allowing herself to reply. "You didn't know that the woman had no right asking you to do such a thing? Weren't you disgusted?"

Her throat tight, the girl simply nodded.

Marie's eyes narrowed. "Were you frightened of her?"

Suzanne nodded again.

"Didn't the teachers ever inspect your billet?"

"Yes. But not when I was putting the ointment on."

Marie's shoulders heaved with anger. "And what else did this woman get up to?"

"Wait till she's back in bed," Aline reached out a steadying hand as her niece swayed. "She's not fit to be up."

By the time Marie and Aline had heard about the porridge oats, mouldy cake and the two girls sharing the billetor's bed, Aline's fountain pen was already busy drafting a fierce letter of condemnation to the head-mistress.

"No wonder the woman never told you you had head-lice," Marie observed. "She knew you had caught them from her. Like the scabies. Thank heavens your mother doesn't know. She'd have fifty fits."

Mummy. Suzanne had closed her eyes and tried to visualise her mother. But despite the irregular, twenty-five word Red Cross messages which arrived, months apart, the three and a half years of separation had dulled the mental image of her parents. If only she had had a photograph to remind her. Of course none of this would have happened if Mummy had got away in time before the Germans landed; no head-lice, no scabies . . . no Fatty Hughes for that matter. Mummy would have made a home and been there when she got home each day from school . . .

Like now? No, surely it would never have become like now! All the interminable family rows, no one seeing anyone else's point of view. Mum constantly complaining and criticising Gran and Auntie. And Gran and Auntie going on about Mum whenever she visited them.

They had been so kind and protective, after the Fatty Williams affair, cooking up tasty meals to tempt her appetite, playing rummy to entertain her, sharing her favorite wireless programmes. They never complained about the extra work, their self-righteous anger given plenty of targets amongst school authorities, billeting officers and billetors, quite apart from Hitler and the Nazis.

"You getting out here, young miss?" the bus driver called down the aisle.

Sue peered out into the darkness. "Gosh, yes! I didn't realise where we were. Seems to have stopped raining." She paid her fare and hurried home down the dark lane.

"Some boy was on the telephone for you," Sarah told her as she took off her mac.

"That'll be John." He of the black, wavy hair, soft, smiling lips and madly attractive blue eyes.

"John who?"

"Harper."

"Where from? What does his father do?"

"They have a pub in town."

"You don't mean Busty Harper from the Kings Arms?"

"That's right. I'll phone him back before supper."

Later, when Richard had fallen asleep and Sue was sitting at the supper table with her parents, Sarah asked, "What did that Harper boy want?"

"For me to go to the pictures with him next week," Sue replied.

"I presume you said no?"

"No. I said yes."

"Then you'd better phone him again and tell him you can't."

Sue sighed, very loudly. "Why ever not?"

"The Harpers are not the sort of people we mix with." Sarah sounded quite adamant. "Anyone want another helping of pudding?"

"Why on earth not? John is very nice. He's a prefect at college," she added for good measure.

"Nevertheless he is not from the sort of family your father and I want you mixing with. Pass your plate."

Sue glanced at her father, who remained silent. "That's

old-fashioned rubbish: went out with the ark. People don't think like that any more."

It was Sarah's turn to look at Greg for support, but none was forthcoming. She pursed her lips. "Well we do!"

"That's only because you were stuck here all through the war, out of touch. You don't realise how society has changed."

Greg felt obliged to jump in before Sarah exploded. "I don't think it has changed all that much. There has always been a social ladder throughout history; wars have never altered that."

"This last one did. Everyone in Britain worked and fought together. They became close pals with everyone else, rich and poor alike."

Sarah was pleased, in a way, that Sue's thinking had developed sufficiently to make such observations; on the other hand, she did not approve of precocious children arguing with their parents. "That may have been so in a time of crisis. Now the war is over and we must return to normal as soon as possible. Now, let's hear no more about it. Just telephone the boy and tell him you'd forgotten you had already made arrangements to do something else."

"But that's not true!"

"No, I know. I only suggested it so he wouldn't be offended."

Sue was furious, not that she was much interested in John Harper though he did give her the opportunity to get 'in' with his crowd. No, what really annoyed her was having her life, her decisions, interfered with. She glared at her mother. "What you are actually asking me to do is tell a lie to suit your social aspirations!"

Even Greg was shocked, so before Sarah got her breath back he ordered Sue to her room.

She marched out of the dining room carrying her plate of shepherd's pie and slammed the door behind her.

The problem of Suzanne was discussed between rubbers over the bridge table with the Martels, at badminton with George and Gelly, Greg's and Sarah's old school friends, and with John Ozanne, Sarah's brother, and Edna. Nothing was said to Marie and Aline – Sarah could imagine her sister saying "Really! Of course we had no trouble with her at all. Such a sweet, co-operative child. Would you like me to have a word with her for you?" She could do without that! Nevertheless, with all the observations and advice, plus pressure from Greg, Sarah was forced to concede that her daughter was understandably resentful of sudden parental authority. "You must give the girl more rein," they all said.

So Sarah said nothing more about the Harper boy, and for the sake of peace Sue cancelled her date with him. Lots of parties and dances were to be held to celebrate the first Christmas since Liberation, and Sarah took Sue into town to buy her first long dress. "We want you to join us at as many functions as you want, dear," she announced.

Sue was duly excited. She took Richard to the shops at St Sampson's to buy presents for their parents and kept him amused making decorations for the Christmas tree.

Marie and Aline accepted Sarah's invitation to Christmas lunch but elected to spend that evening at home. Which enabled Sarah to invite John and Edna to come to supper that night.

"I wonder what the Laurences are doing for Christmas?"

Greg said one day at breakfast. Colonel and Mrs Laurence had been deported to an internment camp in Germany during the war where the Colonel had died. Greg and Sarah had offered to look after their younger daughter Polly, sadly born disabled, and her black nursemaid, Belle, till the end of the war, a hugely successful arrangement all round.

"Nothing much, I imagine. They seldom go out. Let's ask them," Sarah suggested.

"Aren't they related to us, somehow?" Sue asked.

"Yes. Paul Laurence married your aunt, Ethel."

"You mean your sister in New Zealand?"

"That's right."

"I remember playing with Polly before the war. She was sweet, but I was scared stiff of Belle. There were other brothers and sisters, weren't there? Wasn't the eldest one a nancy boy? What's happened to him?"

Sarah studiously avoided catching Greg's eye. Their daughter was even more worldly-wise than they'd reckoned. "Aubry was killed during the war," she said with a straight face. "And Piers and Victoria live in London, I believe."

"Yes. I remember Auntie Aline saying they both 'had bad blood'. Her lovely, old-fashioned way of saying they were rotters. Grandma Alice will be with us, won't she?"

"Of course. And Uncle Andrew and Aunt Maureen."

"And Sybil?" Sue asked hopefully. She had always hero-worshipped her beautiful, blonde cousin.

"I doubt it. You know she married that brigadier she was driving for during the war? They have a vast mansion in Wiltshire and a flat in London. Maureen says she is committed to entertaining his family over there."

"What a shame. I'd so love to see her again."

"You will, but not this Christmas thank goodness," Greg laughed. "Your mother has twelve to cook for on the day without them."

Christmas was a huge success, for everyone, or so it seemed. Marie Ozanne was delighted to announce the sale of Val du Douit to some company represented by an advocate, unaware that the surprisingly happy smiles they had encountered from John, denoted the fact that he and Edna owned the said company. A fact which would have ruined her Christmas, had she known.

Sarah had never been noted for her cooking: pre-war, her enthusiasm for sport had precluded any interest in culinary skills and the past five years of desperately trying to concoct meals from seaweed and horse carrots, cooked over pieces of timber burnt in the sitting room fireplace, had done little to improve matters. However, everyone congratulated her on producing a splendid Christmas dinner, especially the pudding. She lacked the courage to admit that her friend, Gelly, had made it and given it to her as a present.

Greg was happy with the repairs to the greenhouses, and had bought an agency for special pots for tomato plants. Andrew considered it a waste of good money, but realising that Greg did an immense amount more physical work than himself in their greenhouses, had wisely refrained from pressing the point.

Richard was very excited with his second-hand Meccano set and all the books from Santa Claus, and Sue gave him a wooden garage with cars in. Her mother was so pleased with her present of glass bowl and matching sundae dishes, that she insisted on washing them out and using them for lunch. Greg thanked her very much for the book of rude limericks, although some of them raised his eyebrows.

Quite apart from the lovely evening dress, her parents gave Sue a new bike to replace the rattly and rusty old James. But her best present came at teatime. The family was in the sitting room, balancing cups and saucers on the arms of their chairs and plates of Christmas cake on their knees, when the telephone rang in the hall.

Sue hurried out to answer and nearly wept with excitement as David Morgan's voice wished her happy Christmas.

"David! Where are you?"

"Denbigh. Where did you expect?"

"You sound so close."

"I wish I was."

"Same here. When *are* we going to see each other? It's been five months . . ."

"Well, it'll be a bit longer yet. But I think I might be able to come to Guernsey in the summer."

"Ooh! Super!"

They talked about their respective Christmases and presents, mutual friends, and how much they missed each other. Then blew kisses goodbye.

"Who was it?" Sarah wanted to know.

"David," was the gleeful reply.

"David! You don't mean the Welsh boy, phoning all the way from North Wales?"

"Yes!" Sue hugged herself with happiness. "Wasn't that the most perfect present?"

Sarah raised her eyes to Heaven and nearly said, "A shocking waste of money," but managed to stop herself in time. Better not upset Sue unnecessarily.

Gradually as the weeks and months passed, more and more time elapsed between the disagreements and arguments at Les Mouettes. Greg and Sarah were both relieved but Sue, pondering on their relationship, felt this was purely because she gave in to her parents demands all the time. She did it partly to earn their approval, something so obviously lacking from the moment of reunion. She wanted to love them, like she loved David, and for them to love her in return. But her obedience was also to stop Mum's perpetual nagging. And when she elected to disobey, she invented magnificent fairy stories, especially to cover her dates with various boyfriends, even stopping her bike on the way home to run up and down a field, muddying her legs and developing a hot, sweaty look as though she had been playing hockey. Not that she was particularly keen on any of the boys: David was her real boyfriend.

They had met playing football in a cul-de-sac on a housing estate near the railway. At least he was playing with some boys including the one who lived next door to Fatty Hughes, Brian. Piles of coats marked the goalposts, a source of animated arguments about the score, frequent changes of end being demanded as the gradient definitely favoured those playing towards the coats at the bottom of the road.

Suzanne was feeling somewhat adrift, now that Meggie

had left Denbigh to live with her parents in the south of England; plus the fact that, after four months of a sort of family life with her aunt and grandmother, she was back in the hostel while the billeting officer looked for an alternative billet after Mrs Hughes was removed from his list. She knew several of the girls at the hostel, though none were particular friends of hers; there was no one she could feel close to, chum up with. Having spent the first ten years of her life in a warm, demonstrative atmosphere where people touched, walked arm in arm or put a friendly arm round one's shoulders, even hugged and kissed in a genuinely affectionate greeting or farewell, it was hard never to have anyone to touch or be touched by.

"Going to play, Sue?" Brian called, kicking the ball in her direction.

David, tall, blond, blue-eyed and devastatingly attractive, laughed. "Her! Girls don't play football!"

Suzanne, hackles up immediately, stopped the ball with her left foot, dribbled it round two of the other boys and kicked hard with her right. By pure luck it sailed straight through between two piles of coats. She turned to face David, demanding "Who says?"

"Bet you couldn't do that again!" he grinned.

"Could you? Show us."

All the boys laughed. "Come on, Dave, might as well let her play."

"In whose team?"

Thereafter Suzanne joined in quite regularly, making a fair contribution to the games and feeling generally accepted.

Despite David's initial coolness, she was fascinated by him, though she wouldn't have dreamt of showing it, matching his seeming indifference. So it was David who made the first move towards a casual, totally platonic friendship, unaware that a word from him, or a smile, quickened her pulse rate, made her heart thump. The group of teenagers met up most evenings and at weekends, occasionally setting out for picnics on their bikes or taking the short train journey up to the coast at Rhyl. There were other girls in the group both from the County School and from Suzanne's class, and inevitably there was a gradual pairing off, riding together, walking or sitting side by side. David often found his way to Suzanne, though much to her chagrin he sometimes deliberately moved to one of the other girls, invariably the beautiful Welsh girl, Marianne.

It took nearly a year before their relationship developed into something more than casual. Purely by chance the two were the only ones to arrive at the customary meeting point one Saturday, and after waiting awhile they set off on their bikes towards the river. David had heard it was flooding and they wanted to see it cascading under the stone bridge on the Bodfari road. The weather was cold and windy as they stood leaning over the lichen-covered parapet and Suzanne shivered, pulling her scarf tighter round her neck.

The next moment David's arm was round her. "Too cold for you? Do you want to go home?"

That was the last thing she wanted! "I'm okay," she whispered breathlessly, and snuggled closer against him.

His arm tightened.

The pair stood in silence, the river roaring under their feet unnoticed, neither able to think what to say. Then Suzanne felt David's breath on her forehead and the next minute he was kissing her cheek.

68

She was very late for supper at the hostel. "I punctured my back tyre," she lied, red in the face, having let the tyre down before coming in, just in case anyone decided to check. That night, lying in bed in the dark, she relived every moment, every touch, every kiss, hardly daring to believe that the most handsome boy she had ever met should be interested in her.

David Morgan was interested in several girls, and several subjects; he worked hard and played hard, studied, was keen to become an architect and had no intention of becoming seriously involved with any particular girl for years. Suzanne, on the other hand, had at last found someone on whom to centre her affection, to care about and who apparently cared about her, and as the Allied armies swept the German forces back across Europe, she became increasingly concerned about her impending separation from David on her repatriation to the island.

In the event she had been caught up in the general euphoria. Denbigh celebrated VE day in much the same way as cities, towns and villages throughout Great Britain: with services of thanksgiving, parades and, most of all, singing.

Suzanne and David went up the hill to the town square that evening to join their friends and, it seemed, the entire population. Coloured lights lit the area from end to end and loudspeakers relayed patriotic music and hymns. It was a scene Suzanne would never, ever forget. Every detail was etched vividly on her memory, but it was the glorious sound of thousands of Welsh voices raised in harmony, with *Guide me Oh Thou Great Redeemer* and *Rock of Ages*, which brought tears running down her face as she joined in, arm-in-arm with David on one side and a complete stranger on the other.

As long as the euphoria lasted, David figured little in Sue's mind. Letters arrived from her parents, with photographs; she felt guilty that her memory of them failed to match up with the new pictures. Was that long, thin man with a stoop really her father! And who could the white-haired old lady be, with the little boy on her lap? She found difficulty starting her replies – there was so much to tell it was hard to know where to begin – but once she began, her letters went on and on. So with her mind fully focused on getting 'home' again, David took a back seat.

Until now. There was no doubt the homecoming and reunion, however exciting it had been at the time, had not proved an unqualified success. The worst of the problems had been ironed out but Sue could not feel the degree of affection she wanted, between herself and her parents. Sometimes she felt guilt, that it was all her fault: she was certainly criticised enough. Then at other times she blamed Greg and Sarah for their old-fashioned attitudes. So the warmth and affection she had shared with David blossomed in her own mind, becoming the dominant factor in her life, her desire to be with him overriding her love of Guernsey, and her desire to remain in the island.

Therefore, when John Ozanne, her uncle, offered her a full-time job as stable hand at Val du Douit, starting at two pounds a week, she immediately accepted. The offer was more than she could hope to get from Mr Gallienne and was an opportunity to save up, so that within two years she could get a similar job in North Wales. Near David.

"Can I start at Easter?" They were having breakfast at the kitchen table.

"*May* I," Sarah corrected. "And no, you may not. You must wait till the school year ends in July, and give Mr Gallienne ample notice."

Sue bit back an irritable response. Her mother constantly interrupted conversations to correct her grammar – as if it mattered – and also invariably refused all Sue's requests, or so it seemed.

"I agree," Greg said. "What's more, I think it would make more sense for you to study towards a career. Surely you don't want to spend the rest of your life mucking out stables?"

"I don't want a career! I just want to earn a nest egg for my bottom drawer and then get married."

"But you may not find anyone who wants to marry you," Sarah argued.

"I have! David!"

"Don't be silly! You're only sixteen. You can't imagine what you feel for that Welsh boy is anything more than a childish infatuation!"

Sue banged her porridge spoon into her empty bowl and pushed back her chair. "I see there's no point in discussing it. You have no idea what I feel, or what David feels either." She strode out of the room.

Sarah and Greg stared at each other and sighed. "What are we going to do with her?" she asked.

Greg's eyebrows drew together. "I wonder if Edna could use her in the kitchen, in August and September? She's a jolly good cook and Sue could learn from her."

"What a brilliant idea! I'll phone Edna and see what she says."

Edna was happy to comply, and, much to her parents surprise, Sue promptly agreed. As soon as she left school she would work part-time in the stables and the rest of the day in the farm kitchen, where Edna prepared the cakes, gache and scones for her tea house.

"So you've come," Marie remarked, glancing up from her knitting as Sue walked in to the sitting room of the little town house her aunt and grandmother had bought.

"Yes, of course. I said I would." The girl slumped into an armchair, hot and tired from bicycling up the hill. "What are you making?"

"A bed jacket. And what have you been doing, apart from working for *that woman*? We don't want to hear about that!"

"I can't think why not. It's super fun and I'm learning to cook," Sue responded, her square chin, a replica of her father's, uptilted. "I thought you would be pleased." This was a fib. She was well aware of the fury in this house against Aunt Edna and the fact that she and Uncle John had secretly bought the farm.

"What makes you think there is anything the woman can teach you? She can't cook to save her life."

Sue also realised that though Aline was saying nothing, it was *she* who had made such remarks to Gran in the first place, goading her to repeat them. Much as she enjoyed working for her uncle and new aunt and was angered by these spiteful comments, Sue was determined to keep cool. "If that's what you want to think, that's okay. But I don't agree with you. Anyway, I'm going to see if Auntie needs any help in the kitchen with tea."

Over the teacups and hot Guernsey biscuits, the two ladies were regaled with stories about David Morgan, and the fact that he was coming over to stay in two weeks' time. It was obvious that he didn't meet with their approval either, despite never having met him, but seeing the girl's excitement they wisely resisted the temptation to make adverse comments.

Sue stood on the dockside waiting as the *Isle of Sark* was drawn gently towards the land ties by the huge hawsers being wound onto her capstans, fore and aft. The small, cross-channel ferry was loaded with holidaymakers and it took Sue several minutes before she spotted David and his parents. She was suddenly feeling rather nervous: would they both feel the same about each other after more than a year of separation?

She need not have worried. After the first shy greetings, he took her hand in his to walk back down the White Rock, Guernsey's main harbour, to Greg's car, where both her parents were waiting, and it felt good as they kept turning to smile at each other adoringly.

Sarah had seen Sue's photos of David, several times, but was still dismayed at the sight of the large, handsome boy: how could any normal girl resist him? In the privacy of their bedroom, she and Greg had often discussed Sue's 'infatuation', and each had assured the other that it was 'just a passing phase'. They considered their daughter far too young to form an attachment, and when she finally did they wanted it to be with a Guernsey boy, not one who lived hundreds of miles away. They had even hoped that this meeting would bring an end to the friendship, but seeing them walking together hand in hand, gazing lovingly into each others' eyes, Sarah's heart sank. Though the mother-daughter relationship had been virtually severed by the wartime separation, she was sure the worst problems were over and, given time, all would be well again . . . unless Sue was determined to return to Wales as soon as possible, for good. She turned to smile sweetly at Mrs Morgan.

Apart from their accent which was hard to follow, the Gaudions could not fault the Morgans or their son: the boy's manners were perfect and his keenness to please earned their grudging admiration.

Their reunion was all Sue could have wished for, and more. Strolling along the shoreline at Bordeaux, arms round each others' waists, she had no doubt in her mind that 'this was it'. True love, in all its glory.

"Did you wonder how it would be, meeting again?" she asked.

"Yep. I was scared to death. Our parents seem to hit it off, thank goodness." Then he added, "I thought you might have changed completely."

"But I haven't."

"Your hair's different. You've had it cut."

"Mum laid down the law. I didn't want to. Is it all right?"

"It's okay but I prefer it longer."

"Then I'll grow it."

"Don't do it just for me," he said hurriedly.

"Of course I will. I want it to be the way you like it, darling." It was the first time she'd used the term of endearment and she loved the sound of it. "Shall we sit here for a bit? The ground is quite dry."

It was an invitation to the passionate necking session that followed.

Darkness was complete by the time they returned to Les Mouettes. "You're very late," Sarah commented with remarkable restraint, due to the presence of David's parents.

Sue glanced at the clock on the mantlepiece. "Oh gosh, yes. Didn't realise the time. Sorry about that. Don't let us interrupt your bridge game."

"That's all right, just this once. Now, would you like a cocoa before going to bed?"

They weren't late again, David saw to that, but they didn't need to be. Every day they set off on bikes with bathing suits and sandwiches, spending most of the time on remote stretches of L'Ancresse Common. David was very interested in the German fortifications. The area was alive with them; they would go into the cab of the huge radiolocator on top of a hill and wind the wheel to make it revolve; searchlights still stood on the miniature railtracks on which they had been wheeled out each night. Great gun emplacements were built against large natural outcrops of rock and covered with camouflaged netting, below which were the storerooms, arsenals and gunners' living quarters. And all these battlements were linked by an endless network of tunnels and trenches criss-crossing the Common, hidden under gorse and bracken.

Sue, familiar with these relics of war, considered the explorations an awful waste of time and soon the pair would be lying in the bracken again, necking, surfacing only to eat and finally cool off in the sea.

And the days flew by. "Oh David, I'm going to miss you so much, I can't bear it."

"And I'm going to miss you, too, my love." He was kissing her hairline, a hand feeling the shape of her breast through her cotton dress.

"Am I truly?"

"Truly what?"

"Your love."

"Yes. Of course. You know that."

"You've never actually said you love me."

"Well, I thought it was obvious."

She sighed. "And I love you far more than I can find words to tell you." Her fingers combed through his hair. "Do you suppose we'll get married one day?"

"I imagine so, one day."

Sue sat up, suddenly. "I'm learning the care of horses, and how to cook, professionally. Then, as soon as I'm eighteen, in sixteen months, I'll come over to North Wales, find a job doing either one or the other, and get a flat so we can be together."

"Eh!" David gasped. "But I'll be in university."

"Doesn't matter. I'll make sure I'm not too far away."

"You realise it will be years before I can think of marriage."

"Why?" Sue was disturbed by the tone of his voice.

"Four years at university, then two years National Service, for a start. After that I'll need to find a job and even then I won't be earning enough to buy a house and keep a family."

Sue's heart sank. Not only was her dream of a home and family of her own receding by the minute, but David seemed to be trying to talk her out of the idea. "Dad always says, 'Anyone can do anything they make up their minds to do'."

David found a last, squashed sandwich in the bottom of the haversack and began to eat.

Sue watched and waited but he remained silent. When he had finished she asked if he'd like another swim.

"Good idea." Suddenly he grinned and put both arms round her. "It's not that I don't love you. I do. But I don't think it would be right to make plans which could prove expensive when neither of us has any money."

"I would have, once I got a job."

"And what happens if you get sick or . . . well . . ."

"Pregnant?"

"If we are together for years, necking like we've been doing, well, it won't be long before we go all the way."

The thought caused a wave of happiness to wash over her. She had only the vaguest idea what 'going all the way' would be like, but she was longing for their relationship to reach that stage. However, for now she would have to be careful not to seem too keen; David was obviously worried.

Window shopping together next day in town, Sue stopped in front of a shop full of imitation jewellery. "Look! Isn't that ring pretty," she exclaimed, "and only seven and sixpence."

"Well it is only glass," David eyed the metal ring set with a green stone without much enthusiasm.

"But it is attractive and I love the colour. Shall we get it?"

"As long as you don't think it's a waste of money." He apparently did.

Sue was determined. "We can go halves. Look," she

77

extracted her purse from the pocket of her skirt, "Here's my three and ninepence."

"What makes you think it will fit?"

It didn't. But Sue was not to be deterred. Nor did it warrant a ring box: the assistant wrapped it in a piece of tissue and put it in a little envelope. Sue hoped David might insist on paying for it all himself, but he didn't. She picked up the tiny package and slipped it into her pocket.

"Are you going to put it on my finger?" Sue asked when they were sitting in the back of the bus on their way home.

"Okay. Where is it?"

She opened the envelope, handed him the ring and held out her left hand, indicating the fourth finger.

He smiled at her indulgently. "You want us to be unofficially engaged, do you?"

She grinned and nodded.

"Well it will have to remain unofficial for a very long time."

Never mind. Now at last she was sure of her man. Her mate, married or not, for the rest of their lives.

Mary Ozanne, John's humourless wife who had evacuated to England in 1940, and who had never had any intention of returning to him afterwards, sued him for divorce on the grounds of adultery. Edna was named as co-respondent, but the case was not contested, and just before Christmas of 1946, they were quietly married at the Greffe, Guernsey's register office. Marie and Aline Ozanne, John's mother and sister, were conspicuous by their disapproving absence, but Greg, Sarah and Sue were there with Greg's great friend, George Schmit and his new wife, Gelly, who were in much the same situation. They had a reception at the Old Government House Hotel for more than fifty friends and relatives who were all delighted to see John so happy at last.

John and Edna had plans. Following the great success of the tearoom and garden at the farm, already renowned throughout the island, they intended expanding to small hotel status. More bathrooms were added and the kitchen extended, and Sue was asked to go on a short catering course in England. She was thrilled to accept. The job interested her greatly, she thought it would be good for her intended role of housewife and, not least, it meant being just a little nearer David. Her nest egg was growing, slowly. She continued to exercise some of the six horses John now kept for his riding school and was often beset by the yearning to take an instructor's course, rather than catering – it was bound to be more useful.

On her seventeenth birthday Sue passed the simple driving test in Greg's car, which resulted in a rise in the total of weekly arguments, but gave her parents an added lever for her to accept their rulings: otherwise she was not allowed to use the car.

"I've half a mind to spend my savings on a car of my own," she wrote to David, frustrated by the situation.

"Why not?" was his response.

As though he didn't know it would mean a longer wait for her to go and live in North Wales! He did puzzle her, sometimes.

The catering course in London, during which she stayed with Aunt Gelly's sister in her flat in Fulham, proved extremely successful. Not that Sue got her diploma with exactly flying colours, there were far too many distractions to be enjoyed in the big city, but nevertheless she did learn a great deal.

The ten-week intensive course ended in time for the beginning of the tourist season in Guernsey, where the alterations were nearing completion at Val du Douit. John and Edna insisted Sue should be on a bonus scheme throughout the summer, so that by the end of September her deposit account at Lloyd's was far better than her wildest dreams.

"Thank you, thank you, darling Edna," she squealed, hugging her.

"Not at all. Thank *you*! You really have earned every penny. I couldn't possibly have coped without you!"

"Well, now that the last of the visitors have gone, Edna, do you think I might borrow Sue to help out at the stables, while young Ben is on holiday?" her husband asked plaintively. He had had to take on a boy to cover the extra time Sue was spending in the hotel.

Sue arrived next morning in jodphurs. "Who needs exercising today?" she asked hopefully. She had not had more than half a dozen rides throughout the summer.

"Thunder hasn't been out for a few days." John began.

"Who?"

"Oh, haven't you met him yet? I bought him from a riding stable in the Vale two weeks ago. They said they had more horses than they needed, but I suspect they found him too skittish for beginners. You'll need to be careful."

Thunder, a sixteen-and-a-half hands chestnut, took some persuading to allow this stranger to mount, but was perfectly docile and responsive as they walked up the lane to gallop across the top fields. The wind was gusting to gale force, blowing a confetti of leaves from the tall elms and flattening the drying bracken on the hedge banks. Hatless, Sue's hair streamed out in the wind, like Thunder's black mane and tail, horse and rider enjoying every moment.

"Would you like to go down to a beach for a sand gallop, old chappie?" she asked, patting his neck and standing in the stirrups as Thunder's gait slowed to an easy canter. It would be a fairly long ride, but she was sure Uncle John wouldn't mind.

Thunder tossed his head high and whinnied.

"Okay. We'll go through that gap and join the lane farther down." Fortunately it was unnecessary to worry about gates as cows in Guernsey are always tethered and there is little fear of them wandering, so Sue and Thunder would be able to rejoin the lane below the bend without her having to dismount.

Jim Cotterill was having a hard time with the bread delivery van that morning. Three times it had failed to start so, after leaving the Queripel's loaf on their kitchen table, he elected to coast the rest of the way down the lane in the hope of building up sufficient speed to start her in gear.

Thunder was negotiating the muddy slope from the field down onto the quiet lane when a huge, brown monster leapt round the bend at him, jerked, roared and hooted. The horse reared in fright and fell back onto his hocks as his hooves slid in the mud. Sue slipped off over his tail and rolled flat on her face while, in his frantic effort to get up, Thunder's large, iron shoe was planted in the small of her back as he sprang to bolt away.

Until that moment the entire ludicrous incident had seemed to Sue to be happening in farcically slow motion. She had wanted to laugh as she slipped helplessly out of the saddle over his rump, and imagined Edna's amusement when she returned with mud all over her face.

Then an agonising crash of pain in her back swamped her body, and thoughts and vision blurred through clouds of increasing darkness as she lost consciousness.

Chapter Four

Trapped

There was no question of slow motion in Jim Cotterill's mind: it all happened so suddenly it was difficult to explain to anyone what had occurred. Admittedly, he had only been thinking about trying to spark the van engine into life when the horse slid into sight as he rounded the bend in the lane. The reason he hooted, which he wouldn't normally do near a horse, was that he was anxious not to stall the van again as he braked and the wheels slewed off the track. Watching John Ozanne's wild niece slide off her mount, he muttered, "serve her right" under his breath, half amused at the sight, half angry as his motor died away again. However, when he saw the animal's iron-shod hoof smash into the girl's back, humour and anger turned to horror. "Aw my Gawd!" he shouted, wriggling out of the van into the hedgerow, dashing across to Sue's inert body. Better not to turn her if her back's damaged, he thought. But she's got to breathe. Reluctant to touch her, he drew the mass of tumbled hair back from her face, buried in mud. "Aw my Gawd!" he repeated, looking desperately up and down the lane for help, but not even the horse was in sight. Gingerly, he slid a hand under her head to lift it slightly, then seeing the mud-clogged lips drew a well-used red handkerchief from his pocket and attempted to clear both nose and mouth. He felt a faint puff of air against his fingers and gasped with relief. He was loathe to leave her lying there but after minutes of indecision he elected to hurry down to Val du Douit Farm to the Ozannes.

Edna was in the kitchen, baking, when she heard boots clomping across the yard and a voice shouting, "You there, Mister Ozanne? You there? You better come quick, it's your niece!" and the baker almost fell through the open door, puce in the face and panting.

John was in the stables; Edna rang the emergency bell they'd fixed up from the kitchen and within half a minute he was dashing across the yard, and while Edna called St John Ambulance, John raced up the lane ahead of Jim's fat legs.

Sue opened her eyes and stared at her mother in bewilderment. She began to draw a breath to ask what was happening but stopped, screwing up her face in pain. "Uh! I can't breathe!" Her voice was barely a whisper.

"Don't try," her father ordered. "You're just waiting to go into X-ray to see what damage you've done."

Sue tried turning to face him, but winced again. Then someone stuck a needle in her arm.

Later, Sue heard her mother saying, "You have a badly bruised back and a fractured disc, but they can't find any sign of bone fracture. They will keep you here in hospital overnight and bring you home in the morning, if all is well." Which manoeuvre proved equally as painful as the X-rays had been, despite the injections.

And almost as bad as the ministration of the physiotherapist. Long and sinewy, brown and bouncy, he skipped into the house a few days after her return and called her "My poppet". She learned afterwards that he gave all female patients the same title as he was hopeless at remembering names. Two weeks after the accident he ripped the huge strapping of adhesive plaster off her back, creating even more exquisite agony, and declared, "There, my poppet! Your uncle Joe says you may now sit up with your feet over the edge of the bed, just for a few minutes."

Listening from the hallway, Greg and Sarah raised their eyes to heaven. 'Uncle Joe's' jolly visits were becoming increasingly hard to take.

Sue didn't manage to sit up for more than thirty seconds before pleading to lie back again. "However long is this going to take?" she demanded.

"Until all the gel from inside the fractured disc has been drawn back into place or dissolved, it will continue to press against your spinal cord causing pain through all the nerves in your torso, my poppet. You listen when your Uncle Joe tells you how lucky you are that no vertebrae were broken."

"But how much longer will I have to lie here? A week? Two weeks? I've got to get back to my job."

"And what is that?"

"Partly stable work and exercising horses, and partly helping in the tearooms and guesthouse."

'Uncle Joe' shook his head. "Well, the disc seems to be mending quite quickly, they usually do, which means you should be back on your feet, in the next week or so.

But, my poppet, I am not satisfied that the disc itself is in its correct position."

"What does that mean?"

"That the least jerk, or even standing on your feet for more than a few minutes at a time, could force it right out of position and put you on your back again for several months. We must not run the risk of this becoming a chronic condition. So," he gave her a friendly wallop on the side of her leg, "No riding, no mucking out stables and no standing up for more than five minutes at a time until I tell you you may."

"When will that be? Not another two or three weeks?"

A quiff of long, brown hair flopped over his face as he shook his head. "No. Absolutely not. You'll have to wait a minimum of six months."

Sue grinned up at him. "You're pulling my leg!"

Solemnly he shook his head again. "Seriously. I mean it."

"I don't believe you!"

"If you want to be sure of ever leading a normal life again, my poppet, you had better start believing me," he said, "right now!"

She did. But it wasn't easy. She felt so trapped!

Sarah continued to feed her with an invalid cup, both desperately trying not to laugh, knowing the pain it would cause. Sarah would gaze out of the window to avoid catching Sue's eye and consequently produce a fit of choking or spill soup down the patient's neck. Sarah's shoulders would start to shake, Sue would splutter, trying to laugh backwards to ease the pain and Greg would bound in from the kitchen with a stern face to tick them both off . . . with hilarious results.

It was a time of family unity and happiness. Despite Sue's pain and frustration, she revelled in her parent's constant, loving attention: Sarah was delighted to have total charge and control of her daughter; Richard had his big sister lying helplessly at his mercy, ever available to invent stories for his amusement; and Greg, who loved peace and tranquillity above all things, came in from work each day, no longer dreading another feud, ready to enjoy his family.

Tentatively at first, mother and daughter began to talk. In rebuilding their respective lives after the war, they seemed to have had no time to discuss the previous five years in depth; incidents had been related, glossed over and forgotten, neither willing to admit, let alone share, the other's emotional traumas or physical deprivations. Sarah knew that Sue had had some good billets and some bad, but now she had time to probe for details she began to comprehend the loneliness and unhappiness Sue had suffered. Her eyes filled with tears, and seeing them, Sue held out her arms to hug her mother, as she hadn't done for years.

Lying, listening to Sarah explaining how she cooked tiny, wrinkled potatoes over bits of burning greenhouse timber in the sitting room fireplace, and bought seawater from a tank on a handcart because there was no salt and the public were no longer allowed on the beaches to collect their own sea water, Sue was able to picture it all in detail and understand her mother's worries about feeding her family, especially little Richard; no wonder her hair had turned white, and Dad had become so thin.

Sarah passed on some of the details to Greg, at night

when they were in bed. "Poor child. At least we had each other and Richard, she had no one."

"No wonder she came to centre her affection on David," Greg whispered. "She had a big void to fill in her heart."

"Yes," Sarah sighed. "I dread her going off to live in Wales again, especially now we are getting to know each other so much better."

"Do you reckon she'll be able to go, after this accident?"

"Not for some time, according to 'Uncle Joe'. I dread to think how she'll react if she is told she has to wait more than year." Sarah reached up to switch off the light. "Anyway, I don't believe she has dared think about that, yet."

Sarah was wrong. Sue had thought about David, the effects of her injury on her job prospects, and the additional waiting time involved. She had also noted the ever lengthening times between his letters, though he had written very promptly on hearing about the accident.

The next letter didn't arrive for an interminable two weeks and the one after that took four, by which time she was up and about, walking quite normally though she tired very quickly. She was watching through the sitting room window as the postman, draped in oilskins, hurried up to the front door through driving rain. The envelopes were wet as she picked them out of the letter cage behind the door and sorted them, and her heart leapt as she recognised David's writing.

"Post!" she called, carrying the bills into the kitchen.

"Hm," Sarah grunted. "Doesn't look very interesting."

She glanced up from the teapot and saw the happy grin on Sue's face. "Though I imagine yours is?"

Sue waved the envelope triumphantly. "At last!"

"Good! Want a cup of tea?"

Alone in the sitting room, Sue settled back in an armchair, carefully slit open the damp envelope then took a few sips of tea before allowing herself to become immersed in David's letter.

Her grin soon became a frown.

'. . . *and so after a great deal of investigation and discussion, Dad has decided to take the job offered in Canada.*

The initial contract is only for two years, so Mum and Dad won't sell the house, just let it, until we decide whether we want to remain there. The firm says they will provide a place in college for me there, which is very exciting, don't you think?'

No! She did not think it at all exciting! Disastrous, more like. She shook her head in disbelief. What on earth was he thinking about, contemplating setting off to the other side of the world without even speaking to her about it. About them. And they were supposed to be engaged . . . well, unofficially. She scanned the remaining pages, then reread the whole letter, twice.

"Your tea has gone cold, Sue," Sarah pointed out when she stuck her head round the door. "Nice letter?"

Sue stared up at her, her face a mask of misery. "No."

"Darling! What is it?"

Sue told her. "And apart from starting 'My Darling Sue', saying they would return in a couple of years at least for a holiday and he hopes we'll see each other then, and ending 'with all my love'," Sue stared into her lap, twisting the pages, "he doesn't mention anything about us." The only scrap of comfort lay in the fact that since the accident she and her mother had become close enough for her to talk about David more openly.

Sarah tried to be practical. "Well, you are both very young to be thinking about a joint future. Though this move to Canada need not necessarily mean a break-up, it could give you the chance to meet other nice boys, over here."

It was not what Sue wanted to hear but she bit back the retort on her lips, accepting that Sarah meant well. She got up and wandered across the room to gaze out at the rain. Two whole years! And no mention of their future! Suddenly she felt angry: how dared he treat her like that? Where was his loyalty and commitment? "Yes," she swung round to face Sarah. "You're right, Mummy. I'm not going to sit around moping for the next two years! I'm going to enjoy myself!"

Post-war Guernsey was full of social fun and laughter. Ten thousand young islanders had joined the British forces and now many were being demobbed, returning to the island in their Government issue de-mob clothes with post-war gratuities burning holes in their pockets. The local British Legion and RAF Clubs were fast enrolling new members; tennis, badminton, cricket, soccer and athletic clubs were swinging into action. The Guernsey Amateur Dramatic and Operatic Society, whose few remaining members had kept going during the war with willing new recruits as The Regal Players, was bolstered anew with dozens of would-be actors and an army of enthusiastic stagehands, scenic and make-up artists; the Choral and Orchestral Society produced concerts. There were dinners and balls, and the cocktail bars did a thriving trade.

Felicity Warwick had been at school with Sarah and remained a firm friend, despite the five years' separation during the war. She had returned with her husband Gus and daughter Anne, to restore their home at L'Ancresse after Todt workers had left it uninhabitable. Sue was her goddaughter; she visited her frequently after the girl's accident, and now, knowing that Sue's activities were still restricted by 'Uncle Joe', asked if Sue would give her a hand with the wardrobe for the next GADOS production. Sue was dubious, especially when she realised that a great deal of sewing was involved, but being extremely fond of Aunt Filly, and with time on her hands she agreed to 'have a go'. At first the sewing and dressmaking lessons seemed tedious, but Filly's natural sense of fun and ebullience soon took over and Sue was well pleased with her achievements as well as enjoying herself.

The biggest bonus proved to be social. She found herself amongst a large group of new friends, young and old, and enjoyed meeting a crowd of people slightly older than herself, who had recently been demobbed. Norton and James had been in the army; Penny was in the WAAFs and Tiny, large, fat and jolly, whose father was a well-known local hotelier, had been an army cook. Sue was fascinated by their casual repartee, their cameraderie and their acceptance of everyone as equals. James, at twenty-one, was youngest, and Penny, who had risen to sergeant, was twenty-five and oldest. Their dry, straight-faced humour was puzzling at first, but soon she was joining in the ribbing, giving as good as she got.

Seeing the leading lady in costume and make-up for the first time, Tiny remarked to her that in the semi-darkness of the auditorium she looked reasonably attractive.

Unfortunately, the fact that the lady did not appreciate the accolade had an explosive effect on Sue, who was adjusting the hem of the gown. "Oh dear, it must be the dust on the floor," Sue apologised, turning the explosion into a sneeze. Then she accidently caught James's eye and had to 'sneeze' again.

The end of play party, attended by everyone concerned in the production, turned into a near riot, once the older and stuffier members had left. "Always improves once we are down to the nucleus," James remarked. "Now we can get down to some serious drinking."

"Well I'm afraid we have to go, now," Filly said.

"Oh, must we?" Sue complained.

"Certainly not," Tiny insisted. "The party's just beginning."

"I promised Gus I'd be home before midnight," Filly told him, "And—"

"How tiresome. Never mind, Sue isn't married to Gus," Tiny put a persuasive arm round Filly's shoulders, "She can stay and we'll see her safely home."

"Super! That'll be okay, won't it Aunt Filly?"

"Come on, Aunt Filly!" James joined in. "Don't be stuffy. Sue'll be safe with us!"

Filly snorted. "That I doubt!" But she gave in with a grin.

Christmas and New Year were fabulous, followed by a

wonderful eighteenth birthday party with her new crowd of friends. Sue was ecstatic: her parents approved of 'the crowd' – they all came from suitable backgrounds – though Greg and Sarah had no inkling of the level of liquor consumed nightly. They raised a slightly admonishing eyebrow when Sue produced a packet of Balkan Sobranies from her handbag, and lit up, but as the happy atmosphere in the house prevailed they agreed to do nothing that might disturb it.

They also agreed that there was safety in numbers. "It is amusing to see so many different escorts bringing her home each evening," Greg remarked, "Even if it is sometimes rather late."

"True. But I think we should insist on her being home by eleven," Sarah suggested.

Greg grimaced. "Or eleven-thirty, perhaps?"

"Before midnight," Sue said persuasively when the subject was broached. Which was finally agreed.

The very next day Norton announced yet another demob party. "It's for Jonathan Martel. He's just come out of the Royal Navy. Arrived home yesterday."

"Where will it be?" Sue asked.

"At the Palm Court. Want a lift?"

For her birthday, Grandma and Aunt Aline had given Sue a gorgeously sophisticated cocktail dress in shot, turquoise silk taffeta with a swathed, off-the-shoulder top and princess-line waist flaring to a full, ankle-length skirt. Sarah thought it was far too grown-up and low-cut for her and guessed, correctly, that her mother had had no hand in choosing it, but short of a massive family row there was no way to stop Sue wearing it to the party. Sue also wanted to put her hair up, but not wishing to push her luck too far, simply curled it and swept it back with combs to the nape of her neck.

"You look terrific, old girl," Norton commented as she got in the car.

Sue knew it was the best she had ever looked but was still delighted when even Penny, in her mannish pants suit, gave a nod of approval.

Jonathan was leaning on the bar counter as they walked in, listening to someone talking in the group round him.

"Here we are," Norton announced. "Sue, this is the rogue we've all been telling you about. Jonathan, this is the infant we've taken under our wing."

Jonathan stood to attention, held out his hand and shook his head, solemnly. "My dear Sue, I hope we meet in time for me to save you from the clutches of this horrible crew. They are not to be trusted, you know, especially with beautiful young ladies."

Sue quickly summed up the soft blue eyes under long dark lashes, the sun-bleached hair slicked back with Brylcreem and exquisitely chiselled features, weathered bronze. She felt the strong, slender fingers grasp her hand, and equally solemnly replied, "Jonathan, you don't know the half of it. Night after night I have battled for my honour, just waiting for you to arrive and protect me."

Tiny snorted and the rest exploded as Jonathan's eyebrows shot up. "That bad! My dear, come to Uncle Jonty," he put an arm round her shoulders, "He'll fend them off."

It was a lovely party. A sort of on-going party, in that day after day arrangements were made to congregate at somebody's house, or in yet another cocktail bar.

"What do you all do every evening?" Sarah asked

her bleary-eyed daughter who was slumped over a late breakfast.

Sue smiled happily. "Talk about the war and what we'll do now. Play bar billiards or liar dice. Eat, drink and be merry!"

"You must bring some of them home, sometime. We'd like to meet them."

"Of course. Sometime." Though she couldn't imagine what for. Mum and Dad didn't drink much. Or play liar dice. They wouldn't relate to the fast service repartee. Good grief, they were almost a different breed altogether. Their world revolved at a totally different pace. Anyway, no one else's parents were ever introduced.

But, she had to admit, there was an even stronger reason to put off bringing them home. Back in her bedroom, sitting at her dressing table, Sue searched her reflection for a clue to her new problem. Opening the top drawer she stared down at David's latest letter and repeated the question in her mind. How could the feelings she had for David possibly be true and eternal love, when the mere sight of Jonathan had such a violent effect on her, both mentally and physically. When his glance, his smile, sent waves of weakness down her thighs. It was a reaction which Sarah would instantly recognise . . . yet how, being so old, could she hope to understand?

Sue lay in the bath, easing the ache in her back. She couldn't get Jonathan out of her mind; pictured his lean, sensitive face in repose, when he was unaware anyone was watching. For all his bravado, laughter and joking, she guessed there was probably a shy, sensitive man underneath.

Sarah was not a fool. She watched her daughter go out

that evening, hair immaculate, a little too much make-up but studiously applied, wearing a smart dress and jacket she had made herself with a bit of help from dear Filly, and she knew the effort was not for a mere, casual friend. Then, a week later when their long-time friends Ted and Julia Martel came round for an evening's bridge, Julia remarked that Ted's brother's boy, Jonathan, recently demobbed from the Royal Navy, had been asking a lot of questions about Sue.

Sarah closed her fan of cards. "What sort of questions?"

"'Did we know of her?' 'What's her family like?' 'Has she a steady boyfriend?' The usual sort of things."

"Are you going to take this trick, sweetheart, or spend the rest of the evening gossiping?" Greg demanded.

Sarah obliged, played a small Club, then grinned at Julia. "What did you tell him?"

"Very nice girl. Charming family but totally committed to a chap called . . . David. Right?" Julia played the nine.

"Er . . . yes. Well, not totally."

Greg frowned at his hand and threw the Jack, which Ted promptly covered with the Queen. Greg's frown deepened. "As soon as this rubber is over, I suggest you girls go off into the kitchen to yatter while the kettle's boiling."

Julia put a hand over her mouth, signifying silence.

"I'll go into the hotel business," Jonathan said, in answer to Sue's question. "Mother has this great barn of a house where she rattles around like a pea in a drum. She says she'd be happy to move into the old cottage beyond the paddock, if it were done up a bit."

They were sitting in his MG overlooking Lihou Island, trying to fend off the freezing draughts whistling in through gaps in the canvas top. It was the first time he had asked her out, "just for a spin", and their conversation was politely stilted.

"Have you had any experience or training in hotel management?"

"I've had a year of keeping things ship-shape below decks. That should be sufficient, I imagine." He had risen to Sub Lieutenant.

Impressed by his confidence, Sue was sure he was right.

A week later he kissed her, long and tenderly . . . and next day he phoned to apologise. "Terribly sorry about that. Shouldn't have had that last 'one for the road'. Quite made me forget myself. Hope you weren't offended?"

"Why are you sorry?" She had enjoyed it; it was only the apology that offended her.

"Well, I mean, you already have a boyfriend, haven't you?"

Sue took a deep breath. "Had. But that was over some time ago." Like two and a half minutes?

"I'm taking Toby for a walk," she called to her mother as she dragged on her coat and boots, hoping the cold sea air at Bordeaux would clear her head. The gale tore at her headscarf and flattened the dog's ears against his neck as they stood above the shoreline watching breakers bursting into clouds of spume over the rocks. It wasn't hard to analyse her feelings. It was simply a matter of fitting all the pieces of life's jig-saw into place. And suddenly they all did fit, very neatly. Fate, God or whatever, had obviously taken a hand. Her accident had seemed like a major tragedy at the time, yet it had brought her a much closer and more comfortable relationship with her parents. Still, the problem of split allegiance, between her family and Guernsey, or David and Wales, had remained. Her parents had told her often enough how sad they would be if she left the island, and what a pity it was she had a Welsh boyfriend. Then Fate removed David to the other side of the world. She had been so miserable, left behind, pining for him . . . failing to understand the obvious. Now it was all so clear. Jonathan, not David, was the man intended for her. Her dearest, darling Jonathan. Mummy and Daddy liked the family and he was a nephew of their great friends. Now, at last, the puzzle would be solved.

Jonathan proposed three weeks later and Sue had no hesitation in accepting. She had sensed it coming and had quickly written her 'Dear John' letter to David, convinced he would be relieved; he had never shown much enthusiasm for a permanent alliance.

"Darling, that's wonderful. But you are only eighteen," Sarah responded cautiously.

"And Jonathan hasn't got a job, yet, has he?" Greg said.

"Oh yes. He's going into the hotel business."

"Really! Well I would like him to come and see me to discuss it before we give our official approval."

"Daddy! That sounds so old-fashioned!"

Fortunately Jonathan didn't share her opinion. "Of course I must see him. I only spoke to you first to be sure you wouldn't be repulsed by the idea!"

The bucket seats in his car were not designed for

lovers, but Sue managed to get her arms round him and indulge in a prolonged kiss. "I'm not entirely repulsed," she assured him.

It was a very relaxed meeting lasting five minutes before Greg and Jonathan joined their womenfolk in the sitting room.

"I told Jonathan we thought they should wait till they had got a home together. But it seems there is a home ready and waiting."

Sarah's mouth formed a large O. "Waiting?"

Jonathan explained about the old family house he planned to turn into an hotel. "And naturally it will be marvellous having Sue to help, after her experience at Val du Douit."

Sarah tried to feel as happy and confident as the young couple, and failed. It was all so sudden! Only weeks ago Sue had been anxiously watching for the postman to deliver letters from David; not that either she or Greg wanted the childhood romance to continue . . . the thought of Sue going off to live in Wales was bad enough, but when the thought occurred of her going to live in Canada the whole concept was appalling. The Martels were a nice family and Jonathan an ideal prospect . . . hopefully. But Sue hardly knew him. He was so much older, a man of the world. Dare she say anything, risk upsetting the relationship between Sue and herself? She looked helplessly at Greg.

Reading her thoughts, Greg said, "Yes. I think it all sounds splendid. Nevertheless I'm sure my wife and I both feel it might be best to announce your engagement on Sue's nineteenth birthday, next January, with a possible summer wedding to follow."

"Oh Daddy! Why? What is the point of waiting a whole year?"

"We want you both to be absolutely sure . . ." Sarah began.

"We are! Aren't we, darling?" Sue, sitting on the arm of Jonathan's chair, gazed adoringly down into the compelling blue eyes.

"I'm sure Jonathan won't mind giving us a week to consider the options, will you?" Greg asked the young man.

"Of course not. Whatever you want." He was most effusive. "But as far as Sue and I are concerned we would like to regard ourselves as engaged, even if unofficially."

Receiving a fractional shrug from Sarah in response to his glance, Greg nodded. "Very well."

The engagement announcement was in the Guernsey Evening Press the day before the annual Liberation Day Celebrations on 9 May, but only after a great deal of argument and arm-twisting from Sue. She was ecstatic, not only because she was well aware of being the envy of most girls in their crowd for landing the most attractive fish in the pond, but also because she was about to realise her dream – soon to start a home and family of her own.

Too soon, Sarah thought, secretly. However Sue's lively enthusiasm was infectious, sweeping everyone along with her in preparation for an August wedding. Clothes were still rationed, so coupons were gathered and hoarded. Mother and daughter paid several visits to Lovell's for bed and table linen and towels for the trousseau. Mrs Tostevin, who had made Sarah's dress in 1929, was too crippled with arthritis to sew anymore, but she had taught her daughter, now married and living at St Sampson's, who accepted the commission to produce dresses for the bride and bridesmaids. There was a very limited range of materials available: Sue fell for a heavy white satin to be made up into a slim, straight pattern with ample train but Sarah and Aunt Filly talked her out of it.

"Far too old and sophisticated for an eighteen-year-old."

Which had actually been exactly what Sue wanted. However she was far too happy and excited to argue, and allowed herself to be talked into a white silk taffeta, with the same material in very pale blue for the bridesmaids – Aunt Filly's daughter, Anne, and Sue's cousins who lived in England, Josette and Marivonne.

"Mummy, do you still have your own wedding veil?"

"Why yes, I think so. Up in the attic, somewhere."

"Let's get it down, then. I'd love to wear it if it hasn't been chewed up by mice and moths."

Sarah was thrilled at the idea.

Filly had managed to obtain two silk parachutes through a friend in London; these were being sold off in hundreds, no longer required by the RAF after the war, and women everywhere were cutting into the precious panels to make nightdresses and luxurious lingerie.

Hand in hand, Jonathan and Sue wandered round his old family home, making plans. "We'll need a decent-sized dining room and residents' lounge," Jonathan said, "and a cocktail bar, too. But that could be quite small and intimate. Possibly Father's old study."

"Wonderful," Sue agreed. Of course she agreed with virtually all his ideas. They all seemed so good. "What about the guest bedrooms? And our own quarters?"

"I thought we might use the dower wing for ourselves. It hasn't been lived in for years, only used for storage, but it would be fun to do it up, don't you think?"

"I've never seen it. Can we go and look now?"

It smelled musty and was festooned with cobwebs, but the bride-to-be was enchanted. "Oh, darling! It is completely perfect." She waltzed from room to room picturing cretonne curtains and chair covers, a dark oak, gate-legged table and log fires; a brass bedstead and patchwork quilt, and copper pans on the kitchen wall. "When can we start work on it?" Her very own home!

Thereafter, they spent every available minute cleaning the place out, painting, hanging wallpaper and scrounging furniture from their families. Sarah went back to Lovell's with Sue, to help her choose curtain materials. The beautiful wooden floors were repolished and scattered with miscellaneous rugs. Sue loved old, traditional styles, Jonathan preferred modern, but it didn't matter as everything was mixed together in haste. Sarah's sensibilities were offended by the medley, but Sue didn't care, it was their home and she loved it. Wedding presents began arriving in the shape of crockery, glass and cutlery. These were assembled at Les Mouettes for display after the reception.

Greg opened the bills with horror, but Sarah didn't bat an eyelid. "We only have one daughter, darling." She kissed his cheek. "This is a one off. When Richard marries it will be someone else writing the cheques."

"Thank God for that!" He landed a playful smack on her behind. "I know it isn't Sue who is stripping the shirt off my back. You are thoroughly enjoying your spending spree, aren't you?"

The crow's feet at the corners of her eyes deepened. "Yes, sweetheart. I am. And I believe you are too."

Every post brought congratulations on Sue and Jonathan's engagement: Sue developed a sixth sense for timing its arrival and dashed to the door to take it from the postman, prancing back through the house to show her mother. "Oh look! A lovely card from Meggie. You remember, my best friend in Denbigh. And a letter enclosed. I'll read it later."

Near the bottom of the pile was a letter with a Canadian stamp – addressed in David's handwriting. Sue hadn't told him of her engagement so it couldn't be congratulations, just a late reply to her 'Dear John' letter.

Sarah watched as the envelope was slit open and waited, hoping the boy had taken the jilting well. Then she bit her lip as a scarlet flush crept up Sue's neck.

"Oh no, Mum!" The girl looked up from the letter, eyes swimming. "I can't believe it. He says he's devastated! He's coming back to talk it over!"

Mother and daughter stared at each other in horror.

"You'll have to send him a cable, telling him about the engagement," Sarah muttered, adding, when she saw the colour drain from Sue's face, "There is no point in blaming yourself. These things often happen when alliances are made so very young. And he would be wrong to expect to you to wait for him for years. Plus the fact that people do change; there is no saying you would even have liked each other when you met again."

"Quite." Sue desperately wanted to believe it, but later, alone in her bedroom, she gave way to tears. Poor, dear David. If only she had known how strongly he felt . . . but would it have made any difference? Could anything have stopped her falling in love with Jonathan? She looked at her fiancé's photograph standing on the bedside table, and smiled. No, nothing. Yet she knew that deep down she would always love David, in a way. She drifted over to the window, watched petunias nodding at each other in the warm wind, and blew her nose. If only she hadn't had to hurt him so, she wouldn't be feeling so guilty.

Back in the kitchen, Sarah handed her a piece of paper. "Just a suggested wording for your cable."

Sue read it and gave a half smile. "Thanks. Yes that looks fine."

"Like me to phone it through for you?"

"Please, Mum. And let's pray it gets there before he leaves."

The click of the garden gate had always prompted happy anticipation, of visiting friends, of exciting mail and, latterly, of Jonathan's arrival. Now the sound filled Sue with alarm that David might turn up, unannounced. Gradually, day by day, she managed to eliminate him from her mind, most of the time, but it was during those moments when she was tired, or couldn't sleep that she remained vulnerable to waves of guilt . . . which she would deliberately turn into anger. After all, it was his fault for not showing more interest in their future long ago.

Apart from which, everything was progressing very smoothly, and best of all there were few disagreements over the wedding preparations, largely because Sue was too happy to be bothered arguing. What did it matter whether Mummy chose a finger buffet reception or a sit-down meal? So long as there was ample champagne.

*   *   *

It had been an excellent season for the tomato trade that year, so, despite the mounting stack of bills, Greg was very happy, especially when the sun rose on the day of the wedding, to shine non-stop until it set over the west coast, and even more so when he climbed into the beribboned taxi beside Sue; she had never looked so beautiful and his chest swelled with pride under his morning suit. Sarah finished arranging Sue's dress so that it wouldn't be crushed and gazed at her daughter for a brief moment before the door was shut. A moment long enough for the picture to be etched on her memory for all time. The low neckline of the dress was gathered into a lace-edged, stiffened ruff, with ruffs on her elbows below puffed sleeves. The fitted bodice met the full, gathered skirt under a wide sash, tied in a bow at the back with ends down to the flounced hemline, from which peeped dainty satin shoes. Sarah's veil was held in place on Sue's head by a cap stitched with seed pearls, matching the graduated pearl necklet and earrings given to her by her groom. Her dark hair lay curled on her shoulders, her green eyes were enhanced with a suspicion of eyeshadow, her lips reddened and her summer freckles dusted with powder. She held her bouquet of summer lilies and stephanotis very carefully, so that the front of her dress would not be creased.

Sarah's mind flashed back to the car in which she herself had been driven to her wedding at St Saviour's Church, Pa sitting beside her, trying to calm her nerves. She sighed. Had that been a million years ago . . . or only yesterday? Of one thing she was sure, she had never looked as lovely as Sue did today.

She hurried back into the house to collect Richard, who

was bored stiff at having to be dressed up in a smart suit during the summer holidays. "Can't I take the coat off? It looks stupid in this weather," he grumbled.

"You look splendid," Sarah assured him, adjusting his carnation buttonhole. She paused to check her reflection in the hall mirror; the matching floral edge-to-edge dress and coat were of pale amber and green polished cotton, the dark green, wide-brimmed straw hat decorated with silk flowers to match. The corsage of orchids hardly showed up at all against her coat, but it was too late to worry about that now: the taxi was at the door, waiting to rush them to the church ahead of the bride.

There was no way Grandma Gaudion could be left at home, so Andrew and Maureen had brought her, no enviable task. Sarah glimpsed the tight-lipped irritation on Marie's face, no doubt at finding herself in the pew behind the older woman whose *sotto voce* queries to her son Sarah coud hear reverberating round the church, though she couldn't actually see her. William and his wife Annemarie, who had brought their bridesmaid daughters over from Cornwall for the wedding, were sitting with Marie and Aline, and soon distracted them with complimentary comments about their outfits. Wisely, John and Edna sat further back than was their right, for fear that his mother and sister would stage an embarrassing scene.

Alone with Richard in the front pew, Sarah saw Jonathan glance at his watch before looking anxiously over his shoulder towards the door. She caught his eye and winked, a reassurance that the bride was on her way.

The bridal car had driven very slowly round the Vale Castle to St Sampson's harbour, allowing Sarah and

Richard to overtake. The pace made Sue restless. She fidgeted with her bouquet, adjusted the veil, smoothed her dress, until Greg took her hand and squeezed it. "Try to relax, my sweet. Only a few more minutes."

Sue smiled at him through the veil, hoping he couldn't read her mind; she didn't want him to realise that she had a recurring nightmarish thought . . . that when the rector asked if anyone knew of any just cause or impediment why these two persons should not be joined together, David would jump up at the back of the church and shout I do! Might he have left Canada before the cable arrived? Could he know which church? What time? Her chest pounded. Her mouth was dry.

Chapter Five

Teenage Bride

Gathering up the folds of her dress, Sue stepped out of the wedding car, feeling almost faint with excitement. The months since meeting Jonathan, their 'courtship' as her mother insisted on calling it, and their short engagement had all flashed by too quickly to be fully assimilated. She hardly dared believe it was actually happening. Why, only six months ago she had still believed herself to be committed to David! The sudden thought made her glance anxiously at St Sampson's Church door.

St Sampson had been Bishop of Dol in Brittany. In the sixth century AD he crossed to Guernsey, landed in the natural harbour which was to take his name, and was believed to have been the first Christian preacher in the island. The church which bore his name was built subsequently on the site of his chapel, in the eleventh century.

Ancient, lichen-covered gravestones stood to the right of the path which curved its way to where the three bridesmaids were waiting in the church doorway. They helped

Sue straighten her dress, arranged the ribbon-edged veil and, led by the choir, followed the bride down the steps to the aisle to the sound of Purcell's *Trumpet Voluntary*. It was a beautiful church, the long, main aisle leading under what had once been the high organ loft and choir stalls, up to a magnificent triple set of stained-glass windows. Sue's hand gripped Greg's arm as she glanced to left and right at the congregation, appreciating their smiles, but with a niggling fear of finding David amongst the sea of faces. That she failed to see him could have been due to the fact that the church was filled to capacity, so with a conscious effort she put him out of her mind and focused on her beloved Jonathan, who was standing a head taller than Norton, his best man, gorgeous enough to turn a girl's knees to water. He was smiling at her, watching as she handed her bouquet to Anne Warwick, and came to stand at her side as they waited for the service to commence.

Sue could hear her heart thumping until they had passed the 'impediment' bit without interruption; then she relaxed.

After the signing of the register the organist gave full throttle to the fanfare opening of Mendelssohn's *Wedding March*. David completely forgotten, Sue walked in stately procession, her fingers laid on the back of Jonathan's hand, out into the midday heat.

Photographs seemed to last forever, all the usual group-ings plus a succession of extras including Sue with her two grandmothers. Though Marie had shrunk even smaller with advancing years she looked very dignified in dusty pink draped with numerous ropes of pearls and a pearl-grey straw hat. Alice was in a soft blue georgette dress and jacket chosen by Sarah and Maureen.

Unfortunately, at the last minute the old lady had discarded the expensive midnight blue hat her daughters-in-law had selected, replacing it with a weird concoction she had found squashed in a dress-box in the attic, looking like a large pile of pancakes and much the same colour.

Sarah had not seen it as she entered the church and now stared at it in dismay. "What on earth happened?" she hissed at Maureen and Andrew who had accompanied Alice.

Maureen grimaced. "I nearly had a fit when I saw her on the doorstep! I tried to make her go back inside and change it for the one we bought her but she'd have none of it. Said the new one was too dark for a wedding and if she couldn't wear the one she had on she wasn't coming."

Sarah shrugged. "Well at least it should inject plenty of humour into the proceedings!"

A buffet lunch was spread on a long table down the centre of the Royal Hotel ballroom. The bride and groom stood near the door with Sarah and Greg and Jonathan's mother Jessica, greeting the guests and receiving their congratulations, while the bridesmaids and ushers and other members of the family milled round the room talking to the guests, sipping champagne and eyeing the food.

There was an early hold-up in the queue of guests when Sue was surprised to see her mother and father leap forward to hug and kiss a middle-aged couple she had no recollection of ever seeing before, together with a line of youths in tow. At last the newcomers were freed to approach the newlyweds.

"Do you remember your Aunt Ethel?" Sarah asked, dabbing her eyes.

Sue stared at the tall, bronzed woman and shook her head. "No, to be honest, but now I think of it I have seen photos of you in one of Mummy's albums. Have you come all the way from New Zealand to be here today?"

Ethel hugged the bride. "I reckoned it was as good an excuse as any for the black sheep to return. And you won't remember your Uncle Paul, either. And these are your cousins David, Michael, the twins, Roger and Tim, and Sam."

After a feast of hugging, kissing and handshaking, the Laurence family moved on into the room where they were set upon by Ethel's brothers William and John with their respective wives. Sarah had invited Paul's mother, Arabella who, together with Marie, had been responsible for banishing their erring young to New Zealand in 1932. Now the two grandmothers, Arabella, tall, beak-nosed and angular, towering over the diminutive Marie, greeted their grandsons and gave the couple an enthusiastic welcome, all the harsh words of the past forgotten. Sarah and John winked at each other as they spotted their sister Aline standing by, tight-lipped with disapproval.

One of the day's highlights for Sue was finding herself face to face with Andrew's and Maureen's daughter; she squealed with excitement and flung her arms round the statuesque blonde beauty. "Sybil! No one told me you were coming! How wonderful. Jonathan, darling, this is my gorgeous cousin I told you about. My child-hood idol."

"A child of sweet innocence!" Sybil's laugh was a low gurgle. "Hallo, Jonathan. I see my little cousin has done very nicely for herself!"

The bridegroom bowed over her hand. "Madam, you are too kind."

"Ah! Do I note the touch of His Majesty's Royal Navy?" Sybil arched an exquisite eyebrow.

"Indeed. The *senior* service," was his prompt reaction to recognising an army type. "Where were you stationed?"

"Wherever the action was. Meanwhile would I be correct in assuming that you were still in your rompers at the time?"

"Yes, indeed. So much easier to swim ashore when the Krauts removed the deck from under one."

Sue loved the repartee but thought she should chip in. "Sybil was driving a general during the war."

"To distraction?" Jonathan enquired, straightfaced.

"Absolutely. But via the altar. Gordon! Come and meet the happy pair."

A man with a white moustache and red face, his immaculate uniform stretched to the limit over his middle, bounced up to the group, grinning. "Hello. So you are Sue. I've heard so much about you!"

"General Banks! Super to meet you, at last."

"Now look here, young lady. None of this damned formality if you don't mind. The name's Gordon. And you, Jonathan, are to be congratulated on landing such a splendid catch."

"Thank you, sir." The groom clicked his heels and bent his neck slightly.

The general scowled. "Remember, we are both members of the family, now. Gordon, please. Tell me, do you play cricket?"

"Yes, si . . . Gordon. Or rather I did, before the war."

"Got a job?"

"Sue and I are preparing to start up in the hotel business . . ."

"Good. Let us know when you open and we'll risk coming over to try you out."

"You'd better bring a jar of Maclean's with you, just to be on the safe side."

The general eyed him from under lowered lids. "Remind us when we book, right?"

"What a great pair they are," Jonathan commented when they had moved away.

"Daddy says he fields quite a good army cricket team. If you could get a team together we might invite them over for some matches. Now I suppose we should circulate."

Greg had invited George Schmit, who had been a family friend forever, to propose the toast to the bride and groom. The amusing speech was received with cheers and clapping, but this was nothing to the noisy acclamation in response to Jonathan's reply which even the loquacious raconteur, Norton, could not cap when he spoke on behalf of the bridesmaids.

The three-tiered cake was cut up and served by waiters and waitresses, together with even more champagne.

A simple yellow cotton dress formed the basis of the bride's going-away outfit, worn with a white straw hat and sandals. They had not told anyone except their parents where they were going for fear of dreadful practical jokes, so after Sue had tossed her bouquet to Anne and the wedding car was driven away in a cloud of confetti, they went only as far as the Regal car park where they jumped into the anonymous, waiting taxi, and were driven back down St Julian's Avenue to the White Rock where they boarded the Sark boat.

"Satisfied with your wedding, my darling?" Jonathan asked as they leaned over the gunwale watching gulls swooping and screaming after the scraps thrown overboard by a crewman.

"Super. I thought it all went off very well, apart from one or two minor matters. Like Uncle Andrew getting plastered."

"And your dear little brother stuffing himself with sausages before the meal even began."

"Mmm. It has been marvellous but exhausting." Sue leaned her head against his shoulder. "I'm glad it's all over."

"Over! As far as I'm concerned the best part hasn't even started."

"You lecherous beast, you!"

If Sue had had her way during the preceding weeks, she would not have been a virgin on her honeymoon. Jonathan's bachelorhood had been by no means virtuous but he was adamant: "I have always vowed I would marry a woman *virgo intacta* and I'm not breaking that vow for want of a few weeks waiting."

And at breakfast on the first morning she admitted she was glad they had waited. "I might have been put off marriage for life, otherwise!"

"It will get better, my love. We do have ten days in which to practice."

They had borrowed the Schmit's holiday cottage, tucked away at the top of a valley, with wonderful views across to Jersey. It smelled of musty wood and creosote, but when the big French windows were opened onto the verandah, the salt-laden breeze fluttering the curtains, there was a sweet scent from the surrounding trees and from the roses which were determined to climb up to the verandah roof.

"Won't you want to continue practicing when we get home?"

"That won't be necessary. We'll be perfect by then."

Sue laughed. "Poor Mummy. If only she realised how inadequate her 'little chat' on the subject has proved. Do you know, she told me it took her and Daddy weeks and weeks before they managed to make love properly."

"*Her* mother's 'little chat' must have been even worse!"

"Grandma has always boasted that Grandpa never saw her without clothes, or at least a nightdress on."

"All I can say is that you are bloody marvellous, considering your background!"

It only rained once while they were in Sark. They walked up to the main 'street' to buy provisions, rambled on the cliffs, ate, drank, made love and slept, adoring every minute, but before the ten days were up they were itching to get home and start work.

Jonathan's mother had moved into the Old Cottage on the property, not far from the farmhouse which stood a few hundred yards inland from Port Grat. Though she appeared at first to be rather fragile, she was in fact tough as nails having survived five years of nursing in a military hospital in England during the war. The couple arrived home to find their dower wing windows open, flowers on the table and a casserole in the oven. "Shan't make a practice of this, mind," Jessica warned from the back door. "But do remember that if you can find anything practical for me to do when you start renovating the house, I'd love to help." Then she disappeared in her neat little slacks and floppy hat.

"Hope you don't mind her coming in as soon as we are back." Jonathan was a little sceptical. "But she's not a bad old stick. She knows jolly well that if she starts interfering I'll tick her off."

"Heavens no! I think she's awfully sweet. And very kind to fix our first meal here."

The builders had finished work on Jessica's cottage in record time, then completed the lesser tasks on the dower wing ahead of the wedding date. Now they started on the alterations in the main house, moving non-load-bearing walls to make four bedrooms into six with an extension into the reroofed barn for two more bedrooms and two extra bathrooms.

"Well have to tap the bank manager for a loan, I'm afraid," Jonathan said, "I hate asking, but it makes more sense to do the job properly from the start."

"Why don't we get the carpenters to make built-in wardrobes? It would save on buying all the furniture."

"Good idea. I'll get them to quote. Would you like to draw up some ideas for them to work on?"

So one wall in each bedroom became a continuous unit with a dressing table set between two cupboards. Sue prowled round auctions and second-hand shops to pick up little antique tables for the bedsides, and a variety of chairs, many of which she renovated and covered herself with the help of Aunt Filly, leaving only the beds to be bought new. They stitched curtains and bedspreads and scatter cushions, and Sue also bought miscellaneous old ornaments and pictures to lend the rooms individual character. The woodwork in all the rooms was white, and the cabbage roses on the curtains and covers matched the pinks and greens of the lightly patterned carpets. "We cannot have plain carpets," Sue insisted, "They'll show every mark."

Meanwhile, life was sweet. First of their group of friends to be married, their home immediately became a focal point for gatherings. Jonathan soon drummed up enthusiasm amongst them to form a cricket team for the following season, and arrangements were made for use of a pitch. Jessica was very popular with the group and was secretly chuffed to be included in several of their parties. The young couple joined a badminton club and played once a week throughout the winter on the courts above the Market Halls.

Having obtained the necessary permission, the lower floor of the barn was turned into a cocktail bar, with store rooms behind. It was duly stocked and officially opened on Sue's nineteenth birthday, 31 January 1949. Filled to bursting with family, friends and licensed traders, it was a fantastic party which a hardened nucleus continued for two days and nights in the dower wing, with fierce liar dice sessions interrupted only by forays into the stores for more beer, and into the kitchen for cans of baked beans, scrambled eggs, bacon and coffee.

Sarah gazed out at her drenched garden through a haze of rain. It had rained steadily for over a week, lowering even further her already depressed state of mind. Greg's additional business with tomato pots kept him busier than ever through the winter months, months during which they had spent most time together in the past. Richard was at school all day and busy with homework in the evenings. Sue was married.

The rift between Sarah and her mother and sister had never healed; Ethel and her family had returned to New Zealand; William and his family were back in Cornwall and John and Edna, at the other end of the island, were busy preparing for next season. And of course her youngest brother, Bertie, had been killed in the war. Their wonderful, big happy family had disintegrated.

Dear God, why? Why did it have to happen? Wasn't war said to unite people against a common enemy? On the other hand, had she even hesitated before marrying and coming to live as far from Val du Douit as was possible in Guernsey, to become part of the Gaudion family? If they could be called a family. Alice was now nutty as a fruit cake, and Andrew regularly drank himself stupid, with poor Maureen haggard with worry and desperately pretending it wasn't happening.

The phone interrupted the inventory of her miseries. She jumped up, eager to talk to someone, anyone. Maybe it was Sue?

It was a wrong number. She paused to look in the hall mirror, recoiling with shock from the grey, wrinkled image of a woman she scarcely recognised; a creature with drooping shoulders and a sour expression.

"Hello Mum. What's for tea?" Richard came through the kitchen grinning, soaked to the skin.

"Don't stand there dripping all over the hall floor! Go and take your things off by the back door. The trouble with you is you don't think! Don't you realise someone has to mop up all the mess?"

Richard backed away, disappointed. "I'll do it."

"No you won't. I know you, you'll just spread it over the floor. Like you do with the clothes in your room. It took me half the morning to get it sorted out, so just make sure you don't go and mess it up again."

The lad, who looked so like his mother with his dark hair and amber eyes, retreated, mentally and physically.

His mother watched him go, hating herself. Why had she turned into such a bitter old hag? "Richard, darling," she called after him.

His bedroom door slammed.

"I'm off to the bank. Want anything from the Bridge while I'm there?" Greg shrugged into his mac.

Andrew looked up from his desk, scowling. "Have you finished replacing the stakes in number four?"

"The boy is doing that. So if there's nothing you want I'll be off."

"'Bye," his brother grunted. Always going off to the bank, running round selling those damned pots. He'd love to know just how much Greg was making off them; there had to be a fair profit for Greg to afford to employ a boy to do the greenhouse chores. When he heard the car go down past the side of the house, he opened a drawer and pulled out a flask of gin. Damn, it was nearly empty.

In fact Greg was making a very substantial profit. Hundreds. Thousands. But it wasn't bringing him much joy. There were three fat cheques in his paying-in book to swell their private account even more, but for what? He wanted to take Sarah away on holiday, to see parts of the world he had only dreamed of till now. But he couldn't

119

see any joy in taking her while she was in such a gloomy, nagging state of mind. It didn't seem to take anything noticable, logical, to set her off; he had only to set foot in the house and she started. And Richard was becoming so withdrawn, argumentative, even belligerent, one had to wonder if she was having a go at the boy when he himself wasn't around.

He sighed, and pulled into a parking space. There wasn't much he could do about it, anyway.

"There you are, Sue, still working! I've been hunting for you. Here," Jessica handed her daughter-in-law a steaming mug, "thought you might like a shot of cocoa."

Sue left her brush on the top of the paint tin and pushed a strand of hair off her face, leaving a streak of white across her cheek. "So kind of you," she took the mug and sipped cautiously, "Oh, super. I needed this."

"I honestly don't know how you two keep up the pace. I never would have believed you'd be finished in time for the beginning of the season, but it seems you'll make it easily, with time to spare." Jessica strolled across bare boards from one end of the new bedroom to the other, remembering how the place used to be before the war, when Jonathan was growing up.

"There is still an awful lot to do, yet. Carpets to lay, curtains to hang, furniture to bring in. I just pray everything fits."

"I bet it will. But it's the catering that would daunt me. Thank heavens you have had some experience at your aunt and uncle's place."

"Mmm." Sue grimaced. "I'm hoping it will be sufficient for me to cope. It's one thing following someone else's instructions, but quite different when you have to make all the decisions yourself." She handed the mug back to Jessica. "Thank you. Now I'd better get this room finished by tonight if I can."

Jonathan's mother hurried back to her cottage through the icy March wind, smiling. She was well satisfied with her son's choice of bride. She only hoped that all the hard work the young couple had put into La Rocque Hotel would earn the success they needed.

None of them need have worried. Every room in the hotel was ready in time to receive the first visitors, who were full of praise for the attractive comforts like ample, big fluffy towels, details like fresh flowers in each room.

Edna had helped Sue draw up a month of menus, to be repeated throughout the season. "Judging by the ratio of criticism to praise, you two seem to have chosen very successfully," Jonathan remarked in early June.

"I'd rather not have any criticism at all!"

"Well it certainly hasn't been worth recording; only three people have registered disapproval and all were obviously professional complainers."

"I hope Gordon's cricket team will be satisfied. Have you ordered a bus to fetch them from the boat tomorrow?"

"Indeed, and to take us all to the field for our matches."

The Bluebird coach just managed to squeeze through the granite gate pillars next morning, with a cricket team of mixed ages from twenty-five to over seventy, all ex-army 'types'. Jonathan's local team were waiting with a big welcome and a hugely successful weekend followed. There were pavilion teas organised by local wives, cocktail parties in homes of host team members and, on the last night there was a gala dinner at the Royal hotel.

"We want to reserve our rooms in advance, now, for next year," Gordon declared as they checked out at the reception desk. "May not be all the same names, but the number will remain at roughly twelve. Now you lot will have to come and visit us. I'll be in touch. But I have to warn you there is no way we can compete with this weekend. It has been truly stunning!"

It was a windless afternoon of blue skies, open windows and doors and the sound of bees humming in the flower beds. Lunch was long finished and cleared, the visitors had dispersed to the beach with buckets and spades, or to nap away the midday heat in their rooms, while Jonathan and Sue kicked their shoes off on their sitting room carpet and lounged back with the token newspapers which never got read.

Sue smiled. "You have always been a severe critic of restaurant food. What do you think of our fare?"

"The cricketers certainly enjoyed it! Plain, simple and good, just like we planned. In fact, I thought the stuffed mackerel today was first rate."

"Did you? I'm glad. I wondered if it might be too strongly flavoured for most people's taste."

"Emmy said the dirty plates came into the kitchen with all the bones picked clean." Emmy, who had worked for Sue's grandmother Ozanne at Val du Douit before the war, was first to apply for the job of kitchenmaid when it was advertised in the *Guernsey Press*. Sue thought she might be unwilling to take on some of the heavy work involved but Emmy had smiled at her indulgently and said, "Try me." And after the first day there was never any question of her not staying.

Jonathan fanned himself with an old menu card. "Feel like a dip?"

Sue yawned. "Yes, but I'm not sure I can raise the energy."

He stood up and grabbed her arm. "Come on, Mrs Martel, you're getting lazy in your old age!"

Wearing swimsuits under their towel wraps, they walked down the hill to Port Grat, crossed the road to the grass and climbed down over the rocks onto the sand. The tide was quite high, warm enough for them to sink into the water without a shiver, and float on their backs, hand in hand, watching the gulls overhead.

Sue could not stop smiling: the happiness was tangible. Solid. And this, the ultimate feeling of unity, was only the beginning of the rest of their lives together. The bliss, the freedom of which she had dreamed for so long.

By the end of August '49, there was no longer any doubt in Sue's mind. She wondered if it had happened that day in late June, when they returned from a swim at Port Grat and it had seemed so natural when they got home, to stretch out on the bed after they had showered the sand and salt out of their hair . . .

"Are you okay? You look green as grass!" Jonathan studied her face with concern.

"I'm fine, thanks. Apparently nausea is often a symptom of my condition." It was the first time she had said anything.

He had begun to turn away but swivelled, blue eyes goggling with excitement. "Honestly? Are you sure?"

"Well, along with the fact that I haven't had the curse for three months, I imagine the nausea confirms it. But I'll go along to old Dr Collard when I have time."

"Time! It's time you eased up, old girl. Put your feet up for Heaven's sake! And you get Collard to come and see you, tomorrow."

"Whatever for? I'm not ill. The only thing that is troubling me is whether we'll be able to afford someone to take over my duties next April when I produce."

"You can put your mind at rest on that score. We are already way up on our estimated profit for the year. A lot of it from bar takings of course, largely due to local trade which will continue year round. So, my darling," he pulled her into his arms, "we can well afford to employ an assistant manager for next season."

Flight Sergeant Terry Simon's family had had a small hotel in St Peter Port before the war. His father, being elderly but a forward-thinking man, had sent Terry down to Jersey to learn hotel work at the Pomme d'Or in St Helier when he left school in 1937. He enjoyed both the work and his workmates, and when a group of them decided to enlist in the RAF early in 1940, Terry went with them, became a rear gunner and survived the conflict without so much as a torn fingernail. Grounded in 1945 when Germany surrendered, he volunteered for work in a catering unit until his demob. Unfortunately, in the meantime the family hotel had ceased to exist, so he returned to the Pomme d'Or for two seasons until, on a day visit to Guernsey at the end of August, he saw an advertisement for Assistant Manager at La Rocque Hotel.

Dressed for his interview that same day, in dark grey suit and spotless white shirt, black hair oiled flat and moustache neatly clipped, he made a favourable impression on Sue and Jonathan, and his apparent knowledge of the catering industry influenced their decision to offer him the job, starting as barman that autumn until taking up full duties next season. A legal contract was drawn up and sent through the mail for signatures, all finalised by the third week of September.

Their minds filled with these business details, building improvements to be completed before the start of next season, and preparations for the baby's arrival in April, neither Jonathan nor Sue had given much thought to the British Chancellor of the Exchequer's current problems. So it was with utter disbelief and horror that they listened to the news at breakfast on the 19th of September and Sir Stafford Cripps's announcement of a thirty and one half per cent devaluation of sterling.

All colour drained from Sue's face as she stared at Jonathan. He gave a long, troubled sigh, then forced a smile. Taking her hand in his he said, "Don't let it upset you, my sweetheart. We don't know yet how this is going to affect us, or even if it will at all."

"But we've just signed a contract with Terry Simon . . . we might not be able to afford him, now."

"Let's wait and see before throwing in the towel."

It was a cliché Sue repeated at Les Mouettes the following week when she visited her mother.

It was almost as though Sarah welcomed the news as a

good excuse for another moan. "Really, this government is totally useless! Why do the English people put up with them? They must have been mad to oust Mr Churchill: he would never have got us into this mess."

Sue tried to divert her mother onto other topics. "Do you think I could have the baby at home, or would you advise . . ."

"Book yourself into the Maternity Hospital as soon as possible. But make sure you explain you want Dr Collard for the actual delivery. It's no good depending on midwives. Some of them are so old-fashioned in their methods . . . really bossy and cruel. I remember poor Mrs Mahy from the—"

"Hallo Richard," Sue interrupted. "Like your new class this term?"

Her brother gave her the latest news from school. Then asked, "Can I have a sandwich, Mum, I'm starving." Sarah sighed, and the boy added "I'll do it."

"No thanks. You'll only leave the kitchen in a mess." She started to pull herself out of her chair.

Sue leapt up. "You stay there. I'll go and do it. What do you want, Rick, Marmite or jam?"

"Both together, please."

"Good decision . . ."

"Absolutely disgusting," Sarah commented.

Richard followed Sue into the kitchen.

"Is she always like this?"

The boy nodded. "Or worse."

"Must be horrible, some days."

"Every day." He slumped onto a chair. "Sometimes I wish I could board at school."

"Ever talk to Dad about it?"

"I tried, once. He wouldn't listen. Said I should try harder to please her."

When Sue arrived back home, she had no idea of which route she had taken, being so distracted over her brother's dilemma. "Thank goodness I'm not living there any more," she remarked to Jonathan. "I think I would go crackers."

"I do feel sorry for Richard . . . poor little beggar."

Sue had developed a close relationship with Edna, during the time she worked for her. She decided to drive up to Val du Douit and discuss the problem. "Do you think Mummy might be sickening for something?"

"It's possible, but how are you going to find out? You can't very well suggest she asks the doctor for a tonic to cure her moods."

Sue laughed. "True. But I might suggest to Daddy that he talks her into it."

"Huh! Knowing your father I can't think you'll make much headway there. But you can try."

Sue drove to Les Marettes greenhouses and found Greg telling his 'hand' what he wanted done next morning. "I'd like a word with you, if you can spare a few minutes," she said.

Greg raised one eyebrow and guided her out of the greenhouse into the office.

"Phew! What a stink of stale booze in here!" She opened the window wide. "Is Uncle Andrew still at it?"

"'Fraid so. But I'm sure that is not the reason for this visit. What do you want to talk about?"

"Mummy." She hitched her rear onto the edge of the desk. "Have you wondered if she might be sickening for something?"

"No. Why?"

"She seems so irritable all the time. Can't say anything nice about anyone or anything. We had become so close when I had my accident, but now we're back to square one. As for poor Richard, he's having a hell of a life."

"Now look here, Sue, that sort of talk is very disloyal to Mummy," he said severely. "And I'm sure Richard is perfectly happy."

"Oh Daddy! Do you think I would have come here today if I wasn't honestly worried about him, and Mummy? It may be partly due to the change – I know she is having a bad time with it. And perhaps the fact that Richard is away at school all day, I'm married and you are busier now, what with your pots as well as the vinery, well, all that could be making her feel depressed and useless." She shrugged. "Whatever. She's making herself miserable and Richard, too."

And me, Greg thought. But he didn't say so. Instead he said, "Mmm. She doesn't seem to be quite her old self, lately. But I cannot imagine what anyone can do about it."

"Get her to see the doctor."

"She'd be furious if I suggested it!"

"Not if you put an arm round her and tell her you are worried that she hasn't been looking very well lately. Ask her to have a check-up, for your own peace of mind."

Greg smiled at her concern. "I can try."

"You might even give the doc a ring and brief him, first."

Greg nodded, then asked, "What about you? How is junior coming on?"

Sue smoothed her skirt over her slightly protruding

stomach. "Couldn't be better. Never been fitter in my life."

They strolled out to her car, together, discussing the state of sterling and prospects for the coming growing and tourist season.

Doctor Walker told Sarah she was very anaemic, gave her some pills and ordered her to rest. Greg was very attentive and Richard was persuaded to be a little more understanding.

"Your father is being so sweet; won't let me lift a finger," Sarah told Sue at Christmas time. "Anyone would think he had been given a good talking-to."

"Oh Mummy! What an awful thing to say! You know he adores you."

Sarah eyed her daughter for a moment, then smiled. "I had even wondered if you had said anything."

Sue contrived a seriously shocked expression. "As though I would!" Adding, "But I do think you should both take a holiday. Why don't you fly off to somewhere exotic like Spain or Italy?"

"We have thought about it, but I'm not keen on the idea of going by air."

"Oh there have been a few accidents, but not as many as on the roads. Everyone is travelling by air, now."

When news of the plane crash near Cardiff broke on 12 March the following year, it finished any chance Greg might have had to get Sarah into an aircraft. "Eighty people dead!" she exclaimed. "I thought the authorities had banned all those Tudor planes."

"Only the Mark fours. This was a Mark five," Sue told

her. "I suppose they should have grounded them all. Now, changing the subject, anyone like a cup of tea? I'll go and put on the kettle." They were in the Martel's sitting room at La Rocque, where Jessica had joined them.

The two prospective grandmothers leapt up as they saw the girl struggle to her feet, saying "I'll do it!" with one voice.

"Why? I'm strong as a horse. Just a bit awkward, that's all. But you can come out to the kitchen and talk to me while I set the trolley."

"Do you ever have problems with your back, now?" Jessica asked, following.

"Occasionally if I'm on my feet too long."

"She really shouldn't be working in the hotel . . ." Sarah began.

But Sue interrupted, afraid Jessica would take this as a criticism of her son. "The hotel has nothing to do with my back, Mummy. I just find myself reading the paper standing up or forget to use the kitchen stool to prepare the vegetables." She filled the kettle and then set tray cloths on the trolley. "Would someone like to butter the gache, please. And I made some little coffee cakes, this morning. They can go on this plate."

Crisis averted, the women returned to the sitting room, Sue wheeling the trolley.

Jonathan tried to make Sue rest. "It cannot do your back any good, carrying that huge load around all day."

"True, it does ache rather more, now. But to be honest I find the worst part is not being able to reach things. Like my shoes, for instance." She pushed a foot towards him. "Could you do that up for me? And I really cannot drive the car any more. I can't get behind the steering wheel."

"Thank God for that! I told you you shouldn't risk ramming the poor chap with it, weeks ago."

"You must stop calling it a him, darling. I don't want you to be disappointed if it's a her." She sighed. "I wish *it* would arrive before Easter."

"What, in less than a week? He . . . I mean it, will have to be two weeks early."

Roderick Oswald Dennis Martel was safely delivered at nine-thirty a.m. on 10 April 1950, Easter Monday, much to his mother's relief. After such an easy and comfortable pregnancy she was shattered by the long, difficult birth, but her spirits were soon lifted when Jonathan arrived in great excitement that afternoon together with Norton, Tiny and Penny, Sarah, Greg and Jessica. She was upstairs in the 'conservatory' ward at the Amherst Maternity Hospital where 'the boys' had smuggled in bottles of champagne and several glasses. Sue was rather alarmed, eyes constantly flickering to the ward door, scared of seeing the ward sister or one of the rattier nurses approaching, but the toasts were long past and the second bottle almost drained when a junior nurse appeared, looking shocked.

"Cor! I wondered what the noise was. You'd better get all that out of sight, quick, or you'll have me shot!" Then aware of the large number of people in the room she asked, "How many of these are yours, Mrs Martel?"

Fate was on their side. The three other new mothers in the room were without visitors, and one immediately piped up, "Some are mine," the call taken up by the other two.

The young nurse's starched cap quivered in disbelief,

but with the glasses and bottles out of sight she shrugged and disappeared.

"Brilliant!" Jonathan laughed, turning to thank Sue's fellow patients, who were bringing out their glasses from under the bedclothes.

"Cheers!" they giggled. "The least we could do."

Life was sweet.

Although the hotel was already open to residents again, and the bar very busy, Jonathan was able to spend ample time with his wife and son, thanks to the good work of Terry Simon.

Roderick was christened at St Sampson's Church on a wet June day, and everyone came back to the hotel for the party. The residents joined in with enthusiasm. John Ozanne and Norton were Godfathers and Sybil accepted Sue's invitation to be Godmother, coming over with the general for the event.

It was Great-grandmother Alice who provided the entertainment. "You've got a lovely boy there," she kept telling Greg, and asking, "Are you planning another to keep him company?"

Averting his eyes from Sarah, who was doubled up with laughter behind a curtain, Greg shook his head and shouted, "No. We don't intend to have any more," down her ear-trumpet.

"Why aren't you sure? I thought there were things you could use . . ."

"NO!" he roared. "You didn't hear right. I said we don't want any more."

Everyone else in the room was silent, listening to the hilarious exchange.

There was an agonised moan from the other side of the curtain.

"It's you that's not very bright, not me!" Alice said severely. "I know all about these things."

Terry saved the day. "More champagne, Mrs Gaudion?"

"Of course," she replied, holding out her glass.

"The only time she ever hears correctly is when she is offered a drink," Sue explained to Jonathan.

"And that without the use of the ear-trumpet, I see!"

"What age is she?" Norton asked.

"Ninety-one. And looks like going on at least another ten years."

"Well for goodness sake try and get her to use a proper hearing aid, before we all die laughing."

"Do you imagine we haven't all tried?" Sue demanded. "She gets furious at the suggestion. Told me she didn't need another maid, last time I raised the subject. And when I finally got the message through she said she had heard perfectly well with the trumpet for the past thirty years and she was blowed if she'd start sticking these new-fangled gadgets in her ears. One couldn't tell what they might lead to." The way she mimicked her grandmother had them all in stitches again.

Sue could scarcely believe how lucky she was when Stephanie was born on 21 January 1952, ten days before her own twenty-second birthday. "I'm so happy," she whispered to Jonathan when he visited her again in the maternity hospital. "A wonderful husband, and two gorgeous children. Plus a lovely home."

"My darling, I'm so glad you're happy. I am, too. And not only because of my beautiful wife and children, but also because the hotel is going so well, bringing in a jolly good income. I reckon we should get plans under way for starting the extension at the end of this coming season."

"We've talked about it enough. Let's call the architect as soon as I'm back on my feet again."

She came home with her daughter in time for her birthday, and was enchanted with all the pictures of Princess Elizabeth and Prince Philip setting off for South Africa. "Aren't they lucky!" she exclaimed. "I'd love to do a safari one day."

"We will, I promise," Jonathan assured her.

"Wonderful!" She watched little Roddy as he leaned over his sister's carrycot and touched her tiny hand very gently with one finger. She smiled contentedly and continued looking at the pictures in the paper. Her mind drifted back to the war years and her desperate loneliness, her longing for home and family. Until David had appeared. She swallowed, and swiftly put him out of her mind because even now, she still felt a niggling sense of guilt whenever she thought of him.

"The boys are coming tonight to celebrate your home-coming. Is that all right with you?"

"Super! I've got a bean jar we can tuck into." She knew they all loved the traditional Guernsey dish of dried butter beans and haricots, cooked in a slow oven overnight with a pig's trotter.

It was a lively party and continued into the early hours, some time after Sue had retired to bed. She half woke when Jonathan climbed under the blankets beside her. The baby was sleeping soundly and she curled up against her husband with a contented sigh.

The news of the death of King George VI a week later, shocked the nation.

The story of Prince Philip breaking the news to the young Queen brought tears to many eyes, including Sue's. "When you think how happy she looked when the King and Queen were seeing them off at London Airport."

"Well she always knew she would be Queen one day," Jonathan pointed out.

"Of course, but not so soon. Not while her children are still so young. Now her home life is finished." She grabbed his hand and kissed it. "I'm sure it's difficult for men to understand how important her home and family are to a woman. It's quite frightening, isn't it, how suddenly, almost at the snap of Fate's fingers, people's lives can be shattered. Changed forever."

"Frightening?"

"Yes. I mean, it could happen to anyone, couldn't it?"

He sat on the arm of her chair and smoothed the hair back from her forehead. "My sweetheart. You mustn't let this make you nervous! Life is good! And it's going to go on being good."

She turned her face up to be kissed, and when he obliged their son joined in, demanding some of the action.

It was a wonderful summer. Terry was an able manager freeing Jonathan to accompany his family to the beach on fine afternoons where they were joined by various friends, relatives and adoring grandmothers. The hotel continued to show a healthy profit and at the end of the season when they closed, workmen moved in to begin the extensions.

It was late one October evening in filthy weather, when Jonathan was returning home from a meeting, that a young speedster lost control of his car when it skidded on seaweed on the coast road. It slid across the road broadside, and hit Jonathan's Vauxhall with such velocity that it was rolled over the low wall and plunged down onto the beach.

The young man jumped out of his vehicle unharmed, ran to the sea wall and looked over onto the darkened beach in horror.

Chapter Six

Emergency

It wasn't the story that Roddy enjoyed so much as the sound of his mother's voice as she read to him. She had to spend so much time with baby Stephanie, nowadays, but in the evening when the baby was in bed it was Roddy's turn to curl up on Sue's knee and relish her undivided attention.

Sue loved 'Roddy's Time', particularly now that the evenings were getting dark earlier. The sitting room was cosy with the curtains drawn and a fire crackling in the grate while wind and rain lashed the windows. Roddy, in pyjamas and dressing gown, smelled sweet and fresh from his bath, hair still slightly damp against her chin as she read another poem from A.A. Milne's *When We Were Very Young*, at the end of which he no longer wriggled and said, "Nuvver one, peese!" He was asleep. She lifted him gently, carried him upstairs to bed and tucked him in.

Downstairs the kitchen clock said seven-fifteen; Jonathan had said his meeting would last about an hour, so he should be in at any minute. She lit the oven to warm the plates and started frying up the remains of yesterday's shepherd's pie.

She hadn't had time to look at the daily newspapers, so when the supper was ready in the oven she sat down with a sherry to read the latest details on the appalling London train disaster which had killed 112 commuters. The conversation she and Jonathan had had after the sudden death of the King came to mind: the way people's lives can be so normal one minute, and without warning totally destroyed the next. She shivered and turned the page. There the headlines were all about Mau Mau atrocities in Kenya.

At eight o'clock Sue was becoming hungry. Where was Jonathan? Sighing with irritation she went to the phone and dialled the hotel bar. "Is Jonathan up there?" she asked Terry.

"No. Haven't seen him since early this afternoon."

"Maybe he's met up with some of the crowd. Never mind."

But she did mind. Dammit, he could have phoned to let her know. Supper would be a dried-up mess! She opened the oven, took out her own portion and sat at the kitchen table to eat alone.

Suddenly she felt sick. It was quite difficult to eat at first, but she felt a bit better when she had finished her meal.

Gary's first instinct had been to jump into his, or rather his Dad's car and go. Anywhere. His legs were wobbly, his arm agony and his breathing was a series of short gasps. And he was terrified of what he had done. But there were two reasons why he couldn't escape: one, it didn't need

138

a qualified mechanic to tell that Dad's front wheel was now square and the axle obviously twisted; and two, a wee small voice of common sense was pointing out that he would be tracked down and publicly shamed for life if he did. Probably would be, anyway.

There was a cottage a little way off down the road. Shaking, Gary made his way to the front door, knocked and a middle-aged man in a Guernsey opened it.

"There's been an accident . . ." the boy gasped.

"I see that."

"Uh?"

"From the blood."

Gary looked down and in the light through the doorway saw the dark stain down his coat, put his fingers up to his head and located a warm, sticky patch.

"Anyone else hurt?" the man asked.

Gary nodded. "A car's gone over the sea wall. No one got out."

"Aw, lordy! I'll go next door and phone for help. Doris!"

A stout lady appeared from a back room, and when her husband had explained she led Gary away to bathe his head. "I'll make you a cup of tea to stop you shaking. It's the shock, love."

He hoped the tea might also give him sufficient courage to go next door and phone his father.

Sue dug another shovelful of coal out of the scuttle to throw on the fire. She was shivering again and it crossed her mind she might be going down with 'flu. She checked the mantel clock with her watch, and frowned: both said eight forty-three. She had been suppressing bouts of worry for nearly an hour, now she was beginning to feel seriously anxious. In her mind she went through all the places Jonathan might be: his mother's, one of their friend's places, or maybe at his Uncle Ted's discussing the hotel extensions, Ted Martel being their architect. But every one of them had a phone, Jonathan would have rung and let her know. He always did. Should she start telephoning? If so, who?

She didn't want to be alarmist so decided to wait till nine o'clock and then telephone Norton.

Ten minutes later, as she sipped a cup of tea by the fire, there was a knocking on the front door. She jumped to her feet, spilling the tea in her haste, and hurried to open the door . . . to a policeman.

"Good evening," he said, removing his cap. "Mrs Martel?"

Speechless with fear, she could only nod.

"May I come in, please?"

She struggled for breath, stood aside and closed the door after him. "What's happened? Is it my husband? Is he all right?"

"I hope so. But I'm afraid he has been involved in a nasty accident."

"Is he badly hurt?"

"I'm not able to say. We won't know till the doctors have finished examining him."

"He's in the hospital? When did it happen?"

"We were called about a quarter to eight, so it must have been a bit before that."

"That's over an hour ago. Why has it—"

"We had to get a crane to lift the car off the beach before the tide reached it."

"Beach?" Sue shook her head, trying to fathom what Jonathan might have been doing.

"The impact sent his car over the sea wall, or so it seems. Hard to tell exactly but we'll be able to see more in the morning, in daylight. Look, ma'am, why don't you finish your cup of tea then I'll run you up to the hospital."

"It's cold."

"Well let's get you a fresh one. Where's the kitchen?"

She stood up, felt dizzy, and quickly sat down again.

The policeman looked at her grey face, picked up her cup and carried it off in search of the kettle.

They took Jessica with them. Terry had fetched Emmy to sit with the children, while Sue collected Jonathan's pyjamas, dressing gown and toiletries. The two women sat in the back of the police car, occasionally patting each other's hand in encouragement.

They were not allowed to see Jonathan, having to be satisfied with the knowledge he was still alive. A man and a youth who had blood on his clothes and his arm in a splint, sat with them in a side room for a while. Only after they had gone did Sue and Jessica learn that the young man was the other driver in the accident.

A police sergeant came in. "Okay, Wilkins, you can go now. I'll be here for a while until we get some news." He turned to the women. "Hello. I'm Bob Entwhistle. I'm so sorry to meet you under these circumstances," he shook their hands.

"We are the Mrs Martels, junior and senior. Wife and mother," Jessica responded. "Can you tell us what happened exactly?"

"Not exactly. But from what we can gather there was a collision on the Rocquaine coast road and Mr Martel's car rolled over the sea wall."

Sue gasped and put her hand over her mouth. "They must have been going at some speed . . ."

"One of them was, certainly. And between you and me it wasn't your husband. However, it's not for me to make any judgements at this stage. Fortunately the sea hadn't reached the shingle where the car landed, and we were able to get a crane on the scene before high tide. Unfortunately your husband was unconscious and therefore unable to help himself."

"Who called the emergency services?" Jessica asked.

"The young lad who was in the other car. Silly young tearaway. I don't know which is scaring him most at the moment, us, the consequences of his actions or his father's anger at having his car wrecked."

"At least he stayed at the scene and got help. That must have taken some courage," Jessica remarked.

Sue nodded.

"Very generous of you to say so, ma'am, in the circumstances. Ah, perhaps we have news?"

The newcomer's white coat and stethescope indicated authority. He nodded briefly at the sergeant and then looked at the women. "Which of you is Mr Martel's next of kin?"

"We both are. This is his mother. I am his wife." Sue's heart was thumping loudly with fear. "How is he?"

"He has multiple injuries, but none appear to be immediately life threatening. We will have to operate to reset a bad break in his left leg tomorrow. The next forty-eight hours are crucial but he appears to be strong

142

and healthy and his heart is good. His wounds are being dressed at the moment and as soon as he is admitted to a ward a nurse will fetch you to see him."

"Could he be put into a private ward, please?" Jessica asked.

"Possibly. I'll speak to Sister. Would you like some tea while you're waiting?"

It had been the worst night of her life.

Returning home with Jessica at four-thirty a.m., Sue knew that sleep would be impossible. The women returned to the hospital next morning, to sit by Jonathan's bed, watching the restless, bandaged figure labouring for breath, praying for him to return to full consciousness. Then, when he did begin to surface and they saw pain twisting the visible parts of his face, they could only wish him the relief of semi-consciousness again.

During the following week, two facts emerged: one, that Jonathan had three broken ribs, multiple fractures of his left leg and damage to two vertebrae, plus severe lacerations to his head and face – and the other, that Sue was pregnant again.

"Which means Stephanie will be only seventeen months when this one is born." Sue and Sarah had paused for a cup of tea before resuming work on the washing, drying and ironing. "Maybe, once Jonathan is home again and I don't have to fit hospital visits into my day life will be a bit easier."

"Any indication from the doctor when that might be?" her mother asked.

"Not yet. They are still concerned that there is no response in his good leg. If there is no improvement by the end of the week they are going to do more tests and X-rays."

Neither of them voiced the worry nagging at their minds, but it was an anxiety confirmed ten days later, when the decision was made to send Jonathan over to Guy's Hospital in London to investigate the damage to his spine.

Sue felt wretched every time she saw his face – removal of the bandages had revealed the extent of the injuries caused by his partial exit through the car windscreen. His nose, eyebrows and one cheek had been slashed, and stitch scars dotted his forehead up into his scalp. For Sue, the trouble was that the pregnancy nausea was activated by this horrific sight, forcing her to struggle each visit not to appear repulsed. She had decided against telling him of the forthcoming happy event until he was stronger.

The building works, meanwhile, progressed slowly. Ted Martel spent considerably more time on site than he was contracted to, but nevertheless there were repeated calls on Sue for decisions – which she prayed would comply with Jonathan's wishes. Terry managed the bar, taking on extra help to give him time for supervision of party bookings and meals. Edna spent two or three days a week organising the repairs and replacements Sue had listed for the guest bedrooms for the following season.

Sue and the doctor accompanied Jonathan on the air-craft to London, and she stayed with Sybil whose flat was conveniently within a short taxi-ride of Guy's.

"Come on, Sue! We're going shopping," Sybil announced one morning. "There's no point in you moping around here all day while the medics are mauling your man. Let's do Harrods."

Sue laughed. "You really are a tonic, dear cousin. Yes, I think a really smart outfit and a new hairdo would be super. Where do you have your hair done?" Now that Sue was adult the fact that Sybil was eleven years her senior no longer mattered: she could enjoy the company of her favorite cousin on equal terms.

They spent the whole day in Harrods, taking coffee, lunch and afternoon tea in their stride.

Tired but content, they taxied home with their spoils.

"Tell me, what are the police doing about the accident?"

"Gary, the other driver, has been charged with dangerous driving. The Inspector in charge says the boy is only thankful he's not on a manslaughter charge."

"I should jolly well think he is! Stupid idiot!"

"Apparently his father had lent him the car on condition he got it home in time for him to go to a Rotary dinner that night, and Gary was already late. I think he was actually more terrified of his father than the police."

That evening at the hospital, the ward sister led Sue into her office, saying the specialist wanted to speak to her.

"What about?" Sue frowned.

"I can't say. Would you like a cup of awful coffee?"

"Thank you." Still frowning she sat on a proffered chair. Jonathan was obviously so much better now, so what on earth . . . ?

The door was swung open by a tall, pinstriped young man. "Mrs Martel?" He held out his hand. "I'm Mr Weston." He sat down beside her.

Sue shook his hand. "How is my husband?"

"I'm afraid the news is not good. His spine is far more severely damaged than was first thought. Thank you, Sister," he accepted the cup of evil coffee, took a sip, then launched into a detailed medical breakdown of Jonathan's injury.

Sue tried to follow it all and when the specialist raised his cup again she demanded, "Yes, yes. But what does this all mean? What is the bottom line?"

The cup was returned to its saucer and he looked her straight in the eye. "The bottom line, Mrs Martel, is that your husband is paralysed from the waist down. There is no chance he will ever walk again."

"Oh my darling!" The big, blue eyes swam as they peered up at her from his shattered face. "They told you?"

Sue nodded, and leaned over to kiss his lips very gently.

"You realise I'll be a useless wreck, a liability for the rest of my life?"

"Rubbish! For the Lord's sake don't take that defeatist attitude," she responded fiercely. "We'll work something out. We'll get you mobile, even if its in a wheelchair."

"To do what?" he muttered.

"To be a husband and father! And hotelier. You can still run things from a chair. Supervise. Make decisions. The only difference will be that the chair behind the desk has big wheels on. So what?" Sue didn't honestly know that she believed what she was saying, yet. But she jolly well had to try and convince them both. Jonathan was still too weak to think positively, to summon up the will to fight.

He closed his eyes. "Husband! Only in name. I'll never be able to play cricket with my son or dance with my daughter at her first ball." He sighed and turned his head away.

Sue wanted to scream at him to shut up. Instead she held his hand and laughed. "Don't be an ass! You'll watch Roddy from the boundary, yelling instructions. And you'll smile benevolently as your daughter dances with her retinue of admirers."

Jonathan opened his eyes, gazed at her, waiting. "Go on. What about us?"

She knew what he meant and gave his hand an encouraging squeeze. "You are going to be amazed what we will achieve together on our nuptial couch, boy!"

At last he grinned. "Okay. I'll believe you, though thousands wouldn't. Did the quack give any idea when we can go home?"

"Soon as we like. But you'll have to return to the hospital till I've got things organised at home. Wheelchairs don't go up steps too easily."

"Or upstairs, for that matter."

"Uncle Ted's coming to see me when we're back. We will discuss what can be done."

"You are going to be extremely busy, sweetheart." He looked worried, distressed for her.

Busier than you realise, she thought, wondering how long to wait before telling him of the new conception. "So are you, honey bunch. So the quicker you get yourself fit the better."

"It's simply not practical." Ted Martel stood in the hallway analysing the construction of the old granite house. He walked through from front to back. "This part has been added to link what was once the shed to the original dwelling. They weren't too fussy about angles and levels, as you see. To straighten things out for a wheelchair we

147

would have to remove load-bearing walls two feet thick, and insert something else to take the weight."

Sue's heart sank.

Jessica was with them. "If it's a matter of cost . . ."

Ted smiled. "No, dear. It's more than that. As I see it, they would be homeless for months, spend a fortune and finish up with a mish-mash. To be honest, one could put up a brand new purpose-built bungalow with no steps to negotiate, for less than the cost of an inadequate conversion."

Jessica looked at her daughter-in-law. "Well? What do you think?"

The thought of exchanging the quaint old dower wing for a modern bungalow was not a happy one. However, she smiled, shrugged her shoulders and said, "You're the expert, Uncle Ted. If that's what it takes, then that's what we must do. We'd better start looking at possible sites. I wonder if we'd get permission to build in the field at the bottom of the road?"

"Wouldn't that be a bit far for Jonathan to get to and from the hotel?" Jessica asked. "What about the area behind my place, where the apple trees are?"

"That would be even closer to you than we are already."

"Indeed. And I don't doubt we may be useful to each other in the coming years." She gave a wry grin. "I'm not getting any younger, you know. I will need someone to keep an eye on me in my old age."

Sue put an arm round her and gave her a hug. "Why don't we put on our coats and take a look?" If it looked feasible she could broach the subject with Jonathan on her visit tonight.

"What will we do with the dower wing?" was his first

question. He wasn't keen to part with it, either, but he accepted that it simply wasn't possible for him to go back there to live. Not ever.

"Use it as an annexe, perhaps, or let it as a self-catering unit. Old places of character are very popular," Sue said brightly. Jonathan shrugged in a gesture of helplessness.

"Do you think we should have a welcome home party?" Sue asked her mother-in-law.

"I wonder," Jessica mused. "Of course we want him to know how much we've all missed him and want him back *in situ*, but perhaps he would rather just be met by you and the children." She cocked her head on one side. "Of course he has always enjoyed a good party. What are your feelings on the subject?"

"Coming home, crippled, is going to be traumatic for him; maybe a bunch of friends and family would break the ice?"

"Good thinking. Right, let's do it. What time of day is he likely to arrive home?"

"I could arrange it for late afternoon. Better not make it an evening do: he's used to early nights at the hospital."

Sue and Terry organised drinks; Sarah boiled a ham and made bowls of salad, Jessica made soup and boozy desserts and Edna and John provided homemade bread baked in an old furze oven on cabbage leaves, along with round pats of Guernsey butter. Norton assembled their group of friends who arrived with balloons and a huge cake iced with the words, NOW PERHAPS YOU WILL LOOK WHERE YOU ARE GOING IN FUTURE! Sarah goggled at it in horror when she saw it, but Sue laughed and assured her that Jonathan would enjoy the teasing.

149

The ambulance arrived at five o'clock.

"You're looking very smart," the patient observed as an ambulance man pushed the wheelchair up the wooden ramp Sue had asked the carpenter to make. "Is this in honour of my homecoming?"

"Of course, my darling." Sue bent and kissed him briefly, turned to the ambulance men to thank them and took over the handling of the chair.

"Sure you can manage, ma'am? Wouldn't you like us to get him into the room for you?"

"No thanks," Sue responded hastily, not wanting strangers to witness the coming scene. "I can manage from here on." And she busied herself in the hallway, removing his hat and rugs until the men had gone.

Then she opened the sitting room door.

"Welcome home!" everyone shouted together.

Sue watched anxiously as Jonathan's mouth fell open in astonishment, and sighed with relief as a big grin spread over his scarred face.

He looked up at her, eyes narrowed. "You little demon, you!" Then to the crowd in general added "Any flipping excuse for a party, huh?"

At first, everyone was painfully aware of the livid scars on his face, but they were soon forgotten as the ribbing and leg-pulling progressed.

Jonathan laughed a lot, obviously enjoying himself – much to Sue's relief – and when he wheeled himself into the dining room, saw the cake and read the message thereon he gave a great shout. "Who the hell's idea was this?" he swung round to stare at Tiny, the huge, ex-army cook, now turned hotelier. "Yours I suppose."

"Trouble with you navy guys," Tiny growled, "when

you get into a car you imagine you still have the width of an ocean to play with."

"At least I don't drive round the island regularly widening all the roads," Jonathan said solemnly, referring to the big man's tortured car. "Though in your case," he added, eyeing Tiny's girth, "it is understandable."

The room rocked with laughter as the banter continued. Then everyone queued to help themselves from the buffet laid out on the dining table.

"No thanks, I'm quite capable of helping myself," Jonathan responded to offers to serve his meal.

They sat around in various rooms with plates perched precariously on their knees while Terry circulated topping up glasses. While some of the girls cleared the empty plates, Sue and Jessica served coffee and liquers.

And the noise level continued to rise until nearly ten o'clock when Norton raised a hand. "I think that wheelchair is beginning to look a bit shaky. Sue, why don't you get your old man out of it and give it a rest?"

Gratefully, Sue winked at him as the other guests took the hint and began collecting their coats.

"Great party, Jonathan. You must do this again, sometime," Penny said, straightfaced, as she led the guests out into the teeth of a gale.

"No way! I don't wish to be accused of dominating the action! It will be your turn, next." He returned her kiss, shook hands with the boys and allowed his mother and mother-in-law to kiss him, too, as they collected up their dishes and left.

He was waiting by the fire when Sue came back in after locking the front door. "To repeat tonight's well-worn phrase, 'a great party', darling." He took hold of her hand and held it to his cheek.

"Did you enjoy it?"

"Enormously. But I am jolly tired."

"Okay. Bed it shall be. You'll have to tell me exactly what to do, and how to do it. I haven't a clue about nursing but I'm a willing pupil."

"Then I'll make allowances, just for tonight."

Despite finally falling into bed very late and completely exhausted, Sue woke bright and early next morning after a solid sleep. Accustomed to early hospital hours, Jonathan was awake early, too, wanting to be dressed and have his breakfast.

Sue had planned a reasonably restful day, so that Jonathan could become acclimatised to the new routine, but before she could open the subject he proved to have plans of his own.

"I want you to phone Terry and ask him to help you get me into the hotel. I want to see what's happening with the extensions."

"Tomorrow. You must be tired out after coming home from the hospital, and walking into a rather rowdy party." She was concerned that his recovery should continue unheeded.

"Now," he said, without looking up, "It may be raining again tomorrow."

Somewhat surprised by his tone, and reckoning an argument would probably tire him more than doing what he wanted, she shrugged and said, "Very well." Maybe he would feel better when he saw how well the alterations had progressed.

She was wrong. "Hmm. I can't see it's necessary to have all these extra interior walls," he grumbled a quarter of an hour later, as Terry helped navigate the chair round the builders' rubble. "What's this one for?"

"That's between the corridor and the resident's bar," Sue explained.

"What corridor? Where does it lead?"

"To the loos and to the residents' telephone. And through a door at the end to the garden."

"Why on earth have a corridor there? Makes the whole room smaller!"

"It's against regulations to have toilets opening directly from a public room," Terry told him.

"Rubbish! What about the bar at the Trefoil?" referring to a local pub.

"They had to put a lobby inside both Gents and Ladies, then a washroom before you reach the loos," Sue said. "Far more walls and doors than this."

"I want to see the builder as soon as possible. And why haven't these windows been glazed yet?"

Sue's heart sank. Nothing seemed to please him.

After lunch and a sleep, in the warmth of the sitting room, with Stephanie on his knee and Roddy playing with a wooden lorry on the hearthrug, Jonathan was more relaxed. He shared some of Jessica's gache with the baby, and Sue's chocolate sponge cake, brushing away the crumbs with a laugh. "What a treat to have homemade food again, and drink out of proper china cups instead of those awful thick ones in hospitals." He smiled appreciatively at his family. "It is good to be home at last."

That night when the children were in bed Jonathan asked for a whisky.

"Are you sure you should? You had a lot of champagne yesterday. Won't it clash with your medication?"

"No! Of course not."

Again to avoid an argument, Sue gave in and poured him a thin one in plenty of water.

"Now, I've been thinking." From the canvas bag suspended from his chair he took a notepad and pen. "I've made notes of all the things we must do and plan. Obviously my physical contribution to the hotel is limited by this damn chair, so you will have to take over some of my responsibilities." He flicked over the pages. "Between you, you and Terry will have to be the available management presence, much of the time, to iron out residents' problems and queries. I know this won't apply before we open next Easter, but we must be well organised in advance." He paused to savour another shot of whisky.

Sue took the opportunity to interrupt. "There will be a hitch to that arrangement I'm afraid . . ."

He raised his head, frowning. "Oh, what?"

She took a deep breath. "Our next baby is due in June." She knew she should not have waited so long to tell him, but the moment had never seemed right: now she had no option. She prayed he would be as thrilled as when she had told him about Roddy and then Stephanie. Smiling, she waited . . . and was totally unprepared for his violent reaction.

"Shit!" The notepad flew across the room just missing a porcelain vase on a small table. "How the hell did that happen? You stupid cow! All the notes and planning I've been doing for the past couple of weeks are for nothing!" He drained his glass and banged it down so hard Sue feared it would smash. "Shit!" he yelled again, "What a

154

bloody waste of time and energy." He glared at her. "I wondered what you were grinning about just now, you damn fool!" His eyes narrowed. "You couldn't possibly have imagined I would welcome the news, could you?"

Shocked, eyes swimming, Sue nodded, speechless.

"Then you are even more stupid than I thought. It has to be the worst possible thing to happen to us, barring my accident." He picked up his glass and held it out towards her. "You'd better get me another drink."

Hours later, after undressing, washing and coping with Jonathan's other needs before easing him into his temporary bed in the dining room, Sue climbed wearily upstairs, checking the children before getting to bed herself. Though utterly exhausted, mentally, physically and emotionally, it was impossible to sleep. She didn't merely feel hurt – she was totally shattered. What had happened to Jonathan? Why was he behaving like this? Why blame her for being pregnant when he knew perfectly well they had both enjoyed an occasional, impromptu risk? And the hotel extension too; he had approved the plans before work had ever started. What had changed him so much? Was it the fact of being crippled? But the accident had happened over two months ago and he had never spoken to her like that when he was in hospital . . . why he should start now was beyond her. She searched her mind for anything she could have said or done to upset him, triggering this evening's display of uncharacteristic behaviour. At one-thirty she gave up, crept down to the kitchen to make herself a mug of cocoa. Before carrying it up to her room she peeped in at Jonathan; he lay sleeping peacefully, mouth slightly open, his usual gentle snore in rhythm with the rise and fall of his chest. She smiled.

Poor darling, it must be torture to come home in that state, knowing it was for life. She must try to understand and not react badly when he became aggressive.

After reading a while and finishing her cocoa, Sue turned out the light at two-thirty and was asleep in seconds. And at three o'clock she was woken by the electric buzzer by her bed. Dragging on her dressing gown she hurried down to see what Jonathan wanted.

"Water, please."

"Here it is, darling, on the table beside you."

"No point putting it there if you don't tell me."

Sue opened her mouth to say she *had* told him it was there, and made sure it was well within his reach . . . but changed her mind. "Anything else, my love?"

He turned his head to give her a brief, wan smile. "No thanks," then closed his eyes.

"You'd better get a girl to come and work full time; she can look after the children while you're working up at the hotel. If you train her well, she will be able to act as the new baby's nanny, then you'll be free to get back to the hotel as soon after the birth as you can." Jonathan was sitting in his chair at the dining table which was pushed against the wall opposite his bed. Papers were strewn across it, bills, receipts, invoices, bookings for next year all jumbled up together.

"I'll have to leave off at feeding times."

"The baby can go straight on bottle feed, can't it?"

"I'd prefer to feed it myself . . ."

"Well it won't be possible, will it? Now will you pop over to the site and tell the foreman to come and see me. I want some of these invoices explained."

"Okay. Give me five minutes, I've got something on the gas at the moment."

"Well turn it off. It can wait."

Biting her lip but without another word, Sue did as she was ordered.

The new bungalow was ready for them by the second week of the new year. Jonathan had shown no interest whatsoever in its design or construction, leaving all the details to Sue. Every possible thing to help his mobility had been thought of: ramps, wide door frames, the height of shelves and counters in the kitchen, a special bathroom in which he could use the bath, basin and loo with a minimum of help. Door handles were at the necessary height. A team of removers, supervised by Sue, spent a full day transferring furniture the four or so hundred yards from the dower. Jonathan insisted that the dining table and his papers be left till last, and then had had himself taken up to the hotel bar.

Greg, Sarah and Jessica took charge of their grand-children for the day, while Edna and John, Emmy and Anne Warwick helped find new homes for the china and glass, linen and clothes.

"I'll make up your bed and the children's cots," Edna insisted from behind a pile of cardboard boxes. "Emmy, you go and put on the kettle and make tea for Mrs Martel; she's going into the sitting room to put her feet up for ten minutes."

"But I—"

"Suzanne! Do as you're told. I've never seen you look so tired, with those deep dark rings round your eyes. Go on!" Edna could be quite fierce when she chose.

Sue put an arm round her shoulders and gave her a hug. "All right, you old bully! Just to please you," and dodged through the boxes to her new, comparatively characterless, sitting room. She knew, of course, that she wasn't complying simply to please her aunt: she was exhausted.

Over the Christmas and New Year period Jonathan had occasionally apologised after a particularly bad outburst of temper, and smiling, Sue said she understood. When asked if he approved the facilities in the bungalow, Jonathan was invariably non-committal: he showed no interest. He had agreed they should share their double bed, but from the first night when Sue attempted to put an arm across his chest and cuddle into him, he had fended her off, never reciprocating. Lying awake in the small hours one could invent any number of excuses for his attitude, but Sue never felt they qualified as valid reasons. She would wait until he was sleeping soundly then gently move close enough to feel his warmth. And in the freshness of a new morning, giggling with her babies as their cereals went Snap, Crackle and Pop! she reprimanded herself for being super-critical.

Near the end of March, just two weeks before the hotel reopened for the season, Terry tackled her on an upstairs landing. "Who have you got to run the bar for the guests every afternoon during the summer?"

Sue looked up from the list of jobs still to be done before the first guests arrived. "What do you mean? I thought you . . ."

"Me! And what about my afternoons off?"

"I don't follow you."

"You mean you expect me to work from sun-up until the last guest leaves the bar at two a.m., seven days a week?"

"Oh Terry! Don't be so silly, you know I don't expect any such thing! I'm sorry," she shook her head, "it simply slipped my mind. Of course we must have someone stand in for you. And you must have a full day and a half off every week. Any ideas for an assistant?"

"No. You're the boss, so you do the hiring and firing."

Sue wasn't sure she liked his tone: almost resentful? "I'll have a word with Jonathan about it."

Terry raised one eyebrow, gave a half smile and walked away.

She broached the subject that evening at supper.

Jonathan didn't bother to look up from his newspaper. "Can't see that will be necessary. I'm sure you will be able to sit comfortably behind the bar for a couple of hours in the afternoons while he takes a rest."

"Me! And when do I get a rest?"

"All winter. Ah, there's the doorbell. That'll be Norton. I'm going out for a drink with him and Tiny. Nice supper, dear." He propelled himself into the hallway, took his coat off the conveniently low hook in passing and opened the front door. "All ready, boys. Where are we going?"

Sue cleared the table and sat down by the fire with her aching legs up on a footstool. Not for long: the phone rang.

It was Jessica. "Haven't seen you folks for over a week. I wondered, if you're not busy, whether I might drift up for a coffee?"

"Lovely. I'd love to see you but I'm afraid I'm alone. Jonathan's gone out."

"I'll be there in five minutes."

She arrived before Sue had finished filling the percolator, and one glance at her daughter-in-law was enough. "Go and sit yourself down immediately! You look worn out."

Sue didn't argue.

Jessica carried in the tray, set it on a low table and poured out. "Now, are you going to tell me what you are doing to get so overtired or do I have to drag it out of you with a winkle-picker?"

"I don't feel that bad," Sue began.

"Don't prevaricate. What are you doing each day? What time do you get up?"

"The children get me up at about six-thirty."

"So you wash and dress and feed them, and Jonathan. Go on?"

Sue listed the sorting of household laundry, meals and, with some hesitation, the errands she had to run for Jonathan, before going up to the hotel by nine o'clock.

"For what?"

"Supervising the finishing of jobs and preparations before we reopen."

"I thought Terry was supposed to be doing that?"

"He does some of it. But he also handles the bar work."

"Well what is he, an assistant manager or a barman? He can't be both."

Sue bit her lip. She had never told Jessica the difficulties she was having with Jonathan, ever since his accident. The coffee was already tepid so she finished it, giving herself more time to think before replying. "Jonathan doesn't seem to think—"

"At all! About anyone!" his mother exploded. "I don't know what is happening between you two but whatever it is it isn't good! Now come on. Spill the beans."

Much to her own disgust, Sue burst into tears.

Next morning Jonathan was on the receiving end of one of Jessica's fiercest lectures. "Just because you're in that bally chair doesn't give you the right to pile your daily work onto your wife," she ranted, "Nor onto your assistant manager. You simply must face up to the need for more staff. Now get on with it!"

Inevitably, after she had gone, Jonathan turned on Sue. "I should have known you'd go whining to outsiders the moment I was out of earshot! Who else have you complained to?"

Sue had had one of Jessica's lectures, too, the previous night, all about standing up for herself and for what was fair. "I shall treat that remark with the contempt it deserves," she said, and walked out of the room.

"Bitch!" he shouted after her.

She poked her head back round the door. "Emmy will have great fun relaying your clarion call round the neighbourhood," and quickly disappeared again.

It was apparently a good ploy. Jonathan resisted the urge to vent his frustration on her on a daily basis, even if his resolution was soluble in alcohol at least once a week, and he agreed to employ a barman for the summer. Furthermore, he said Sue could have a nanny for the children *and* breastfeed the new babe.

But he remained cold and distant.

Deborah was born on 2 June 1953 – Coronation Day.

It was a difficult and painful birth. Fortunately, Sue had had time to sleep and recover a little strength by the time Jonathan arrived with the obligatory bouquet and chocolates, and she was able to greet him with a smile. "Sorry to keep you all in suspense so long," she said. "It ended up being a hammer and chisel job."

"What does that mean?"

"It means it was a breech birth," a nurse replied as she handed him a cup of tea. "The baby came bottom first. And your wife has needed a lot of stitches. I'm afraid she is going to find it uncomfortable being on her feet for some weeks."

"Then she'll have to keep off her feet until everything has healed up." He smiled lovingly at Sue.

The nurse was about to joke that he'd have to keep off, too, but stopped herself in time when she registered the significance of the wheelchair.

"Don't worry, darling," he whispered when the crisply starched nurse had gone. "You must take all the time you need."

She was sure he meant it . . . at that moment.

Sadly, the moment passed.

"There are fewer visitors this year, that's why," Sue snapped, when he asked yet again why the turnover had dropped so much behind the previous two years.

"We have never had empty beds before. Dammit, I wish I could spend more time in the place and find out what you're doing up there."

162

"Are you suggesting it's my fault?"

"Well, apart from the past three weeks, you are in charge, now."

"And I suppose if you were able you would go over to England and order people onto the boats to fill our empty beds."

"Don't be childish! Can't you understand the basic principles of business? Like balancing the books? Of course we'll have lean years, but in those years we have to pare down our expenditures. Instead, we have a far larger wage bill than ever. For two thirds the number of guests. Doesn't make sense. Particularly having taken on a qualified chef."

Sue had only been home for two weeks with the baby, and was feeling desperately weary. The girl they had taken on as nanny knew very little about tiny babies, so Sue had to demonstrate, over and over, how to handle her. Also, breastfeeding drained her resources, she was overweight and her hair was badly in need of skilled attention. She was in no mood to accept criticism after all the excessive hours she had put into the hotel, nor was she in any fit state to sustain an argument. "I'll check it all out tomorrow," she promised.

After her bath and feed next morning, the baby threw up over her clean cot. Then the washing machine wouldn't work and Emmy couldn't remember what to prepare for lunch. Having ironed out the household problems, Sue hurried up to the hotel as fast as the lingering pain would allow and found a chambermaid in tears in a vacated bedroom.

"It's not me, ma'am, what lost them sheets. I packed 'em into the laundry boxes like you said, but I 'aven't 'ad time to check the list since they came back. Not with all the dining room work as well."

It was almost lunchtime when she reached reception.

"Mrs Paige, with an 'I', wants a meeting with the management," the girl told her from behind the counter.

"What about?"

"Noise from the bar in the evening, I expect. She's forever complaining about it."

"I'll go and speak to Jimmy."

"He's gone, Mrs Martel."

"Gone?"

"Mr Martel came up when you were in the hospital and dismissed him."

"Well, then I will have to speak to whoever has taken his place." Sue wondered what on earth Jimmy had done to get the sack.

"There isn't anyone. Mr Martel said you didn't need anyone else." She blushed. "At least, that's what Jimmy told me last night at the cinema."

One couldn't go on getting all this vital information from a junior member of staff; Sue thanked the girl and hurried home.

"Who is currently managing the hotel?" she asked Jonathan.

"Terry, you and I," he replied.

"But I've been away for three weeks, and even now I can't put in much time. And you . . . are busy . . . looking after the books. Terry can't do everything."

"Terry has not been asked to do everything!" he released the brakes on his chair and shoved himself away from the table. "I can't face any more of that muck. I'm going into the sitting room."

164

Even Sue herself admitted it was not the best Irish Stew she had ever made.

A couple of weeks later Terry tackled her in the empty hotel dining room. "Look here, Sue, I can't keep this pace up much longer. I haven't had an hour off since Jimmy left. We have to have a replacement."

"I agree, but it's not up to me. You'll have to tackle Jonathan about it."

"You're joking!" he muttered. Nevertheless he did try.

Sue could hear the argument through the open windows the moment she switched off the car engine outside the bungalow next morning. She was still debating with herself whether to go in or not, when Terry emerged through the open door, puce in the face. He stared at her for a second before turning to hurry away.

It was the last time she ever saw him.

Jonathan had sacked him.

Chapter Seven

In Sickness and in Health

A huge flower arrangement in a basket stood in the empty fireplace. Sue stared at it in amazement. "Where on earth have those come from?"

Jonathan gave her a sly grin.

"Darling! Why?" she hurried to give him a grateful kiss.

His powerful arms drew her down, he kissed along the hairline on her forehead, nuzzled her ear. "Because I've been such a bastard lately. I don't know how you put up with me, sometimes."

Sue allowed her file of papers to slide onto the floor, as she knelt to put her arms round his waist and rest her head in his lap. "Darling," she muttered, unable to think what else to say, savouring the moment of peace and harmony. Of course she knew it wouldn't last; it never did. She would dare allow herself to relax, love him and believe he loved her . . . then out of the blue would come another storm. Sometimes the climate was just wet and overcast, Jonathan wallowing in self-pity, at others it was close and humid, himself silent and simmering. There were times the bitterly cold wind of his sarcasm knifed through her, but nothing was as bad as the raging storms of undisciplined temper when the air filled with shouts and flying missiles. Occasionally there were warning signs and Sue was able to take shelter just in time, but too often, triggered by some mysterious functioning in his brain, Jonathan exploded, thunderously.

It was so hard to know how to handle it. She had tried ignoring it, carrying on as though nothing was happening; she had tried walking out of the room and letting him rant on alone. Sometimes she would deliberately square her shoulders, adopt an aggressive stance and coldly inform him that she refused to be spoken to in that manner and if he couldn't act like a reasonable human being she would leave him to stew alone until he learned to behave himself. Worst of all was when she was desperately overtired and unable to hold back her own anger, flying at him for being so damned unreasonable, careless of other people's efforts and feelings.

If any of these responses had brought consistent reactions, Sue would have known where she stood. But they never did. However, the fact was that she lived on hope, continuing to believe that Jonathan's attacks of remorse were genuine and that one day, despite his disability, they could return to the happy home life, shared parenthood and working relationship they had so enjoyed in their first years of marriage.

During the winter months a new set-up was organised. What had been a storeroom behind reception was turned into an office for Jonathan, from where he could direct operations. A cement path was laid from the bungalow to the hotel along which he could propel himself and from the beginning of the 1954 season at around nine in the morning, he would unlock his office door and wheel up to his new desk. The door remained open so that he could see and hear all that went on, check who passed through the foyer or rang at reception.

Molly Machon was due at the reception counter at nine o'clock, too, and had she not had the most gorgeous head of long, blonde hair swinging silkily over her shoulders, and violet blue eyes twinkling coyly under fluttering lashes, no one doubted she would have been sacked on the spot by her ill-tempered boss any day of the week, for arriving anything up to half an hour late. But in Jonathan's eyes she could do no wrong.

In contrast, Sue who was in the hotel kitchen by seven-thirty each day to supervise early morning teas and cope with visitors' queries regarding beaches, buses, hairdressers and tar-removal, and provide weather forecasts while breakfast was in progress, was in constant line of critical fire. With guests safely dispatched on their chosen pursuits and the chef taking over in the kitchen, she helped the waitress/chambermaids change bedlinen and towels, clean and tidy the rooms and replace filched toilet rolls. Tar and toffee had to be removed from carpets, curtains rehung after being torn off their hooks and water mopped up from under flooded basins. She had to check every room to see that sticky fingermarks were polished off windows and mirrors and, on one occasion, rescue a favorite teddy bear which had been stuffed head first down a lavatory and flushed halfway round the bend.

And in the middle of these tasks, Molly would appear. "Mrs Martel! The boss wants you in his office!"

Stupidly, Sue used to drop what she was doing and hasten downstairs, only to be tackled about some trivia which could well have waited for hours, even days. Now, on this particular day well into the season and increasingly irritated by Molly's tone of voice, she decided to dig her heels in. "What does Mr Martel want me for?"

"I couldn't say." Molly examined her nail varnish.

"Well find out and let me know if it's important. Tell him I am very busy."

Two minutes later the girl reappeared. "He says it is."

Sue straightened, rubbing her aching back, and pushed the hair out of her eyes. "What is what?"

"What he wants you for is important."

"What is it?"

"Don't know!"

"Well go back and find out and let me be the judge of whether it's more important than this!" She waved the lavatory plunger at Molly.

The girl didn't return, but when Sue finished upstairs and went down to the office, Jonathan was in a foul mood.

"Where the hell have you been?" he demanded.

"Sshh!" she tilted her head towards the open door.

"I will not sshh! What's the matter with you? You know damn well I cannot get upstairs to you, yet you refuse to come down and speak to me. Twice I've had to send that poor girl upstairs . . ."

"Stop shouting and tell me what is so important that I have to come running to your summons."

"I have to know whether rooms eight and nine are

booked for the last week in August," he snarled. "I've had an enquiry this morning . . ."

"And you couldn't ask Molly to check with me when she came up?"

"No! I wanted to ask you myself, for the simple reason that you have no business pencilling in bookings unless they are confirmed."

"If you had read the pencilled note you would see that they promised confirmation by today if they wanted to keep it." She snatched the pile of post from by his elbow, and withdrew a sheet. "Here! Here is your confirmation along with their deposit." Her anger dissipated and she grinned at him. "Just try opening the post when it arrives, my love. It will save us all a lot of hassle."

"There wouldn't have been any bloody hassle if you'd come when I sent for you. Silly bitch!"

Molly was smirking at reception as Sue left.

Many people in Guernsey were still enjoying the post-war party spirit. The hotel cocktail bars were full night after night, with reunions and camaraderie, men and women returning after demobilisation and the younger set eager to hear their stories. Despite the previous year's devaluation of sterling, many islanders were prospering: builders were busy repairing and replacing all that the Germans and Todt workers had destroyed, scrap iron merchants were keen to rip out all that remained in the German fortifications, hoteliers and shop keepers were benefiting from the 25 per cent Purchase Tax imposed in Britain which did not apply in the islands, encouraging tourists to spend – and smuggle. Growers couldn't keep up with the demand for their produce.

Greg was very pleased with the returns at Les Marettes Vinery . . . and his brother Andrew took all the credit; Greg just smiled and ignored him.

Andrew lived in a constant state of depression. Everything was wrong. "Have you seen that awful construction they're putting up in the Truchot?" he grumbled.

"I thought it was rather nice, with the stone facing."

"Facing! Why can't they build properly in solid granite? And another thing. Where's all this compulsory States Insurance going to get us?"

"Security in our old age."

"Bah! Ought to be left to the individual what he does with his money. I don't agree with it."

"There have been a lot of changes since the war and I cannot say I like all of them. But we have to move with the times."

"Bah!" Andrew repeated.

"The boss says will you come down to reception, quickly!" Molly shouted at her from the top of the stairs.

Sue hissed with annoyance and stuck her head out of the linen closet. "What for this time?"

"He didn't say!"

Once again Sue had the urge to send the girl away with a curt message, but at that moment two guests emerged from their room and greeted her with charming smiles. So she responded in kind and followed them, and Molly, down the stairs. Once in the office she closed the door before saying, "Well? What do you want me for?"

Jonathan looked up from the papers on his desk. "Eh? Oh yes. That Nanny of yours just rang to announce a crisis. You'd better find out what it's all about."

Sue turned the phone round on his desk and dialled. "Nanny?" She listened, her face expressing concern.

Jonathan was watching her. "What's the matter?"

"Sshh!" she frowned at him. "Yes, of course you did right. I'm coming over." She replaced the receiver in its cradle. "It's Roddy. He's passed out! He has been complaining his head hurt for the past couple of days."

"Oh God! Come on we must get home!" The wheelchair spun away from the desk. "On second thoughts, I'll only hold you up. You go, sweetheart. Quickly. Phone me if there is anything I can do at this end." He looked distraught, and so helpless.

Sue bent over him with a hasty peck on the cheek. "Try not to worry, darling. I'll call as soon as I know anything," and she dashed out of the office.

At home, chaos reigned.

Stephanie was screaming with delight as she chased the cat round the house. Deborah was screaming with fury at being ignored and Nanny was on the verge of hysteria, while Roddy lay on the sitting room sofa, white as a sheet, not moving.

"Have you phoned for the doctor?" Sue demanded.

Nanny jabbered incoherently.

"Control yourself. Have you telephoned . . . ?"

The girl burst into tears.

Sue smacked her on the cheek. "Stop that! Pull yourself together and answer me!"

With a gasp of surprise the girl nodded. "Yes, ma'am. They said they would try to find him."

Sue grabbed the phone and dialled the surgery. "I want a doctor immediately! This is an emergency! Then send an ambulance and we'll get the child to hospital."

Within five minutes the bell could be heard coming up the hill. "Nanny, make yourself a cup of tea, now. Then give Debbie a bottle and stop Stephanie teasing the cat."

The ambulance men were very efficient, and soon they were all bouncing back down the road, Sue sitting in the back of the vehicle holding Roddy's hand.

Doctor Collard was waiting as a nurse wheeled the boy into the examination room on a trolley and having phoned Jonathan to say where they were, Sue was left sitting on a hard chair in the passage, biting her thumb.

"I have decided to admit him, Sue," the doctor told her half an hour later. "Three of us have had a look at him and we would like to do further tests. From what can be adjudged so far, we none of us see his condition to be of immediately serious concern, but agree he should be kept here under observation. They are taking him straight along to the Children's Ward and perhaps you would go down there to see him installed. Sister will advise you as to his requirements."

It all seemed so coldly clinical. A thousand questions came to mind, but she guessed the doctor would simply ask her to await the answers in due course.

Roddy looked so small, pale and pathetic, lying in the big, starched hospital bed. His blond hair was damp and tangled, his eyes opening, rolling towards her, questioning, and closing again as his lips quivered. At least he was conscious.

She took a taxi home and found all was peaceful. Stephanie was having her nap, Deborah was sitting in her pram bashing the toys strung in front of her on a piece of elastic, and Nanny was peeling potatoes for her lunch.

Upstairs, Sue grabbed a holdall and stuffed it with Roddy's pyjamas and dressing gown, a pair of slippers, a toothbrush, his teddy bear and two favourite books. She threw the bag into the car, drove round to the front of the hotel to park while she rushed inside to tell Jonathan what was happening.

"My darling!" he held out his arms and she went to him, hugging him briefly before pulling away. "Keep your pecker up, old thing," he kissed the palm of her hand. "The little man will be okay. Now off you go, and don't worry about a thing here."

Roddy tossed about in his bed, constantly checking his mother was still by his side, but saying nothing.

Sue read him a story, not knowing if he was listening until he squeezed her hand and whispered, "More."

A nurse brought her a tray of tea and sandwiches, which reminded her she hadn't eaten anything since seven that morning, six hours ago!

The staff told her to try to encourage Roddy to drink, and even eat if he could. He lunched on Bovril and jelly, and by teatime he asked for two sandwiches, one paste and one jam.

"He is a much better colour, don't you think?" the staff nurse remarked.

"Yes. But I wish we knew what the problem was." Sue smiled down at him and stroked his hair.

"Maybe we'll know more tomorrow. Now don't you think you should get home and rest? It's past six o'clock."

Roddy looked up with a miserable expression.

"I'll wait till bedtime and lights out, if I may. You won't mind if I go home to bed, will you darling? I promise I'll come back in the morning."

The child turned his face away, with a reluctant nod.

Nanny was in the sitting room reading, the two girls obviously asleep, judging by the lack of noise.

"Mr Martel home yet?" Sue asked.

"He came in looking for his supper. But when I said you weren't back yet he went out again." She returned to her book and her bar of chocolate.

Sue went into her bedroom, realising for the first time as she glanced in the long mirror, that she was still in the working clothes she was wearing when Nanny had phoned for her that morning. She stripped off, longing to run down for a dip in the sea, but stepped under the shower instead. Jonathan hadn't returned when she finished, so she hurried up the path to the hotel.

He was in the bar. "Where the hell have you been all this time?" he snapped.

"At the hospital! Where do you think?" She was in no mood for this.

"It's nearly eight o' bloody clock . . ."

"You yourself told me there was no need to hurry back!" she hissed, aware of stares from residents still enjoying their aperitifs before going in to dinner.

"Quite. But I didn't tell you to stay away indefinitely!" he snarled.

"I couldn't conceivably care less what you did or didn't tell me. I did what I considered necessary," she retorted, loud enough to be heard right through the room, "for which I do not require your permission." She turned to order a drink, and realised Molly was standing behind the bar. "Hallo! What are you doing there?"

Molly looked at Jonathan.

"Jimmy has gone down with flu," he said, "so as you weren't here I had to ask Molly to step into the breach." He was red with anger.

"Splendid!" Sue smiled, thinking that the girl looked

far more like a barmaid than a receptionist. "I'll have a half of bitter, please." Then to her husband, said, "I don't feel like cooking tonight, so I'll eat here in the dining room. Will you join me?"

"Possibly."

Sue moved away, smiling at the hotel guests, acting as though she was quite unmoved by the scene. But inside she felt winded. It was hard to believe Jonathan's moods could change so quickly, especially in this instance with Roddy in hospital!

As on many previous occasions, Jonathan remained too furious to bring himself to apologise for his outburst.

The doctors concluded that Roddy was suffering the infant equivalent of migraine, prescribed microscopic amounts of pheno-barbitone, much to Sue's alarm, and the boy was soon running around at home as though nothing had happened.

Sarah sat watching him from her deckchair on the lawn. "Isn't that typical of kids. They worry you stiff with sudden illnesses and flaring temperatures and by the time you've dosed your nerves to cope with the situation they are completely recovered and you are a shattered wreck!"

"Thank goodness you were around, Mum!" Sue smiled appreciatively.

"I didn't do anything!"

"You moved into my hysterical household with your calming influence. That was more help than you realise."

Sarah glanced over her shoulder to see if the nanny was in hearing before whispering, "That girl is next best thing to a disaster. Doesn't she drive you potty?"

"Yes. But a real, qualified Norland Nanny is so expensive. Jonathan won't hear of us having one. Anyway, I never wanted anyone else looking after my kids; every year I dream of a hugely successful season which would allow us to take on adequate staff so I could return to being housewife and mother."

"I know, darling. Frankly, I just don't understand how you keep up the pace. You look worn out."

"As long as I have you on the end of the phone to moan to when I get fraught, I guess I'll get by." She reached for her mother's hand and they sat side by side, fingers entwined, for several minutes.

Both women laughed when they sighed contentedly at the same moment. Both knew they were happy that the rift between them caused by the war, was healed.

Two weeks later, Stephen Martel, junior partner to his architect father Ted, dropped in for a drink on the way home. He was surprised to find Sue behind the bar. "Got a new job, then?"

"Not new, exactly. Our current barman's flu turned to pleurisy. I'm standing in until he's fit to come back to work. What are you drinking?"

"A pint of bitter, thanks."

She was aware of him watching her as she drew the beer up from the barrel in the cellar.

"How are you? How is your back coping with standing there by the hour."

"Fine, thanks." She had no intention of boring him with the truth: that her back was agony by the end of each evening, there was a lumpy, varicose vein swelling in her right calf, and though she fell into bed exhausted each night, she seldom slept for more than three hours at a stretch.

Stephen's eyes narrowed. "Have you looked for a temporary barman, or are you doing it yourself from choice?"

It was nice of him to show that much interest. "No. And no again. Jonathan doesn't think it's worth getting someone in. Well, it is nearly the end of the season."

"But the bar is open to non-residents all year round. If you want someone to fill in, I don't mind doing two or three evenings a week. Not Fridays, though. That's my badminton night."

"What a kind offer. I'll speak to Jonathan about it. We'll pay you, of course."

"No, no . . ."

"It would have to be a business arrangement. Family favours too often end in rows!"

"Okay. If you insist. What are the hours?"

"Flexible. The bar is open all day to residents during the season. I take over from Molly at four-thirty and stay on till closing."

"Surely it isn't necessary to have the bar open all afternoon?" he tried to sound casual, but he was boiling inside. What the hell was his cousin Jonathan playing at? Couldn't he see that Sue was grey with exhaustion?

"I tried to talk himself into closing for two or three hours but he wouldn't hear of it."

"I'll be here tomorrow by six unless I hear to the contrary." He took a long draft of beer. "Now tell me, how is Roddy?"

Sue was relieved at the change of subject. Much as she

appreciated other people's concern, it did tend to arouse self-pity . . . which made it even more difficult to cope.

"Jonathan's accident seems to have changed his character quite dramatically," Steven remarked that night at dinner.

"Hardly surprising, I suppose," his mother, Julia, said as she placed spoonsful of cauliflower in white sauce neatly on each plate beside the lamb chops. "But in what way do you mean?"

"He works Sue into the ground. The poor girl is on her feet from seven in the morning till midnight."

Ted picked up his knife and fork. "Well, only on the odd occasion in an emergency, surely?"

"On the contrary! She's been at it seven days a week for the past month, as far as I can gather."

"Steve, dear, that's impossible," Julia frowned at him. She was well aware that her son had carried a torch for Suzanne Gaudion when he was still at school long before the girl ever met Ted's nephew Jonathan. She hoped he'd grown out of it. "Did she tell you that?"

"Lord no! She wouldn't dream of saying a word against Jonty, she's very loyal." Adding, "Too darned loyal for her own good."

Ted and Julia had always been very fond of Jonathan, and had taken a special interest in him especially since his father, Ted's brother, died in his late fifties. They were proud of his war record and of the way he had settled into the hotel business. The tragedy of his accident had affected them both deeply, and Julia was reluctant to listen to any criticism of him. "Well it is surely up to her, isn't it, to say if and when she is overtired?"

179

Steve explained about the bar work. "I've told her I'll help out in the evenings, sometimes, when I leave the office."

Ted looked up from his plate. "That's very noble of you, I don't doubt, but are you sure it's wise? I mean, an emergency is one thing, but you can't keep it up forever."

"I don't mean to. But I regard the current situation as an emergency. You should see how rundown Sue looks at the moment."

Which was exactly what Julia intended to do.

She arranged to meet Sarah in Town for a coffee, three days later, and wasted little time in niceties before launching her case. "How long is it since you've seen Sue?"

"Er . . . not since last Wednesday. Why?"

"How did you think she looked?"

Sarah frowned at her friend. "Tired. Why?"

"Just . . . tired?"

Sarah made a moue. "Well, no, since you ask. She was grey with fatigue. So, come on, what's this all about?"

Julia sipped her coffee. "Steve came home the other evening, saying she was overworking and looked awful. Well, as you know, he has always had a soft spot for her and I guessed he was being over-protective, if you know what I mean."

Sarah nodded across the table.

"But he stressed the point so strongly that I decided to go see for myself."

"That was sweet of you. And was he right?"

"Frankly, dear, I have never seen her look so dreadful. It was about five in the afternoon, before Steve got there

. . . well I didn't want him to see me so I made sure to go early enough. I had made the excuse of taking a note about some phone call, quite unnecessary, of course, and I went into the bar pretending to be surprised at finding her there. Well," she paused to sip more coffee, "she was totally fagged out. And the dreadful thing is that if Steve hadn't intervened and insisted on going in to help in the bar in the evenings, she would have been there for *another six hours*!"

Sarah's mouth fell open. "Oh dear! I feel so guilty, Julia. I have thought she's looked ill for months, but you know what it is, one hates to interfere. And when I mentioned it to Greg he laughed and said I was overdoing the mother hen bit." She didn't add that she had been feeling unwell herself, lately. "Well we'll have to see what we can do. I'll talk to Greg."

"We've booked ourselves in for lunch on Sunday," Sarah told Sue on the phone. "We haven't seen much of you, lately. Maybe we could all take the children down on Port Grat afterwards, if it's fine."

"Lovely idea, Mummy, but I'm afraid Jonathan and I won't be able to come down to the beach. However, we'd love to see you. I'll make sure we all eat together. And of course the meal is on us . . ."

"No no, dear . . ."

"Don't be silly, Mummy! I can't imagine why I haven't asked you before. I'm afraid we've been so busy."

The family lunch party was a great success.

"Do you often have lunch here with Daddy and Mummy?" Sarah asked Roddy.

The child shook his head. "No. We never did before."

"Oh. You usually eat together at home, do you?"

The blond head shook again. "No. Wiv Nanny."

Sue loved watching the conversation proceed between her mother and her son; their colouring was so different, he so fair and blue-eyed like his father, yet already with her mother's determined chin and high cheekbones. "This is a special treat, isn't it darling?"

"How often do you eat together?" Greg asked.

Sue shrugged. "Can't remember the last time. It's very difficult, you see."

"Yes of course. Mealtimes must be awkward. So, when do you spend time *en famille*?"

Sue glanced at Jonathan. "Not much chance in the summer, unfortunately. Far too busy," he told them.

"Really!" Greg turned pointedly to Sue. "What time do you start in the mornings?"

"Seven, seven-thirty."

"And finish?"

"Depends. Six, when Steve helps out in the bar. Otherwise I'm on till closing time."

"And when is that?" Sarah was alarmed.

Sue sighed. "When the last guest goes up to bed."

Greg and Sarah gasped.

"Good grief! That is ridiculous, girl!" Greg retorted. "What are you trying to do to yourself? Commit suicide?" He swung round to face Jonathan. "Can't you stop her?"

"Not easily. When she sees work to be done I'm afraid she does it. But I agree with you. She is doing far too much."

Sarah launched into a lecture on mothering and home-making; on the impracticability of having some young

182

girl who calls herself a nanny, bringing up one's children.

At one stage Sue cleared her throat significantly, caught her mother's eye and tilted her head, very slightly, towards the attentive Roddy.

Sarah ignored the gesture. She had the bit between her teeth and, what was more, Jonathan was agreeing with every word she said.

"I hope you've listened to all your mother's been telling you, darling. You really must ease up," he insisted.

Sue glared at her empty cheese plate. The two-faced liar! How dared he speak like that, after the way he had behaved! Suddenly she realised that, despite all their arguments and upsets in the past, this was the first time she had actually felt, even momentarily, she could hate Jonathan.

The same feeling swept over her again after her parents had left, when Jonathan swung his chair round to face her. "So you've been whining again, I see. Poor, badly-done-by little daughter, been running to her mummy and daddy? Aahh! We are all so sad for you. Silly bitch!" he turned away and propelled the chair out of the dining room.

"What's a bitch, Mummy?" Roddy asked.

Sue thanked Heaven there were no hotel guests or staff left in the room.

That evening, Sue tackled Jonathan about bar hours: buoyed by her parents concern she was prepared to risk another shouting match. They were sitting reading the Sunday papers in the bungalow, leaving Stephen alone to cope with any bar trade. "So few people ever use the bar in the afternoons, it doesn't seem worth being open between two and six o'clock. Shall we try closing each afternoon and see how—"

"No!" Jonathan didn't look up from his paper.

"Why not?"

"I said no! I won't hear of it!"

Sue was not prepared to give up without a fight. "Well we cannot afford extra staff and I'm certainly not going to continue exhausting myself with work I consider unnecessary."

The *Sunday Times* was twisted into a stiff rod in Jonathan's powerful hands before being hurled through the open window. "Shut up! You don't know what you're talking about. I'm the one who keeps the books. I know what is necessary or unnecessary, so I make the decisions. Right?"

Still she stood her ground. "No. Wrong. I am the one who has stood behind that bar all summer, and I know darn well that the gross takings don't cover the wages."

"That's why you are doing it, for nothing."

"Only while Jimmy is ill . . ."

"He's not ill."

Sue frowned. "Well, why isn't he back?"

"I sacked him. He was the sort of unnecessary extravagance you complain about so often."

"And you never told me?"

He sighed dramatically. "I was trying to avoid hearing you make another scene."

Sue stood up and in an ominously quiet voice said, "Very well. Tomorrow I will give Nanny two week's notice, and I will take over as mother and housewife. You can sort out the bar hours with whomever you employ to replace me." She picked up her empty coffee cup and newspaper. "I'm going to bed now. Goodnight."

"Damn you, woman," he screamed. "Come back here."

She closed the door behind her, very gently.

Sue was as good as her word: when she handed Nanny her wages envelope the following day, she gave her a fortnight's notice. The work she had been covering at the hotel, other than in the bar, she redistributed amongst the other staff and, with Emmy helping out two mornings per week at home, she launched happily into full-time motherhood.

"Jonty, darling, I think you and I ought to have a little chat," Jessica told him. "Let's go for a walk in the garden, shall we? Can you manage the chair by yourself?"

"Mother! I'm busy!"

"Of course, dear. But I'm sure you can spare me ten minutes or so of your time."

Jonathan scowled and grunted. But Jessica was standing in the doorway of the office, waiting: he couldn't refuse to accompany her without an argument and he'd had enough of that in the past week. He released the brakes on his chair. "Okay. Lead on."

Molly was left in charge – a role which greatly enhanced her feeling of self-importance. She flicked her long, blonde hair back over her shoulder and smiled as they left.

"Haven't the roses been marvellous this year?" Jessica bent to appreciate the scent of a dark red hybrid tea.

She was stalling, so he followed suit. "In a manner of speaking. I wish that blasted Albertine over the front door didn't make such a mess, though. Rotting petals everywhere being trodden into the hotel." He stopped the wheelchair by a bench seat on an enclosed area of crazy paving, just off the path.

She stood fingering the petals of a hydrangea.

"So what's this all about? What's on your mind?"

Jessica arranged herself comfortably on the wooden seat. "You, my dear. I'm very much afraid you have been making some serious mistakes, lately."

He sighed. "Go on."

"Whether you are aware of it or not I don't know, but you are being very cruel and unkind to Sue."

"Oh God! Don't tell me she's been whining to you, too!"

"No she has not! She hasn't said a single word to me about you . . . or about the way you overwork her and speak to her in front of the residents as though she is dirt!" Which was absolutely true – Sue had not spoken to her on the subject; what Jessica didn't add was that she had been briefed by both Sarah and Stephen about what was going on. Not that she hadn't suspected as much for some time.

"Well, then I'd like to know who the hell—"

"That is not the point at issue. What is worrying me is that if you go on like this both your business and your marriage will collapse."

"Go on like what?" he stormed. "This is all bunkum!"

"How dare you raise your voice at your mother in that fashion! Control yourself! Now you listen to me," she said severely, "Everybody was very upset and sympathetic about your accident and we are all sorry for you being so disabled. However, not even that excuses you for your foul and abusive temper and the way you treat Sue. Everyone has a breaking point, remember, and I assure you Sue is very near hers."

"Really?" he asked with heavy sarcasm. "Well, let me tell you, Sue is fine! She has run out on the business and plays about at home with the children all day, refusing to come back. I came out here with you because I thought you were worried about *my* breaking point! But of course no one thinks about me!" With his powerful arms he swung the chair back towards the path. "I cannot imagine why you are fussing about Sue."

Jessica got up to follow him. "Then you had better get your imagination working a bit harder. Can you remember the last time you took her out for a meal? Or made her think you truly cared about her?"

"More times than I could possibly recall," he snapped over his shoulder, before disappearing round the corner of the hedge.

Jessica turned away to stare, unseeing, at the boisterous sea beyond Port Grat.

Her efforts, however, were not entirely fruitless.

Back in his office, Jonathan slammed the door and poured himself a whisky. His expression was grim, brooding. Bloody women! What the hell was his mother on about, anyway? Sue hadn't done that much . . . He pulled a spiralled notebook towards him, and uncapped his pen to begin a list.

He hadn't got very far when there was a knock on the door and without invitation one of the residents came in bristling with military aggression, moustache quivering. "Now look here, Martel, old chap, we'd like to know what the devil's going on. Huh? Yesterday the wife and I said nothing, thinking our room had been accidently overlooked. But here we are waiting for the luncheon gong, and once again our room hasn't been touched, not even the bed made. And, what's more, not a chambermaid in sight!"

"Damn! How appalling!" Jonathan exploded. "I really am most awfully sorry! I'll get someone on to it immediately!"

"Hrm. Well. Very well then. Er, thank you." Anger deflated, the red face and moustache retired.

Jonathan rang the reception desk and Molly came in.

"Yeah?"

He winced. "Who was doing the bedrooms this morning?"

"Marilyn."

"Where is she now?"

Molly shrugged. "Dunno."

"Well find her and send her to me!"

The blonde stepped back, open mouthed. "Awright!"

'Supervision of daily guest room cleaning', he wrote. That wasn't so difficult. What else?

He was still thinking of the next item when Marilyn arrived. "Molly says you want me."

"Why wasn't Major Potter's room done this morning?"

She hung her head. "Wasn't time."

"Why not? All the rooms are always done, every morning."

"Yeah. But with Mrs Martel not being here . . ."

"What difference does that make. She doesn't do the actual bedmaking and cleaning herself, does she?"

The girl stood on one leg, rubbing the back of her calf with the toe of her other shoe. "No, not always. But she sorts things out what goes wrong."

"What things?"

"Like when the vacuum cleaner don't work. Or when some kid's thrown up on the carpet, like today. Took me ages to clean it up and it don't look too good, yet."

"I see. And what was your excuse yesterday?"

"The flood."

"What flood?"

"Remember the water was switched off while Bert replaced a washer in the kitchen?" Jonathan shook his head. "Well it was. And seems like the people in number four put the plug in their basin, turned on the taps and got nothing. So they left it and went out. There was water everywhere. The carpet was soaked and the bedclothes what hung down off the bed was dripping. Took a long time. I had to strip the bed right off and—"

"Yes, yes. But what difference would it have made if Mrs Martel had been here?"

"Well . . ." the girl spread her hands, "she's the one what sorts out all the problems. There's always something what takes time to fix. She cleans the beach tar off the floors and towels. And she unstops the drains. Last week a little boy in number six broke a window. That had to be seen to. And she's good at putting the legs back on the beds . . ."

Jonathan held up his hand. "Okay, Marilyn. That's enough. You can go." He sat gazing at the blank lines on the notebook for a long time, remembering other mini-dramas Sue had coped with; not just upstairs, either. Neurotic chefs, clumsy waitresses, explosive boilers . . . and the pump bringing beer up from the cellar, which went on strike at least once a week.

There was no one in the bar after lunch. Molly was

sitting on a stool reading a weekly magazine of Love Stories when Jonathan wheeled through the door. She didn't look up, and he went out again, sat in the foyer looking out of the open door. Finally, pursing his lips, he rolled the chair out onto the path and headed for the bungalow.

He found Sue playing on the lawn with the children. "Hallo!" he called.

"Daddy!" Roddy rushed across the grass to hurl himself onto his father's lap. Stephanie waddled after him.

"What are you playing?"

"Injuns. Mummy made us a wig . . . wiggy . . . tent wiv rugs. Come an' see!"

The 'wigwam' was suspended on string from a tree branch, and pegged out with meat skewers. Jonathan peered through the door flap and saw cushions, bakelite plates and mugs. "Having a picnic tea in there, were you?"

"No! We was eating bison for lunch," Roddy corrected him. "Mummy and me shot it wiv our bows and arrows."

His parents grinned at each other.

"Feeling better, dear?" Jonathan asked.

She wanted to demand 'than what?' Instead she nodded. "It's lovely out here with the sprogs. I must try to do something about the garden for next year."

"Why don't you get Bert to help you. The hotel garden needn't take all his time."

"True. Okay, I will." She couldn't help wondering why he was being nice, and waited for him to start again trying to persuade her back to the hotel.

But he didn't. "Seems ages since we had any free time

together," he reached for her hand. "Why don't we go off to a restaurant for dinner one evening? Like to?"

Which made her even more suspicious, but she responded with enthusiasm. "Love to! Where have you in mind?"

The evening proved a great success.

For the first time Sue had an opportunity to wear the dress Aunt Filly had made her last year: a floral cotton with a wide, square neckline and deep-flounced skirt cut so full it flared and swayed as she walked.

"You look lovely!" Jonathan said as she pirouetted for him in the hall while they waited for the taxi. "Why haven't I seen that dress before."

Sue was so thrilled to be going out she had no wish to tell him why he hadn't seen it. She had suggested the Restaurante Belle Vue on the Esplanade, the only place she could think of which was convenient for wheelchairs.

Jonathan was almost his old, charming, witty, decisive self, ordering Sue's favourite aperitif without asking her, discussing the menu and choosing for them both before ordering a bottle of Sancerre to accompany their first course and an expensive Pauillac to follow.

"We'll be pie-eyed by the time we get through both bottles," Sue commented, wondering if at last his mental frustrations were fading – like the scars on his face.

"Excellent. It's time we got a bit tiddly together."

"But I can feel this martini hitting my knees already!"

He picked up her hand, turned it over and kissed the palm. "I've been too pre-occupied to notice how tired you were. Now I want to see you relax and enjoy yourself."

The martini had lowered her guard. Instead of meeting his words with dubious, if silent, cynicism, she allowed herself to wallow in them, purring a response to the gentle pressure of his fingers on her own.

The Cocquilles Meuniere were tender as cream, and likewise the duckling under its crispy skin. They nibbled cheese while finishing the Pauillac, then had a bowl of late strawberries each, with fresh Guernsey cream.

They knew the taxi driver quite well; fortunately he was accustomed to helping Jonathan in and out of his wheelchair and into the car because Sue announced her own legs could not be relied on.

Falling into bed together, giggling, they kissed, and stroked, and kissed again. Jonathan had lost none of his old technique, taking her winging through the mists of passionate love until, with a deep sigh, she relaxed every muscle in her body and drifted into a sweet, dreamless sleep.

Chapter Eight

Lost and Found

"I was wondering if Mummy could come up for the day on Wednesday," Sue told her father when he answered the phone.

"I know she'd love to, dear. But would it be possible for you to come here instead?"

"Could do. Any particular reason?"

"Only that your mother has been a bit off colour, lately. I've tried to persuade her to get the doctor but she refuses." Greg didn't add that he had been very worried by Sarah's recurring bouts of sickness and diarrhoea. He didn't want to cause alarm.

When Sue arrived on Wednesday morning with the three children, Sarah was looking perfectly fit though she had lost some weight.

"You getting into shape for a bathing beauty contest?" Sue joked.

"I'd certainly need to. I couldn't get into my swimming costumes of a few years ago when I tried them on in the spring."

Sue eyed her mother's figure objectively. "Hmm," she grunted, "They'd fall off you, now. Have you seen the doc lately?"

"Two or three months ago when I twisted my ankle. Now," she smiled at the children, "Are you all hungry? Come and see what Grandma has for your lunch."

The little ones were excused from the dining room when they had finished eating and dashed outside to play in the autumn sunshine, leaving Sarah and Sue to chat over their coffee cups.

"Have you been out for another meal with Jonathan, *à deux*?" Sarah asked, remembering how happy Sue had looked a few weeks ago.

"Er, no. We seem to have been so busy, recently." Sue flushed: Jonathan's snarling response to her suggestion that they repeat the outing, still hurt. She had loved every minute of that evening and believed he had, too, until last week when he had told her in no uncertain terms that as far as he was concerned it had been a disaster . . . boring beyond belief!

Sarah knew that Sue was fibbing. The season had not been good and there were few autumn guests this year. Normally she would have challenged Sue for the truth, but unfortunately she was feeling queasy again . . .

"What's up, Mum?" Sue got up in alarm. "You've gone a funny colour!"

"I think I must have eaten too much, dear. If you'll excuse me a minute I think . . ." Sarah doubled up in pain. Her legs felt weak and she knew she was going to retch.

Sue helped her to the bathroom. "I'm leaving the door ajar. Call me if you need help."

Afterwards Sarah allowed herself to be led into the bedroom to lie down.

"You stay put, Mummy. I'll clear up. The kids are quite happy in the garden." But as soon as she left the room, Sue picked up the phone and dialled the surgery.

"I want to operate," the doctor told Greg two months later. "I've done every test and examination possible, and apart from establishing that Sarah has a large unidentifiable lump in her abdomen, I cannot make a more accurate diagnosis without going in to see what it is."

Cancer was not a word to be spoken out loud: one knew about it, knew it could attack different parts of the body in various forms, and one could, when asked, disclose that the patient had a stomach problem or a bad leg or a blood disorder, but doctors knew that neither the patients nor their relatives wished to hear the dreaded word.

Greg nodded at the family doctor who was both physician and surgeon, carefully avoiding eye contact. "I am sure Sarah will want you to do whatever you think best. As always, we are in your hands."

Sarah came out of hospital in time for Christmas, looking and feeling worse than when she went in, despite assurances from the medical staff that the problem had been removed and she should soon begin to feel better. She was determined it should be so, and the doctor had no intention of telling her, or Greg, that her womb and colon were distorted by a massive carcinoma.

"Your mother is looking much better today, don't you think?" Greg smiled encouragingly at Sue a week later.

"Yes. Ever so much. Aren't you pleased with your progress, Mummy?"

"Indeed!" Sarah enthused. "I'm longing to tuck into a good Christmas dinner." Her skin was a dreadful yellow-ish grey, drawn over the sharply defined cheekbones. Her hands were wrinkled claws.

In their hearts all three guessed the truth, yet none were prepared to admit it yet, even to themselves.

The big act carried them all through Christmas. Greg supported Sarah out to the car and drove her and Richard to Port Grat, where they stayed at Hotel La Rocque over the festive season and into the New Year. The residential part of the hotel was closed until Easter, though the bar remained open to locals as usual, so they had the whole dining room to themselves for a family party. Ted, Julia and Stephen joined them, and Jessica, who spent a lot of time sitting with Sarah. Edna and John came, too, the latter taking occasional turns behind the bar with Greg. Without the seasonal staff Sue was in charge of cooking, which was considerably easier than putting up the decorations with the dubious help of her children. It was hard to feel the Yuletide spirit, blow up balloons, pin the paperchains to the picture rails and hang baubles and tinsel on the Christmas tree, without the thought that this must be her mother's final Christmas bringing a lump to her throat. Edna insisted on helping in the kitchen and when he wasn't out with friends, Sue's brother Richard helped entertain the little ones. They adored him, followed him like sheep and Roddy in particular mimicked his every move and word: not always appreciated when these were some of the more popular and prevalent used by Richard's peers at Elizabeth College.

Greg was given the honour of carving the turkey on Christmas Day. Everyone else had a task, and Sarah and

John were reminded of their own upbringing at Val du Douit, when Marie had ruled the household.

Marie and Aline had declined the invitation to join the party, but accepted the offer of Boxing Day lunch. As had old Alice, Greg's mother.

Sarah joined in the fun, laughing and joking, and hoping her almost non-existent appetite went unnoticed. It didn't, but no one was foolish enough to comment.

So many Christmases had passed, so similar in format that it was hard to recall which was which. But Christmas 1954 was one that Sue would never forget.

Jonathan had made a New Year's Resolution. "I need more independence," he told Sue, "So I have ordered a custom-built car and shall learn to drive it. I hate having to rely on other people to get out and about."

Sue couldn't think of a reply. He was the one constantly nagging about expenditure, and a special car for him would cost the earth. Then she decided she was being mean; why shouldn't he have a car of his own, regardless of expense. Anyway, apart from the deposit, they wouldn't have to pay up till it was delivered several months hence, by which time they might well be into a bumper season.

"This place is a mess," Sue commented, looking round the bar at the blotched wallpaper and chipped paintwork. "We must get it redecorated before we reopen for the season."

Jonathan nodded. "Definitely. But we can't afford professionals. We'll have to do it ourselves."

Sue frowned. He was using the term 'ourselves' rather

loosely: what he meant was *she* would have to do it, herself. "I don't know when . . ." she began, thinking about his expensive car.

"You'll have to bring Debbie here with her playpen while you work, and spend less time round at your mother's."

"I can't! I feel guilty enough as it is, about being there for such a short time each day."

"Oh for God's sake! She's going to die whether you are there or not. Tell your father to get a nurse in. He can afford it." He swung the wheelchair round and left the room.

It was hard to believe anyone could be so cold and callous! There were a dozen retorts on the tip of her tongue . . . but what was the point? How could one possibly argue with that kind of mentality?

She elected to hang the new paper over the old, stained one. The drinks and glasses were moved into the dining room, using it as a temporary bar, leaving her free to get on with the job uninterrupted. Richard sometimes dropped in to help at weekends, mainly to pick up extra pocket money secretly removed by Sue from her housekeeping purse when Jonathan wasn't around. Stephen came too, happy to work for nothing other than easing Sue's burden.

The late winter and early spring was a sad period for them all, seeing Sarah's weight rapidly dwindling. Her skin was like parchment, yellow and wrinkled way beyond her years.

"Dad, do you think we should try to persuade Aunt Ethel to come over, soon?" Sue suggested. "Much better that she arrives while Mummy is . . . still *compos mentis*."

There was a lot more grey in Greg's hair, now, his eyes, dull and sad, had sunk deep into their sockets as he looked up at her from his chair. "You don't think she's going to get better?"

Sue's lower lip quivered. "No, Daddy, I don't. Nor do you. Hm?"

Greg shook his head. It was the first time they had spoken about it. "You're probably right. But if Ethel turns up here, don't you think your mother will smell a rat?"

"I think Mummy has guessed the truth, anyway. But if not I'm sure she would want to know."

"Why?"

"When one . . . goes before one's time, there must surely be things you want to say to people. Unfinished jobs and plans you'd like to hand over to someone else."

Greg rocked to and fro in the creaking armchair for a few minutes before muttering, "The doctor hasn't said anything specific, you know."

"When is he coming again?"

"Tomorrow."

"I suspect the only reason he hasn't spelled it out is because he knows it is something you don't want to hear. But I think for all our sakes you should ask him, point blank."

They heard the bedroom door open and Greg's sister-in-law, Maureen, joined them.

"Hello," Sue greeted her, "Haven't seen you for ages. How are you? How is Uncle Andrew?"

The two women pecked cheeks. "I'm extremely well, thanks. Wish I could say the same for your uncle. Is that a pot of tea you have there?"

A few minutes later Sue returned to her mother's bedside.

The following day the doctor confirmed what the family had already guessed. "Yes, I knew as soon as we operated last year," he told Greg. "We were able to remove very little because it involved some of her vital organs. Frankly, I am surprised she has hung on so well."

Greg took a deep breath before asking the burning question. "How long do you reckon she has?"

"Three, maybe four weeks." He put a sympathetic hand on Greg's arm. "I'm so sorry, old chap. But she is becoming very weak. I doubt she'll be with us much longer."

Greg spent a long time in the privacy of the bathroom trying to plan, between bouts of weeping, how to tell Sarah the news.

He need not have worried: the moment she saw his freshly dried cheeks and swollen eyes, she knew. "I only wish we'd been told sooner, my darling. Then we could have spent more time together doing some of the things we've been meaning to do for years and never got round to. Tell me, did the doctor give you a guess how long I have left?"

"Three or four weeks."

She smiled. "I suppose we must be thankful for small mercies. I mean, just imagine how awful it would have been if I'd fallen under a bus and we had never had the chance to say goodbye."

She rocked and comforted him while he wept in her arms.

Sue was trying to be all things to all people with mixed

success. Nurse to Sarah, comforter to Greg, painter and decorator in the hotel, and psychologist-cum-pacifier to Jonathan, while attempting to run her own home and be mother to her children. She was constantly tired. If only it had been possible to have an occasional break, she thought, but having married a man a few years older than herself she had lost contact with her school friends who had married in their own age group and were referred to by Jonathan as 'puerile'. It would have been helpful to have a friend her own age to compare notes with, about babies, washing powder, men, and how to make the Yorkshire pudding rise in the oven. And she would like to have a friend with whom she might to go to the theatre or cinema, but the only possible young women were married, and she had no intention of inviting herself along without a partner.

Jonathan, of course, was uninterested in any form of entertainment or socialising other than greeting customers in the bar. He had taken to drinking quite heavily, shortening his temper even more, especially after whisky. There were days on end when he didn't even stay in the bar, but wheeled himself home to sit brooding with bottle and book. Sue was seldom at home with him in the evenings, taking the opportunity when the children were in bed to get on with papering the bar, or visiting Les Mouettes to be with her mother.

"Why don't you take Sue out for the evening, sometimes?" Stephen suggested to him. "I'll keep an eye on things here."

"What the hell for?"

"Well . . ." Stephen was staggered at his cousin's reaction, "I thought it would be nice for you both."

"Then you thought wrong, old chap. I hate going out to see some amateur play or fake war film. Bores me rigid."

"Fair enough," the younger man tried to keep his tongue under control. "But what about Sue? Doesn't she like a break now and then?"

Jonathan swung round and glared at him. "For Chrissake, Steve, you're as bad as my mother! Look, if you think she needs a night out, you take her. But not yet," he added, "she's dawdling over that decorating enough as it is."

Stephen picked up a glass and began polishing it, furiously.

Not that Sue actually felt like a night out, anyway. Sarah was on her mind constantly, while she was wielding a paintbrush, or at home with the children her mother would never see grow up; whispering prayers as she drove down to Bordeaux, or weeping as she drove back. Amazingly, she felt most cheerful when sitting beside her mother, chatting, or reading to her, the dying woman was always so bright and smiling, even when the pains were very bad.

Sarah had never been a deeply religious woman; she knew her Bible reasonably well; she believed in God and felt free to speak to Him without the ceremony of formal prayer. She loved books both fictitious and factual, on religious subjects and now that she was too weary to read she loved to have Greg, Sue or Richard sit reading to her.

She was less interested in newspapers. "Always full of declining morals, death and destruction about which it is too late for me to do anything. I leave your generation to put the world to rights, after I've gone," she would tell Sue.

Almost as though prompted by some telepathic message, she insisted on getting up and dressed on the day that, unknown to her, Ethel was due to arrive from New Zealand.

"I don't believe it!" Sarah exclaimed when her eldest sister walked into the sitting room. "Where have you come from? Did you just drop out of the sky?"

"Yes, literally. Well almost. Fortunately the plane didn't actually fall but landed quite comfortably." Ethel sat down on the settee beside Sarah to hug her.

"You mean you came by aeroplane?"

"Yes. Why not?"

"I suppose if you'd come by boat . . ." Sarah began, then stopped. "Tea, someone. And something solid for the girl to eat before we start on the champagne!" She turned to look at her bronzed and healthy-looking sibling. "You haven't changed much since last I saw you. And still looking as though Ma had an affair with a black man!"

"It's summer back home, remember?"

"I'd meant to come out and visit you," Sarah said wistfully, adding in a more strident tone, "I'll be very disappointed if you haven't brought lots of photographs."

"Hundreds. I'll just go and fetch them." Ethel hastened out of the room . . . and collapsed on to her bed in tears.

One of Sarah's many regrets about dying at fifty-one was being denied the joy of seeing Richard and her grandchildren grow up. Richard would be fifteen in June and was already a tall, handsome lad. She and Greg were not sorry the boy was showing no interest in the tomato industry. It was certainly lucrative, at the moment, but was endlessly hard, tiring work with long hours, and they were happy that he spent so much of his spare time at the boatyard with George Schmit, though slightly worried about his friendship with Gelly's nephew, Michael Smart. There was something about the older boy that neither of them liked.

One of the highlights of Sarah's life, now, were the visits of her grandchildren. Roderick was a serious child, often preoccupied with his own thoughts and imagination, but nevertheless very open, friendly and polite for his almost five years while, in contrast, the beautiful three-year-old Stephanie bounced through her days with vigorous, noisy passion. She adored everyone and had no doubt everyone adored her, and her idol-in-chief was young Uncle Richard. Sarah loved to witness the child's big amber eyes gazing into Richard's face as he helped her with a simple jigsaw puzzle or read her a story; the fact that Richard would invariably choose a book which interested himself and was often way over Stephanie's understanding, mattered not. At twenty-one months Deborah already had a mop of wavy, red hair and deliciously enchanting green eyes. Sarah often sighed, wondering if she, too, would develop into a raving beauty.

Through sheer will-power and determination, Sarah was at the family party to celebrate Roderick's fifth birthday. She gave him a bicycle and a surfboard and a wonderful set of Meccano.

"Mummy! Daddy!" Sue admonished, out of Roddy's earshot. "That's far too much. You really are spoiling him!"

"Just think of all the birthdays to come when I won't

be giving him anything," Sarah replied in a practical tone of voice. "I've put by a good stock of gifts for the girls, too. They are out in the garage, waiting for their coming birthdays and Christmas."

Sue watched through the window where Richard was holding Roddy on the new cycle, then had an idea. "Why don't we have an unbirthday party next week for the girls and you can see them receive their presents?"

Sarah shook her head. "A lovely thought, dear, but somehow I don't think I shall be around, then. I hope not," she added with a sigh.

"Oh Mum! Are you feeling very ill?"

Sarah nodded. "Yes. Rotten. I shall crawl back to bed as soon as we've had tea." She said it with a smile, determined not to reveal just how difficult it was, despite the pillows, to sit there on the settee, or how dreadfully wearying was the sound of her beloved grandchildren's happy voices. "Don't look so sad, my dear. My father and my brother, Bertie, who was killed in the war, you remember, they are waiting up there for me. I'll never be far away from you all, watching to see you behave yourselves. It is God's will, and who are we to question His decisions?"

Next day, Marie and Aline arrived, unannounced.

Greg was worried lest they upset Sarah, but Marie had her heart set on seeing her youngest daughter one last time. "You stay here in the sitting room with Aline," she ordered him, while I go and speak to her."

Sarah was half awake when her mother walked in and managed a smile. "Hello, Ma. I'm so glad you've come."

Marie sat on a chair beside the bed and took Sarah's

hand between her own. She sniffed, and her eyes were brimming. "I only wish I'd come before. It's what they call nowadays a character flaw, that I'm so bad at saying sorry." She sniffed again. "Ten years wasted, when we could have been good friends." She groped in her handbag for a hankie as tears began to trickle over her wrinkled cheeks.

Sarah pulled Marie's hand to her lips and kissed it. "It was all a silly misunderstanding, Ma."

"It's never too late to make up, is it?" Marie murmured.

"Well, in this case it's been a damn near-run thing!"

The two women hugged and had a little giggle together.

"Do you want to see Aline?"

"Yes, of course." She was so tired, but felt she must perform this last duty. Aline approached the bed, tongue-tied, but Sarah held out her hand. "Come and sit down, a minute. I'm so glad to have the opportunity to say goodbye to you."

Looking distressed, her sister shook her head and mumbled, "I can't think why. We never got on, did we?"

"We found it difficult to understand each other. But we are older and wiser, now. I'm so glad you are able to go on looking after Ma. She's eighty-four now, isn't she?"

"Coming up eighty-five, but she's tough for her age." Aline swallowed hard. "Is there anything you would like me to do for you?"

Sarah stared at her for a moment, then nodded. "Do you think you you could persuade Ma to patch things up with John and Edna?"

Aline's eyes widened. She had made a life's work of

being the family troublemaker and now her sister's dying wish was for a total role reversal. She flushed to the roots of her hair. "I could try . . ." she said hesitantly.

Sarah smiled. "Now? Will you go and ask her now?"

Aline got up slowly and left Sarah to doze quietly.

Marie didn't hesitate. "Where is the telephone?"

Twenty minutes later John and Edna walked into the sitting room at Les Mouettes to find his mother chatting quite amiably with Ethel, the daughter she had banished from the island nearly a quarter of a century ago. The diminutive family matriarch promptly stood up and said, "Come," and marched ahead of them all into Sarah's bedroom.

Sarah opened her eyes to see them standing around her bed; her siblings John, Ethel, Aline and William who had flown over from Southampton that morning, plus Edna, Greg and Sue. "Seems like it's a day for saying sorry, doesn't it?" Marie smiled. "Well, first of all John. Come here and give your mother a hug."

John had answered his mother's summons, but had had little idea what it was about. He looked round the group, open mouthed, then willingly did as he was told. "Ma! I'm sorry you've been so upset by what happened."

She hugged him back. "My fault. It was none of my business. I didn't know how things were between you and Mary . . . and Edna. Can we all be friends, now?" adding, when she saw his nervous glance at his wife, "yes, that means you too, my dear." She held out an arm and Edna hurried round the bed to be kissed.

William, Aline and Ethel joined in and they gathered close round Sarah, who closed her eyes and smiled.

"I don't believe heaven can be better than this," she whispered.

For the next three days Sue, Ethel and Greg scarcely left Sarah's side. The doctor came each day to administer painkilling injections, which kept her very drowsy, but she was able to open her eyes one last time as Greg leaned over the bed to hold her frail body which was now only skin and bone. "It's time for me to go, now, my darling. I love you." She continued to doze fitfully until nearly midnight, then with one last shuddering breath she slid into the after world.

"Why don't you fly out to New Zealand with me for a break?" Ethel suggested to Greg, "When the funeral and everything is over."

"Sweet of you, but no. It's the beginning of the season and I can't leave the tomatoes to grow themselves."

"Why can't your brother cope for a few weeks?"

"Afraid he hasn't been well, lately." No point in telling her that Andrew was in a semi-permanent state of intoxication.

"What are you going to do, then?"

"Oh, Richard and I will muddle along together for the time being. One doesn't want to make any hasty decisons one might regret later." He continued to feel dazed, walking through each day like a zombie.

St Sampson's Church was full to the door on the day of the funeral, in spite of the pouring rain. After the interment the family and close friends went back to Les Mouettes for tea; Marie and Ethel tended to be a bit weepy and tried to console each other, while Sue and

Aline kept themselves occupied playing hostess, pouring teas and handing round plates of sandwiches and cakes.

Everyone remained very solemn until old Alice, who had not been taken to the funeral, asked, "When is the cake going to be cut?"

"What cake, Mother?" Greg bellowed into the infamous ear-trumpet.

"A fruit one, I suppose, with icing. Come to think of it, who's birthday is it, anyway?" Unlike the sombre clothes of all the mourners, the ninety-six year old had appeared in bright green and red chiffon and the same delapidated old hat she always dragged out of a box from the attic for Special Occasions.

"No one's birthday, Mother. We've just come back from Sarah's funeral."

Everyone sat in embarrassed silence.

Except Alice. "Come back?" she frowned at him. "Where from did you say? I didn't know you'd been away. Off gallivanting again?"

Sue accidently caught Ethel's eye and their lips twitched. Richard snorted in his effort not to laugh.

The bosom of Marie's black dress, heavily draped with pearls, began to quiver. "If Sarah can see and hear us now, she'll be helpless with giggles," she commented.

Which somehow broke the ice. Everyone started laughing and chatting . . . much to Greg's relief. They all remembered how full of merriment Sarah had been, how tickled she was by her dear, deaf mother-in-law's misinterpretations.

"Was it something I said?" Alice asked innocently.

No one could think of an answer.

*　　　*　　　*

Like everyone else who had witnessed Sarah's suffering, Sue had prayed for to her die. Yet the fact that she was gone remained unreal. Impossible to assimilate. "I keep thinking of things I want to tell her," she said to Aunt Filly, when her mother's old friend came to help repair some of the hotel sheets. "I feel perfectly normal and emotionally in control, then suddenly it hits me below the belt."

"Me too. And I felt the same when my own mother died."

"Does it get better?"

"In time. Gradually the body blows become more infrequent." She bit off a last thread. "There, that should look a bit better. By the way, how is Jonathan, lately?"

"Okay." The reply lacked enthusiasm.

Filly raised an eyebrow. "Oh?"

Sue had always had a special affection for this bouncy little blonde woman and, longing for a confidante, was tempted to tell Filly at least some of her worries. She wanted to talk about her marriage, if it could be called that; her husband and his coldness. She felt the need to share some of her miseries. But would poor Filly want to be burdened with her problems? Or might she be so shocked that she would never want to come to the hotel again? Dared she reveal that when he heard that Sarah had died, Jonathan had merely said, "That's a relief. Now perhaps you'll get on and finish restocking the bar." What was the point in making Filly hate him?

Filly listened to the silence, guessing what was going on in Sue's mind. Finally she spoke out. "Bottling it up isn't good for one, you know. You need to talk it out of your system. Doesn't have to be with me, but do find someone. He's getting worse, isn't he?"

Sue lifted her head, frowning. "How do you know?"

"Silly girl. I wasn't born yesterday. It is perfectly obvious to anyone with a grain of sense."

Sue got up and looked out of the window. "Please don't think I don't want to confide in you. I cannot imagine anyone better but why should you have to listen to my woes?" She sighed. "You know, though half of me wants a shoulder to cry on, the other half doesn't want to even think about it, let alone talk about it."

"Playing ostrich? Burying your head in the sand?"

Sue turned round and shrugged. "Something like that."

"Next fine day, why don't you and I take a trip to Herm?"

Sue grinned. "Love to, if I could think up a good lie to tell Jonathan."

"Would he mind you going?"

"Mind! He'd use it as an excuse to drink and shout abuse for at least a week," Sue replied, voice thick with resentment.

Filly packed up her sewing box. "We'll say next Tuesday. That will give you time to dream up some story."

The hotel profits for 1955 were no better than the previous year. "Hardly get any repeat bookings like we did at first," Jonathan remarked as he pored over the ledgers on his desk.

Sue had been aware of the fact for the past couple of years – not even Gordon's cricket team came anymore – but what could she say? "If only you'd stop making embarrassing scenes in front of the guests? If only you weren't so rude to the staff that most of them walked out by mid-season, to be replaced by the useless drifters who'd been sacked by at least three other hotels in the first three months?" No one could tell him that he should stay out of the bar and thereby stop upsetting the local trade with his sarcastic remarks. Unfortunately. The hotel's reputation had slumped, not even Norton and Jonathan's other service friends used the bar, nowadays.

"Trouble is, you're never around to keep an eye on the staff. And you know I can't get upstairs to check what is happening." Jonathan glared at her. "If you don't want us to go bankrupt, you'd better stop playing with the kids all day and do some work."

Sue had heard it all before, but since her wonderful day in Herm with Filly at the beginning of the season, she had felt much calmer. More able to ignore the perpetual jibes. But nevertheless, she was depressed. Life was miserable; Jonathan's moods unpredictable; the children overhearing his furious outbursts, which always upset them. She left the office without speaking, going out to sit on the bench overlooking Port Grat.

Why? She kept asking herself. Why is this continuing to happen year after year? She didn't notice the sunshine or the view. Her mind's eye was focused on images she had created during the war, of home and family. And afterwards, when the atmosphere between Sarah and herself had been so bad, there had been the dreams, the determination to marry David and build a home and family of her own . . . David! Dear God, David? Was this some kind of Divine Retribution for abandoning David?

Molly was off, sick, so Sue agreed to man the bar for the evening, as soon as the children were in bed. She ran along the path through icy November rain and stomped the wet from her boots on the kitchen floor, hung her mac over the door and left the brolly open to dry out. The first person she saw in the bar was Stephen. "Hallo, stranger! Haven't seen you for a while. What brings you here?"

"Aunt Jessica told Mother that Molly was away so I thought I might make myself useful." The only group of customers were at the far end of the bar with their glass tankards of bitter.

"Terribly sweet of you, but don't tell Jonathan. That will put Jessica back in the doghouse again!"

Stephen scowled. But when his cousin wheeled himself up to his usual bar table, likewise querying his presence, he said, "I hadn't seen you all for a while so I thought I'd pop down for a drink."

"Excellent!" Jonathan beamed. "What will it be? A G and T? Sue! Fix the man's drink, will you?"

The group of customers were discussing the appalling weather, then started complaining of the approaching Christmas.

"My old lady loves dressing up and waltzing off to dances and parties," one volunteered, and it was obvious he didn't share her passion.

"Most women do," another observed. "Isn't that right, Jonty?"

"I wouldn't know," he responded. "You'd better ask the wife." He tilted his head towards Sue.

"Well, Mrs M, what do you reckon?"

Sue grinned at the man. "Definitely. Most women love to take off their pinnies and put on their glad rags. Makes a girl feel human."

"Right." He nodded at his friends. "And how often does Jonty take you out and show you off?"

There was a horrible hush.

Jonathan took a swig of whisky. "Trouble is, old man, I'm not much use on the dance floor. In fact there are precious few places without step and stairs that I can get to without a crane – or an attentive team of navvies." He finished with a laugh, so his audience joined in.

"So," the talkative member of the group persisted, "When Mrs M wants to go off for a jig, who takes her?"

"Whoever she likes!" Jonathan's hands were spread with great bonhomie. Adding with a wink, "Or whoever will have her! Talking of which, I see we are invited to some do at the Royal next Thursday, darling. Why don't you get someone to take you? What about you, Stephen?"

Stephen and Sue were both flushed with embarrassment, not least because of the lie Jonathan was acting.

"Er, yes. Yes I'd be delighted, if Sue would like to?"

"Of course I would." Sue's mind was spinning. She had not attended a social function for ages . . . months . . . years? It would be wonderful, even worth the inevitable snide remarks and reprisals later? "To be honest I'd love it," she declared boldly.

It was a Charity Dinner and Ball in aid of displaced persons and refugees. On hearing of the forthcoming event, Filly had 'discovered' the ideal dress in her wardrobe – an unlikely story as she was half Sue's size, but Sue overcame any scruples when she saw it. The deep coral lace dress had cap sleeves, a low neckline, nipped waist and a full skirt which flared to her ankles. And with it was a matching bolero-length jacket fastened with pearl-cluster buttons.

214

"It's fantastic!" Sue exclaimed. "But what on earth was it doing in your—"

"Sshh!" Filly interrupted. "Ask no questions and you'll be told no lies! Now, what about shoes?"

"I have some plain gold courts."

"Perfect. And evening bag?"

"Yes."

"Fine. And you must use your mother's squirrel coat. She would want you to," Filly added, seeing the doubt cross Sue's face.

Stephen was quite overawed when he saw her. "Suzanne! You look marvellous," he exclaimed.

"You don't look so bad yourself!" He was immaculate in dinner jacket and black tie, his straight black hair combed flat for once. He had a strong, square chin which contrasted with the gentleness of his eyes. There was no doubt he was extremely handsome.

Jonathan saw them off, Sue waiting in dread for some biting sarcasm. But there was none. "Enjoy yourselves, you two! I won't tell you not to do anything I wouldn't, or there would be no point in you going! Look after her, Steve, and bring her back in one piece. She's not a bad cook when she puts her mind to it and might be hard to replace."

They all laughed, and Stephen's sports car did a mild wheelspin as it roared off into the dark.

Stephen knew nearly everyone there. Sue did not. He introduced her to several of his friends and they split up for a while as waiters circulated with trays of cocktails and canapés.

They were seated opposite each other at dinner, at the long flower-decked tables arranged in the dining room.

215

"I've always been very fond of the Royal," remarked the bald, overweight gentleman who sat on Sue's left. "Do you come here often?"

"No. But my mother did, in her day." Realising her gaffe immediately, and seeing Stephen cough explosively into his table napkin, Sue spent the next ten minutes trying to avoid eye contact with the latter. She turned to the young man on her right, saying, "The paté is delicious; how were your roll-mops?"

"Simply super. I say, don't you think you should let me help you pin your corsage?" Every lady had had a little spray of carnations waiting on her napkin.

Sue wanted to tell him to keep his lecherous hands off her bodice; instead she murmured "It really is terribly sweet of you to offer, but I think that that particular shade of pink would look simply ghastly against the coral, don't you?"

He nodded reluctantly. "Yes. I suppose you are right."

When they returned to the ballroom after dinner, Uti and Tilly Walgrave, friends of Stephen's, asked them to share their table near the tall, curtained windows, and no sooner were they seated than Uti asked Sue for a dance. He was shorter than herself but an excellent dancer.

"Why are you called Uti?" she asked as he whirled her round the floor in his firm clasp.

"For some God forsaken reason my parents elected to christen me Uhtred, after some ancestor I believe. It's been the bane of my life. I hope you think Uti sounds fractionally better."

Sue giggled. "Quite definitely," she assured him. She liked him, and his wife: very bright, happy, natural people. They continued dancing through several breaks.

"Mind if I cut in, Uti?" Stephen took Sue's hand while they stood in the centre of the ballroom. "You've commandeered my partner for long enough."

"I'll relinquish her only if I can claim another dance later!" Uti said, pouting playfully.

"Hey! Doesn't the lady get a say in this?" Sue asked indignantly.

Both men peered round the room, straight-faced. "I see no ships," Stephen quipped.

"You rotten beggar!" she exclaimed. "You wait!"

"Willingly," Stephen laughed as he swept her away, leaving Uti to find out who had claimed Tilly.

They were natural partners: Sue found she could read his every touch. He loved the way her skirt flared out as he twirled her through the old-fashioned waltz. She loved his gentleness, even when he was teasing.

Stephen let his gaze wander over her hair, down her neck to her shoulder. She had left her jacket on the chair with her purse, so he was able to watch the small muscles ripple under the golden skin of her arm. He bit his lower lip, trying to control his thoughts.

"Funny to think we've known each other for years, yet this is the first time we've ever danced together," Sue commented, just for something to break the silence . . . and quell the dizziness which threatened to throw her off balance.

"You're wrong, you know."

She glanced up, one eyebrow raised.

There were smile lines at the corners of his deep grey eyes. "You don't remember the Hall's Christmas party in 'forty-seven!" he accused.

"Oh, yes I do. Were you there?"

He feigned indignation. "How could you forget the gangly youth in a suit several sizes too big for him, who stood in a corner most of the evening . . . until a beautiful princess took pity and asked him to dance."

"Oh? And who was that?"

"You can't guess?"

She gave a shy smile, and nodded.

Apart from a lively foxtrot with Uti, Sue danced all evening with Stephen. They shared extra bottles of wine with the Walgraves, and when the girls went off to powder their noses, Sue took the opportunity to explain to Tilly why Jonathan couldn't take her to dances. "I'm afraid he bullied Stephen into bringing me here tonight."

Having watched the pair dancing together, Tilly wondered if Jonathan had a clue what he was doing.

The lights were dipped low for the last waltz. Sue felt Stephen's mouth against her forehead, and pressed closer. Her mouth filled with saliva, her knees trembled. His lips were kissing her hairline. Their feet scarcely moved.

The orchestra signalled the end of the evening with the National Anthem, as the lights went up. Sue and Stephen stood side by side, fingers entwined, secretly, within the folds of her skirt, both flushed with excitement . . . and alarm.

Tilly and Uti waved the little sports car out of sight, then turned to stare at each other, heads to one side, questioning.

"Why are we coming up here?" Sue asked as the car wound round the bends of the Val de Terre – in the opposite direction from home.

"I need time," he replied briefly.

"What for?"

"To think. And perhaps tell you how much I have loved you for years."

Huddled into the fur coat, Sue could feel her heart pounding. His words were sweet, dangerous music. "Stephen!" her voice shook.

The car sped along to the turning off to Jerbourg Point and swung into the car park at the monument, facing back towards the lights of Town. Switching off the engine Stephen turned to stare at her in the silent darkness. Reaching for her hand he kissed the tips of her fingers, then they were in each other's arms.

Chapter Nine

Accords and Discords

Jonathan turned over in bed with a vigorous snort and
Sue was grateful for the gentle breathing which at last
replaced the heavy snores. Not that the snoring ever woke
her but when, unable to sleep, she lay gazing up into the
darkness hour after hour, the racket became unbearable.
What did she feel for Jonathan, now? It was very difficult
to assess for her moods changed, like his. There were
times when she hated him, wanted to get away as far
as possible from the snarls and sarcasm. There were also
times when she felt she still loved him . . . or was she
only in love with a memory, of the way he used to be?
It seemed she had being living on hope for years. Hope
that he would get better, mentally if not physically. The
latter she could cope with, the moods were different. There
were those precious moments when he was loving, caring
and thoughtful and she dared to let herself believe that
this was *it*, the beginning of the rest of their wonderful
lives, together with their three children. Which made it
all the more painful when the sweetness ended abruptly

in a volley of curses, for no apparent reason. So what else did she feel? Pity. Lots of pity which frequently turned to anger. And pity was no replacement for love.

Was it really only three years? Three years of lying in the darkness imagining the feel of Jonathan's arms round her, loving and caressing her . . . the way it used to be. Tonight, for the first time, the mirage was of someone else's arms, conveying her with passionate urgency towards . . . what? She could feel Stephen's love wrapping her in a silk cocoon, where her emotions might lie safe for evermore. Yet it must remain only a dream. She could never abandon the children, for of course, as the innocent party, Jonathan would be awarded custody of all three of them by any divorce court. But would she ever think of abandoning Jonathan himself? He was her husband, father of her children, her partner in sickness and in health for the rest of their lives. She must push Stephen away, out of her mind . . . out of her life. If she did not, every time they met from here on, he would be an emotional threat.

They did meet again. Both Stephen and Sue realised they couldn't just walk away from their feelings without an explanatory goodbye. The venue was Le Noury's Restaurant in the Arcade, where they were able to sit over coffee pretending to the world it was an accidental meeting. In fact they were the only customers upstairs, where the tables were already laid for the town's business people to come in for lunch.

"This is going to be very difficult," Sue whispered, not for fear of anyone overhearing, but rather because she didn't want to hear the words herself.

Stephen's eyes focused across the table on her face, unaware of the untamed hair drawn back in a rubber band, the lack of make-up and the dark circles round her eyes, seeing only the young woman he had loved from a distance all his life, whom he had held, for a brief hour in his arms. He nodded. "Yes, very, very difficult." He glanced across the room to the top of the stairs, but no one had come up since the waitress had delivered their coffees, so he reached for her hand. "But it has to be done. You cannot go on suffering this living hell. I love you, my darling Sue."

She closed her eyes and shook her head. "You don't understand. I . . . we cannot . . ."

His eyebrows drew together in alarm. "What? What are you saying?"

Sue looked down at the hand clutching hers on the checkered tablecloth; he was squeezing her fingers so tightly his knuckles were white. She bit her lip, trying to hold back the hot tears stinging her eyes. "It is impossible."

"Why? You don't regret what happened the other night?"

"No. I know I should, but I don't. The tragedy is that we can't repeat it. Ever."

His mouth opened and closed. "Seriously? Never?"

She couldn't speak. Staring out of the window over the heads of the shoppers below, she groped in her bag for a hankie, and blew her nose.

"I'm sorry. I thought you felt the same way . . ." he began.

"I do, unfortunately. At least, I think so. But we must be sensible. I mean," her fingers scratched viciously into

222

her scalp, "Steve darling, nothing can ever come of this but misery."

"You mean you still love Jonty. You don't want to leave him."

"No! Yes! I don't know. But I do know I love my children, dearly. I couldn't possibly leave them. They need me as much as I need them. And Jonathan needs me, too."

He sipped his coffee; it was getting cold and tasted awful. He fondled her hand, turned it over and covered her palm with his own. "We could meet from time to time . . ."

"No, darling. It would only be to tempt ourselves, mentally and physically. And I don't know about you, but frankly I don't think I could bear to go on seeing you, not without cracking up."

"I don't know which would be worse: resisting temptation or facing the fact of never seeing you again." He gasped at the painful thought. "Oh God, Sue darling."

"Sshh! I can hear people on the stairs. Come on, let's go. The quicker the better. Long drawn-out goodbyes are always painful. You can walk me down to my car on the pier."

He followed her down, watched her smiling at the lady behind the counter as he paid for their coffees, and stumbled out to mingle with Christmas shoppers.

"But Sue, there is so much to talk about!"

"I know. The discussions could last throughout every day of the rest of our lives. We could make them last forever."

"What about the bar? What will you tell Jonty?"

The gulls were wheeling and screaming overhead as

someone emptied a bag of bread scraps on the slipway in front of Woolworths. The December wind cut through Sue's overcoat, piercing her skin like icicles. She stopped as she reached her car, shivered, and opened the door. "I shan't say anything. You can telephone him and say you're sorry, but something has cropped up and you can't come in any more."

"Something like what?"

She shrugged. "Stephen, I don't know. You're an architect, invent something," she was sobbing. "I love you. I'm trying to be strong. Goodbye." She got into the car.

He held the door, about to say he would see her at Christmas . . . but her misery, the pleading look in her reddened eyes stopped him. "Goodbye, my dearest love," he whispered, and watched her car edge off the pier into the traffic, till it passed the States Offices and out of sight.

Christmas came and went. Part of it was really good, like watching the children's faces as they put out a drink and mince pies for Santa Claus and his reindeers, and found sooty footprints next morning on their bedroom floors; and seeing them tear open their presents with squeals of joy. The bar was closed all Christmas and Boxing Day and Sue was happy to build up a good fire in the sitting room and dining room as soon as the turkey was in the oven. The children were awake early and continued noisy all day, so Sue worried that they would get on Jonathan's nerves, causing an outburst. But he remained quite calm, drank little, and even played snakes and ladders with Roddy.

When the children were in bed on Boxing evening, Sue

produced bowls of soup and a large plateful of turkey and ham sandwiches. She and Jonathan had a glass of sherry each, followed by wine, then port with hot mince pies.

"Another pie?" Sue offered the plate to Jonathan.

"Mmm! They're good. And another drop of port, please."

She took one for herself before settling back in her chair with a contented sigh. "What a lovely Christmas it's been."

"You think?"

"Indeed. Don't you?"

He shrugged. "If you like that sort of thing, I suppose. Personally I thought it rather boring."

Her heart sank. "Oh. Did you? I thought it was lovely, being in our own home with our little family."

"You've always had an obsession about home, haven't you?"

"It was because of the war and not having a real home for five years."

"Nor did I. I was in the navy, remember." He glanced up at an old ship's company photograph on the wall, and added, "Wish I'd never left."

"I'm glad you did leave. Being a sailor's wife isn't much fun, especially when one is shunted around with young children."

"Agreed. But then I would never have married." He looked up at her. "I'm a lousy husband and father. I'd have been much better off living aboard with a steward to look after me."

There were a thousand things she might have said, but none that wouldn't have started a row. So she got up and silently removed the dirty dishes.

Alone in the kitchen with the washing up, Sue found herself wondering what Stephen was doing.

Gradually, over the next six months, it became easier for Sue to keep her mind off Stephen. Her moods fluctuated from deep depression when it was difficult to motivate herself into any activity, to frenetic bouts of industry. Despair at the state of the hotel would drive her to stripping out bedrooms and redecorating them herself, whenever Emmy was available to keep an eye on the children, or reorganising the bar to better efficiency and revitalising the menus. All this would work well as long as she continued to supervise it, but the moment she took her eye off the ball everything lapsed again.

"Can't you watch what the chef is up to when I'm not around," she begged Jonathan one hot July day.

"He works better when he's left to himself. He hates it when you interfere," was the only response. "Your trouble is you haven't enough to keep you occupied and you keep inventing things, upsetting peoples' routines. I think it's time I got hold of Steve again to take you out."

"No!" she said sharply, and he looked up in surprise.

"Why not? You are becoming very scratchy and snappy again."

"I . . . I'd rather go out with you."

"But I don't wish to take you out." He shrugged. "Oh well, forget it."

She breathed a sigh of relief.

Roddy's first end-of-year report arrived from the little preparatory school he attended near L'Islet. 'Roderick is unco-operative and frequently disrupts the class.' 'A pity Roderick is so uninterested in every aspect of school

226

work.' 'Roderick often picks fights with the other children.' 'Roderick uses very bad language at times. This should be discouraged at home.'

Jonathan had opened the post in his office. He sent Molly to find Sue and tossed the folded sheet of foolscap across the desk as she came in. "You'd better read that."

She scanned through the teachers' comments, frowning. "I don't understand it! I'll have to go and see them. Find out what's been happening."

"I would have thought it was pretty bloody obvious what's been happening. You are just not being a proper mother, are you?"

Maybe she had failed in some respects but she was certainly not going to shoulder all the blame. "He never hears me use bad language!"

"Nor me!" Jonathan retorted. "Not unless you have provoked yet another row. As is your wont."

"I never provoke rows. You just develop a foul temper when you've been drinking!"

"Oh! So now you're saying I'm an alcoholic!"

"I am saying no such thing! I've read that alcoholics cannot help their addiction, but you are not addicted, just moody and bloody bad tempered . . ."

"There you are, swearing again!"

"It's darn difficult not to when trying to hold a reasonable discussion with a fool!" She stormed out and slammed the door, aware she was being very petty, but needing a release for her anger.

Miss Parkinson agreed to see Sue that afternoon. Afterwards Sue wasn't sure she had made any headway, but the elderly woman seemed very sympathetic, possibly because she knew of Jonathan's disability. Sue left in no mood to go straight home, so she drove out to the old German stone-crusher at L'Ancresse. The afternoon was hot and sunny, the sea in L'Ancresse Bay like glass, so she left the car and walked north to the Buttes, out onto the high rocks so popular with the amateur fishing fraternity.

There were no fishermen there that afternoon, she was entirely alone. Gazing down through the clear water at drifting seaweed and rocks whose colours were enriched as though lacquered by the sea, she longed to dive in, taste the salt, feel the relaxing weightlessness. Tempted, she glanced around, checking no one was in sight, then whipped off her blouse and skirt, kicked her sandals onto the rocks, eased herself down to a ledge near the water and plunged in.

It was incredibly warm. A slight swell gently rocked her as she lay drifting on her back watching the gulls riding effortlessly on soft currents of air so high above her they were mere specks, like tiny flies. Swimming across a gully, she clambered out onto a hot smooth rock and lay sunning herself, loathe to go home to the noise, problems and discord.

Sue had no idea how long she had been there when she heard a voice calling. "Hallo! Anyone there?" Sitting up in her bra and panties to peer over the rocky spur which hid her from view, she wondered whether or not to respond. There was a man standing with his back to her, peering across the water.

"Hallo! Anyone there?" He leapt down onto a lower level, out of sight.

Damn, she thought. He must have seen my clothes and thinks I've drowned. Better let him know I'm here before he calls the rescue services! "Cooee! I'm over here!" she shouted, at the same moment as hearing a loud splash.

A minute later the man appeared swimming towards her rock.

Sue tried to shout that she was perfectly okay, but he was doing a fast crawl, ears under water most of the way, and didn't hear her. She didn't want to stand up – the water had made her white undies quite transparent – so it wasn't until her would-be rescuer drew himself up at her feet that she recognised him, and gasped.

It was Stephen.

Sue couldn't stop laughing, almost hysterically. Stephen was chuckling too, sitting beside her in his sodden underpants.

"Was this meeting fate?" she asked, "or a most amazing coincidence?"

"I would like to claim the former. But in reality, having heard you repeat how much you used to love this place, I have taken to coming here, just to feel . . . spiritually closer to you."

Without thinking, she reached out to touch his hand . . . and then they were kissing, clasping each other. They could not release one another, until she felt his fingers unhook her bra. Then she panicked, pulled away and dived head first into the water, Stephen close behind. The effect of their dives was inevitable: having already lost her bra, the force of the water now dragged her panties down to her ankles, and removed Stephen's underpants.

Sue knew as he caught her and felt their naked bodies move against each other, that there was no turning back now. She rolled into his arms, both submerging as they kissed, surfacing with laughter, gasping for breath. "Supposing someone comes and recognises us?" she spluttered.

"They can't. We're cut off by the tide." He drew her around the rocks, away from the shore, to a submerged shelf on which they could stand, and took her into his arms again, their bodies pressed together.

Years had passed since Jonathan's accident had robbed him of any chance of a normal sexual relationship. Sue felt Stephen's hardness and felt faint with need of him. Far from resisting she could only help his advance, crying, laughing with excitement as she leaned her back against the smooth granite and their bodies melded together.

"What the devil do you think you're playing at?" Jonathan roared as she came in the back door. "Haven't you got a watch? Do you realise it is nearly seven-thirty?"

"Terribly sorry about that." Sue smiled apologetically. "Got cut off by the tide out at the Buttes. Terribly silly thing to do." At least it was the truth, even if only a half of it.

"What the hell were you doing out there? And what have you done to your hair?"

"In answer to your first question, I was indulging in an outing, as you would call it, and to your second, there seemed little point in just sitting there waiting for the tide to recede far enough for me to get back, so I had a swim."

"You just happened to have your bathing suit in the car when you went to see Miss Parkinson?" he sneered.

"No. I swam in my undies. Now," she grinned at the children who were sitting round the kitchen table listening in awe, "What stage are we at?"

"I've given them their supper."

"No you didn't, Daddy!" Roddy exclaimed. "I did! You just told me what to do." Then for some inexplicable reason he burst into tears and ran out of the room.

"See what you've done," Jonathan snapped, and wheeled himself off to the sitting room.

Four-year-old Stephanie was sobbing quietly.

Sue tried to put her arms round her but the child shrugged her off. "What is it, darling?"

"I don't like it when you make Daddy angry," she replied, and turned up the volume.

Debbie, sitting in her high chair, watched and listened, eyes widening by the minute. Gradually her bottom lip came out over the top one, quivering in preparation to join in the protest.

It wasn't until later that night when everyone was in bed, that Sue realised she hadn't felt the least bit guilty: not for what she and Stephen had done, not for being late, nor for the children's distress; if Jonathan hadn't made such a scene they would have been perfectly happy. Thinking about it, she was convinced God would understand. He knew how hard she had worked both at home and in the hotel, trying to cope with Jonathan's moods, trying to protect the children from his recurring outbursts of anger. He knew how many times she had walked away from a potential argument leaving Jonathan crowing in triumph, simply to avoid subjecting the children to more discord. Okay, so she had committed adultery, breaking one of His Commandments, but He alone knew how much she had tried to put Stephen out of her mind, and how painful it had been never seeing him. Till their accidental meeting this evening.

Before parting, they had promised to meet again. Well, God might not approve of that, but having now broken her marriage vows for the first time, did it really matter how many times she repeated it?

Stephen was at Jessica's cottage one evening that autumn when Sue dropped in to match some darning wool. "Auntie had run out of catfish so I've brought her some," he explained.

"It is so kind of him," Jessica smiled fondly. "You really are such a thoughtful person. Tell me, when are you going to get yourself a wife? It is time you were married. Don't you agree, Sue?"

"Definitely," Sue agreed, avoiding eye contact with him.

"Well what is stopping you? Can't you find a girl you could love?"

"I have," he responded involuntarily, then reddened.

"You have! Oh wonderful. When are you going to bring her round to see me? What is she like? Have you proposed?" Jonathan's mother was overjoyed with the news of her nephew's romance and the thought of another family wedding.

Sue and Stephen glanced at each other.

"I can't propose, unfortunately . . . ."

"Why ever not?" his aunt demanded, catching the brief exchange between them.

"Because she is already married."

Jessica looked from one to the other as they held their breaths, waiting, wondering if she had guessed. "Oh! Dear me. Oh, Stephen! How careless of you!" Then turning back to Sue she asked, "And you knew about it?"

Sue had never felt more confused. "Er . . . yes. Stephen has confided in me."

"Well I'm glad he has had someone to talk to. I know this sort of thing happens . . . so tragic. But, Stephen dear, one cannot go marching in breaking up a happy marriage just to gratify—"

"Okay, Auntie. I know. But I didn't come here for a lecture. Believe it or not, I do know right from wrong, but there are always more facets to these problems than might first appear." He put an arm round her shoulders. "Now will you stop worrying about me and pour that cup of coffee, or do I have to go home without it?"

"Want any help with the dishing up?" Sue asked her father's new housekeeper.

Mrs Birch was vast, filling the small kitchen with acres of quivering pinafore. "No, thank you, Mrs Martel, I can manage." Which was just as well: there wasn't enough room for anyone else in there.

Lunch was served in the dining room, Greg and Sue sitting together at the far end of the table near the window. He carved the pork and Sue added vegetables to the first plate before passing it through the hatch for Mrs Birch.

"How are you getting on, Dad?" she asked as they began their meal. "Is this one working out all right?" She tilted her head in the direction of the hatch.

He grinned. "A good deal better than the first one: she was a walking disaster." He lifted the glass jug. "Water? And what about yourself? You've looked much more relaxed, lately."

Sue watched as he filled her tumbler, then sipped, stalling her reply. "Fine, thanks," she said casually.

Greg stared at her. "That is not an answer. I want to hear how you are coping."

She longed to tell him the truth. She wanted him to know that she had been meeting Stephen secretly at least once a week for nearly three months . . . and that as long as she could continue to lie in his arms while he filled her, body and soul, with his love, she could cope with anything . . . But Dad was old fashioned. Could he ever condone what she was doing? Could he even begin to understand? She remembered her mother telling her years ago, how much she had dreaded the impending sex act, and how long her father had had to wait before it finally happened, months after their wedding. Sarah had been his adored, ideal woman: what would he think of his daughter craving sexual love with someone other than her husband, even knowing Jonathan was unable to do anything about her need.

"Well, I am much more relaxed than I used to be," she replied, truthfully. "When Jonathan is having one of his bad days, I find I can handle the situation far better. Maybe because the children are a bit older."

"Bad days? You mean when he is in a bad mood?"

"Ye-ss. But some days he complains of not feeling well." She shrugged. "Of course he always did. If I had backache, his was much worse. When I had morning sickness he would tell me that he frequently suffered nausea but *he* didn't make a fuss about it." She laughed, "But then I'm told that all men suffer far more than their women ever do."

"Told, no doubt, by some malicious female!"

"No doubt. Actually he can never manage to digest this sort of thing," she added, crunching into a delicious piece of pork crackling. "Mmm! Your Mrs Birch has done this to a T!"

"She certainly cooks like an angel. Her meals are divine. Only trouble is she samples so much she has difficulty bending, so the cleaning leaves much to be desired."

Mrs Birch came in to replace the first course with a delicious apple crumble and a bowl of custard.

While they tucked in, Sue said, "By the way, how is Richard? I hardly ever see him."

A slight frown crossed Greg's face. "He spent most of the summer holidays working at Schmit's Boatyard."

"And that worried you?"

He grimaced. "Not the fact of working there, that's fine. But I have a feeling he is getting very keen on the boat scene."

"Why shouldn't he?"

"Your mother and I always hoped he'd go on to university. He's quite brainy you know."

Sue laughed. "I'll never forget seeing that report of his when he got one hundred per cent marks for mathematics. My brother! Do you know, once, during the war, I got exactly eight marks out of a hundred for arithmetic!"

"You little devil! You've managed to keep that dark for years." He glanced at his watch. "George said he'd pop in to see me after lunch. Seems to have something on his mind."

They were drinking their coffee in the sitting room when Greg's old schoolfriend arrived, with his wife. Gelly, who had been at school with Sarah and Filly, had remained in the island during the war, and George's then wife, Margery, had gone to England. The five-year separation had left George bereft and he and Gelly had drifted together, married after his divorce and continued the close friendship with the Gaudions.

Sue stood up when they came in. "I'll press on home and leave you to your business," she said.

George was looking unusually serious. "No, don't go. I'd prefer you to stay."

Puzzled, Sue dropped back into her chair and waited.

George had never been one to beat about the bush. "It's about that lad of yours, Greg," he scratched his bald patch. "Has he said anything to you about his plans?"

"Plans? What plans?"

"At the beginning of the holidays he started talking about boats and engines, and reading my yachting magazines. He always enjoys the work, however filthy it might be, and I was only too pleased . . . that is until he started talking of it as a more permanent career." He looked at Gelly, who gave him an encouraging smile. "Well, I know how you want him to complete his education, so I felt it was only fair to try and discourage him."

Greg and Sue were trying to follow the story, but with difficulty.

"And did you succeed?"

George snorted. "I thought I had. But it seems I only succeeded in making him think I didn't want him working for me! Next thing I know, he's been offered a job with another yard."

"Where?" Greg prompted. "When for?"

"As soon as he can leave school."

"Have you said anything to him?"

"I haven't tackled him, yet. You see, I thought it best to speak to you first."

Greg was stunned. "Richard is at school right now."

"Tomorrow's Saturday so he'll be at the yard. Why don't you come round about nine-thirty and we can both talk to him? I mean, I don't want to interfere, but I feel partly responsible."

Greg shook his head. "Of course you're not. And I would be very grateful if you were there. He'll probably take more notice of you."

Late that evening Greg telephoned George, who was already in bed. "Sorry to call so late, but they do say troubles don't come singly. Afraid I won't be round in the morning, after all. I've just had a call from my Ma's nurse. The old lady has died."

Apparently, Alice had been sitting in her chair by the fire after supper, looking through an old family photograph album while the nurse was pottering in the kitchen. When the latter went back to start getting the old lady ready for bed she found her sitting very peacefully, head to one side, dead.

"Oh, I am sorry, old pal," George sympathised, "but she has had a good innings. What age was she?"

"Just two years short of her century. As you say, a good innings."

Greg was immediately involved with funeral arrangements, and sat back after his supper on Saturday evening with a great sigh of exhaustion, the newspapers on his knee, unread, the old dog, Toby, asleep at his feet.

"Dad?"

Greg opened his eyes to see his son peering at him round the door. "Yes?"

"I wondered if you could spare a minute; I need to talk to you."

"Yes of course. Come on." Greg sat himself upright, trying to get his mind into gear. "What's on your mind?"

The sixteen-year-old youth looked drawn and serious as he lowered himself awkwardly onto the edge of the armchair opposite his father's. He was almost as tall as Greg, his legs and arms long and coltish, out-growing his trousers and sleeves. Like his father his features were strong, but the amber eyes inherited from his mother were dark and troubled as he tried to find the right opening words.

Greg saw his plight. "If it helps, I do know what has been going on at the yard."

Richard's jaw dropped. "Uh! You do? I mean . . . what do you know?"

"Uncle George has been round. He tells me you seem keen to start a career in the boat business." Greg was glad the boy had come to him, rather than the other way round, but wished he might have chosen a better moment.

Richard grinned. "Yes, that's right. I'm not sure why, but I'm afraid Uncle George doesn't want me . . ."

Greg held up a hand. "Wait a minute, lad. Let me explain."

So Richard sat back, listening, the smile gradually leaving his face when his father insisted he should remain at school to take A-levels to get into university. "What on earth for, Dad?" he protested.

"So you can get a good job."

"I don't need a degree for the job I want. It would be a total waste of time. It would gain me nothing; whereas if you let me go straight into a yard I'd be a fully qualified marine technician at the age I would have graduated."

"Young people nowadays need to get away from the island and see the world." Greg started on another tack.

"I can do that on holiday."

"Not the same thing. One has to live abroad for a while."

"We chaps often talk about this at school. Several want to get away, but I always argue that I love the island and the sea; I have no desire whatever to 'get away'. Guernsey has everything right here: every imaginable sport and hobby, splendid libraries, it's own Orchestral, Choral and Dramatic societies. Artists and writers from all over the world choose to come and live here. You and Mum have had a super life here with your sport and bridge and trips to Herm and Sark in Uncle George's boat. Dad, what would I want to go away for? It's all encapsulated here within our shores!"

Greg rubbed a hand across his forehead. How could one possibly argue with such eloquence? "Very well, I'll think about it. But in the meantime, don't go signing up for a job with anyone else until I've discussed the matter with Uncle George . . . after Grandma's funeral."

Why, oh why did problems and dramas always come at the same time?

And that wasn't all.

The Martel family were at the kitchen table having breakfast on Tuesday morning when the phone rang.

"Dad!" Sue exclaimed on hearing Greg's voice. "What do you want at this hour?"

Jonathan listened, waiting.

"Oh Dad! No! What happened?"

Another pause.

"What a terrible shock for poor Aunt Maureen. Yes, I realise he had it coming, and better for him this way than just continuing to deteriorate."

Jonathan frowned, straining to hear above the children's chatter.

"They do say these things happen in threes. Let's hope this is the last of the series. Of course, you're right. It has been awful for Auntie, living with his problem these past few years. He has been no use to anyone, least of all himself. She has had to look after him like a baby."

Roddy and Stephanie began fighting, and by the time Jonathan sorted them out Sue returned. "It's Uncle Andrew," she whispered, bending over his chair so the children wouldn't hear.

"He got blind drunk again last night and apparently drove into a granite gatepost near La Rochelle corner."

Sybil came over to the island as quickly as she could to give her mother moral support. She arrived in time for Alice's funeral on Wednesday afternoon, but there was no 'wake' held afterwards . . . No one felt like it, not with Andrew's post-mortem pending.

General Sir Gordon Banks, Sybil's recently knighted husband, arrived at the weekend and proved a tower of strength, helping Maureen through the formalities and officialdom. When she thanked him he gave her a casual hug. "Must be honest, Mother. I'd do anything for an excuse to get over here; just love the place." He also loved calling her Mother, she being just four years his senior. "Do you know," he went on, "I just wish I could retire over here."

"Do you really, darling?" Sybil looked up from her magazine. "Seriously?"

"Unquestionably! I cannot think of a better location for one's declining years!" He noticed the two women glance at each other. "What? What?"

"Nothing really," Sybil acknowledged Maureen's nod, "Except that Mummy and I were speculating, earlier, on what is to happen to Les Marettes, the Gaudion family home, now that Grandma has gone."

Sir Gordon's eyes narrowed. "You scheming minx, you! I suppose you want me to find out who owns it, now, and buy it."

"That shouldn't be difficult," Maureen pointed out. "My mother-in-law left the house to Andrew and the vinery to Greg. Which means that I now own the house, so the advocate tells me."

The General turned from Maureen to raise a bristling eyebrow at his exquisitely beautiful wife, then gave a broad smile. "I can see we have some serious thinking to do!"

Jonathan did some serious thinking too, during the following year. Doubts and certainties had been battling in his brain since Deborah was born in '53, and his moody reactions had frequently been expressed in anger and resentment against Sue. Too often he felt embarrassingly guilty – more often than she knew – but he was loathe to let on; if she knew, it would make him feel even more of a worm than he did already.

He despised his useless body. All his life his masculine image had been of prime importance, particularly in the navy. The sports at which he had excelled at school, particularly athletics and boxing, were continued into service life, with concentrated training. He prided himself that he could out-run, out-box and out-swim anyone, plus out-drink them afterwards. Now he could only look down in anger on his useless legs. He hated his dependence on Sue: she had to assist or perform for him so many of his mundane and intimate daily chores as well as being mother and housewife . . . plus all the work she did in the hotel. It placed her in a superior, dominant role – which was probably why he was unable to stop himself criticising, nagging, trying to diminish her in front of the staff and hotel guests. He had not felt so badly about his outbursts as long as she had fought back with anger and resentment to match his own; but for the past year she had been insufferably sweet and submissive. No amount of sarcasm or shouting could cut through her calm, happy smile. Nothing riled her, however hard he tried. And the more he tried the more he hated himself. Worst of all, he had never managed to eradicate from his mind her telephone conversation with her father when the latter rang with the news of Andrew's death. Sue's sympathy for Andrew's widow and talk of the relief from degradation and anxiety Maureen would feel henceforth, caused him nightmarish comparisons with their own situation. Admittedly Andrew had been a chronic alcoholic, as well as exceptionally unpleasant with it; and unlike himself, the older man had had no excuse for the way he treated his wife: fate hadn't put him into a wheelchair in his mid-thirties. But at least Maureen had had a forlorn hope that one day the drinking might stop. Sue knew full well that her husband could never get out of his wheelchair and walk, never make love to her properly or take her for walks on the cliffs, romp on summer beaches with the children or dance with her at Christmas parties.

Never, ever again. Yet he was the one who complained, shouted, blamed her for all the problems. However hard he tried he was powerless to stop himself. The anger and resentment would grow in his gut like a cancerous balloon, expanding until it burst.

And in the past year, alongside the anger, another emotion had started growing: pity. Sympathy! Sadness for Sue herself! Suddenly he was seeing their situation through her eyes, almost as often as through his own.

Sir Gordon and Lady Banks bought Les Marettes from Maureen soon after Alice's estate was wound up. The general had opted for early retirement and while he remained in London to complete his final duties in Whitehall and organise the selling up of their place in Wiltshire, Sybil spent most of her time in Guernsey with architects and builders, modernising the old family house.

Sue was delighted that her favourite cousin would be coming back to live in the island, especially now that the difference in their ages had shrunk with maturity. Although Aunt Filly had always been a close friend and confidante, it was much easier to talk with beautiful, sophisticated and worldly-wise Sybil.

Even so it took time and courage for Sue to reveal her secret. Several times when she knew Sybil was in the island, she had driven round to Bordeaux with that intention, only to lose her nerve at the last minute – until the bright July day when she had arrived with the children to find Maureen waiting, eager to take the youngsters down onto the beach, leaving the two young women to enjoy a peaceful cup of tea.

Sybil had negotiated with Greg to move the packing sheds further away from the house, thus giving her a reasonable area of back garden. To the back of the house she had added a lovely modern kitchen and a large conservatory with new Lloyd Loom table and chairs with colourful cretonne cushions, and big double doors opening onto a paved patio. Which was where they had escaped from the builders' chaos to sit with their tea tray.

"How do you manage to look so bright and cheerful all the time?" Sybil asked, handing Sue her tea.

The question had come right out of the blue and without hesitation Sue told her, "By taking a lover." And proceeded with the story.

Lady Banks sat smiling, nodding so gently that the long blonde hair, which curled softly over her tanned shoulders, and the huge green earrings which matched her dress, hardly moved. And when Sue fell silent she reached out to take her hand and said, "Oh Sue, my dear, I'm so glad. So pleased for you. Not that it is a solution, but it does ease the torment, doesn't it?"

Sue had thought for a minute before replying. "I have never quite thought of it that way . . . but yes, I think you're right. Steve does make my life a lot happier, but I feel very guilty about him: I have the awful feeling I've ruined his life."

The alterations at Les Marettes were finished and the Banks' moved in late in October. It was no surprise that Sybil's architect, Stephen Martel, just happened to call when Sue was having lunch with them one day: the simultaneous visits had become more than coincidental. After coffee, Sue had to drive off to collect the children from their respective schools, take them home and give them their tea.

Jonathan was waiting for them, the meal laid on the kitchen table – fingers of Marmite toast, biscuits and a glass of milk each. And a fresh pot of tea for Sue and himself.

"Sweetheart, how lovely! What a super surprise!" She bent to kiss his cheek before removing Debbie's coat.

"It's nothing, really. I should do it far more often. One of the few tasks I can manage." Though his arms and shoulders were immensely strong, the muscles developed from wheeling himself all the time, the price was high: pain in his back steadily increasing particularly in the cold and damp of winter.

"Look, Stephanie! Your favourite!" Sue helped the child onto a chair.

The five-year-old took some toast and said "Thank you, Daddy."

Her father smiled, noting how like her mother she was growing, with her dark hair and wide grin. Only the eyes were different, amber like Sarah's had been.

Sue sipped her tea, wondering what was going on in Jonathan's mind. He had had more and more of these nice, helpful moods, lately: was it possible that he knew about Stephen? Might he be scared of losing her, trying to make it impossible for her to leave? Or even hoping to rebuild a loving relationship again?

Love. She had loved three men in her life – all passionately. First David, whom she had let down so badly. Then Jonathan whom she had adored, and continued to do so long after his accident and change of character. She supposed she loved him still – sometimes as friend and companion, at others as one might a difficult and belligerent child. But no longer as a lover.

And now she had Stephen.

Jonathan wheeled his chair round the table to wipe Deborah's face. He loved her red curls tied in bunches behind each ear – the same colour hair as his father's had been – and he loved the sparkling green eyes. Sue's eyes as they were when he had first known her . . . eyes which had dulled over the years, no doubt with pain and disappointment.

Dear God, what had he done? He turned away and reached for the teapot, asking himself the same questions that never left him, nowadays: what could he do about it? What was he capable of doing, that could ensure a normal and fulfilled family life for Sue and the children?

Of course he knew the answer. The only question was when?

Chapter Ten

Turn of the Tide

"Suzanne! Can you come?" The ringing telephone had interrupted the nine o'clock news and Aline's voice sounded strange.

"Now?" Sue glanced down at her old housecoat and slippers.

"It's your grandmother. She's passed out."

"Have you called the doctor?" Sue was reluctant to answer the summons unless it was really necessary.

"Yes. But I don't know what to do while waiting."

Sue grunted in exasperation: Aline could be so helpless when she chose. "Okay. I'll be there in ten minutes," she said, and ran into the bedroom to change.

"Poor you!" Jonathan smiled sympathetically when she explained. "Why couldn't she call John? He is her brother."

Sue grinned. They both knew the answer to that one.

Aline was waiting at the door as Sue came up the path. "The doctor's still here making phone calls. I'll have to remember to knock the charges off his bill when it comes. Anyway, you're too late. She's gone." Slowly and dramatically she shook her head.

"Where? To the hospital?"

Aline tilted her head sadly to one side and put an arm round her niece. "I know it is hard to assimilate, but you must try. Your grandmother has died."

"Oh no!" Why on earth couldn't the silly woman say so before? She moved on down the hallway into the sitting room. "Where is she? What happened?"

"Her body is in the kitchen. She went out there to make us some cocoa. She was a long time and I nodded off in my chair."

Sue ground her teeth. Typical of her aunt to let an old lady in her eighties wait on her. When the doctor finished with the telephone she called John, who left home immediately.

Aline was not pleased to see her brother, allowing him into the house with grim reluctance.

Sue was glad to leave her uncle to cope with the morticians and with Aline's crocodile tears: she couldn't erase the vision of her aunt reappearing after a visit upstairs, wearing Granma's pearls and a diamond brooch.

Nor, several days later, seeing her wear them at Marie's funeral.

Months later, when Christmas was all over, Sue told her cousin Sybil that it had been the best ever. All the family were congregated under one roof, except, of course, for Sarah, Andrew and the two grandmothers. "And Jonathan was wonderful," she added.

"It was sweet of him to get us all to stay the two nights in your hotel. And it was so thoughtful of him to take my mother under his wing, so to speak, and he started teaching her bridge." Sybil enthused. "Do you know, she has taken to it like a duck to water."

"So I gather. Dad says Aunt Maureen plays a decent hand, and coming from him, that is really something!"

"It was splendid that your Uncle William brought his family from England. Annemarie is a hoot."

"And what a surprise to see Aunt Ethel as well, with her lot. You may have remembered them from our wedding?"

"Were you not expecting them?"

"No! Jonathan arranged it all behind my back. As a Christmas treat."

"How extraordinarily kind!" Sybil exclaimed, wondering once again what had brought about Jonathan's metamorphosis.

"Yes," Sue acknowledged. "The only one missing was Aunt Aline."

"What happened to her?"

"She probably guessed John and Edna would be with us, so she made other arrangements! Spent the day with a family called Mitchell."

"The retired bank manager who's wife died last year?"

"That's the one. His sight is not too good so he gets Aline to drive him around, I believe."

"I think it is remarkable the way Jonathan is able to drive himself, now. Amazing how the manufacturers can produce a car entirely hand controlled."

Sue smiled. "Yes. Wonderful. He felt terrible when he couldn't get about under his own steam."

Jonathan was quite pleased with himself: he felt sure that

Sue had no inkling of his secret. He looked at the calendar on his office wall – February already.

"Sue, darling!"

She slid round behind the reception desk into the office. "You want me?"

"Saw you pass by and wondered if you could spare some time. There are a few things I'd like to discuss with you."

"I'll be right with you when I've put this pile of sheets in the linen cupboard."

He had a large box file open on the desk when she returned. "I've taken these cuttings from magazines," he said, passing her a clipful of printed papers. "Our kitchens desperately need updating. What do you think of those?"

Sue studied the adverts for magnificent stainless steel ovens and worktops, refrigerators and gadgetry. "Beautiful. But somewhat outside our price range at the moment, don't you think?"

"We could get them on hire purchase."

"And pray for enough profit this coming season to meet the instalments?" She grimaced at the thought.

"I don't want you . . . us to take on any extra worries, but if we can follow up some other ideas I've had, maybe we can upgrade the hotel this year."

Sue listened as he began to outline his suggestions, stunned that they were only suggestions, having become so used to his dogmatic decisions. What's more, he was making sense. He wanted to aim advertising at more local trade, offering snack meals in the bar, thereby keeping a permanent chef busy through the winter, rather than taking on a new one each summer. "And packed lunches for the visitors," he added.

"Could we have an arrangement with a car hire firm and get a small percentage per booking?"

"Brilliant idea." He wrote it down on his list.

Sue hardly dared breathe in case she woke to find she'd been dreaming. Jonathan had been much easier to live with for the past few months, but this . . . he had never sought her opinion or agreed with an idea of her's since his accident, and suddenly he seemed unable to fault her! She looked up and found he was watching her.

He smiled. "I've written this over a carbon so we can keep a copy each. Then we can add to it whenever a thought occurs and compare notes, later." Seeing her surprise as he handed her the top copy, a wave of guilt stained his face and neck red. God, what a swine he had been in the past . . .

Sue thanked him, mumbled something about lunch, and bolted. She wanted to find a corner where there was no chance he might find her, read her thoughts. Upstairs, she shut herself in one of the bedrooms, stood at the window watching the thin dusting of snow melting on the lawn, her mind dazed by a tangle of conflicting emotions. What was going on? Why, after making her life hell for eight years, was Jonathan being so . . . nice? What had brought about the change? Not that it was new. He had had phases of being his wonderful, charming old self all along; but they never lasted more than a day or two, or maybe just an hour! Now, apart from a few minor bouts of irritation he hadn't really lapsed since well before Christmas. He was almost his old self again: charming and lovable! Except that she no longer loved him.

It was her turn to experience a wave of guilt, remembering how their lovely Christmas had been shared with

Stephen. And his parents, and Jessica, of course. And Dad and Aunt Maureen, Gordon and Sybil. Twenty-seven of them all together. And apart from the children, she had been more conscious of Stephen's presence than all the rest put together.

Oh God! Am I very, very wicked?

"Your Aunt Aline is on the phone, Sue!"

"Can you finish cutting your sausages, Debbie?" Sue asked, wiping her fingers on the dishcloth.

"'A course I can," the little redhead frowned indignantly.

Sue hurried into the hall. "Hello, Auntie. How are you?"

"I'm fine, but I want to see you. I've something I need to ask you about. Can you come round for a coffee tomorrow morning?"

"Er . . . yes, I suppose so. What is it?"

"I'll tell you when I see you. Goodbye."

Sue puzzled over her aunt's call all evening and arrived at the house in town still mystified. She assumed it had something to do with Grandma: the old lady had only been gone four months.

Aline had the percolator on the stove and a tray laid with cups and biscuits. "Leave your coat in the hall," she said, "and come and sit down."

Sue did as she was told and waited.

"Bertrand has asked me to marry him."

Sue nearly dropped her coffee. "Marry?" She managed to stop herself commenting that, at fifty-seven, it might be a bit late to start thinking about wedded bliss. "Who is Bertrand?"

"You know, Bertrand Mitchell."

The banker! "Oh yes. I know of him but we've never met." Over the rim of her cup she studied her aunt's superbly cut navy-blue suit and matching blouse with white spots, the wide bow tied at her neck; the shapely nylon-sheathed legs and navy and white punched-leather shoes. Aline's grey hair was drawn back with soft waves into a French roll, new diamond stud earrings matching Grandma's diamond crescent brooch. She looked marvellous, could be absolutely charming . . . and was the world's worst troublemaker! "Did you accept his proposal?"

Aline gave a coy smile. "Well, I didn't say no, but nor did I say yes. I wanted to speak to you, first."

"Me! Why me?"

"Well you are a married woman, and I thought you would be able to advise me." A flush of deepening colour rose into her face. "Bertrand is a charming man, very wealthy and very fond of me. But he is seventy-six, you know, and I was wondering if he might be likely to want . . . well, you know, *that sort of thing*, after we were married. You see he was married before and accustomed to . . . that sort of thing, whereas never having been married myself, well I don't know that I would want to start."

The picture in Sue's mind made it very difficult to keep a straight face. "You mean you would only want to marry him for companionship?" And his unlimited wealth?

Aline stared at the carpet, nodding.

Sue, still only twenty-eight, also found difficulty in imagining a doddery old gentleman having the strength and energy to overcome Aline's virginity. Then it came

253

to mind that at least at her aunt's age they wouldn't need to worry about contraception! Arranging a serious expression on her face, she said, "Why not ask him?"

"Oh! I couldn't do that!" Aline turned puce.

"You wouldn't have to get technical. Just say that if you did marry you would need to have separate beds, or you would never get any sleep." Then it occurred to her she might have worded her advice a little better.

Aline and Bertrand were married two weeks later. Sue never did discover what the marital arrangements were, but it did not take her long to realise that Bertrand had known all along exactly why he wanted to marry. He required someone to do his shopping, cooking, washing and cleaning. Someone to nurse him in his declining years.

The car swayed, buffeted by the wind. Rain lashed the windows. Sue shivered and snuggled closer to Stephen. They were parked on Vazon Headland where the pounding of the breakers vibrated up from the rocks below.

"Want to go back home now?" Stephen asked, nuzzling her hair.

"No. But it is getting late, so I must." Sue tilted her face up for his kisses, desperately clinging to him. When she pulled away it was with a sigh of misery. "Parting is always the worst part, isn't it?"

"Almost as unbearable as not having the opportunity, never meeting. Oh, darling, must this go on forever? Will there ever be a chance for us?"

Sue fastened the buttons on her mac and retied the scarf round her head. "Don't," she muttered in the darkness, "I cannot bear it. The worst part is that Jonathan is being so good, now, that he makes me feel more and more guilty every day. It didn't seem so awful when he was giving me hell, but for the past few months I could hardly fault him."

"I'm glad, for your sake and the children's, but not for mine." He peered through the water on the windscreen at the faint lights across the bay.

"I keep telling you we should break this up to give you a chance to find someone else."

"I keep telling you I don't want to."

"But I will never be free. Ever."

He drove her back to her car which they had left a mile down the road, and they pecked briefly before going their separate ways.

Sue brooded on the cards Fate had dealt her as she followed the west coast road. Her thoughts drifted back to the war years: all the hymns and songs they had sung at school assembly about peace and freedom. Freedom! Was this freedom? Or would God continue to punish her for jilting David for the rest of her life? But there never had been any freedom, even before she met Jonathan; she had hated her mother's attempts to dominate her.

She smiled into the darkness. Poor Mummy. It was only now, with Roddy approaching the age she had been when she left the island in 1940, that she could truly understand in depth just how her mother must have suffered, having her then only child wrenched away from her. Thank God they had made up their differences before she died.

At Cobo the sea was cascading over the wall, flinging stones and seaweed across the road, so she had to divert inland to avoid being hit. Her 'alibi' was Sybil, and there would be no excuse for sea damage to the car between her cousin's house at Bordeaux and the hotel at Port Grat. She hated the lies more now than ever; hated answering Jonathan's questions about Sybil and Gordon, dreading he might have telephoned to speak to her and been told some story to cover her inability to take the call . . . a story she wouldn't know or be able to back up. The last thing she wanted was to hurt him; he would be devastated if he ever found out.

Yet was there any way she could ever break with Stephen?

"Let's go down to Jersey for a weekend with the children." Jonathan and Sue were sitting either side of the fireplace, reading the newspapers.

Another first! Sue smiled at him, "They would love it!"

"Wouldn't you?"

"Of course I would. Wonderful idea. What made you think of it?"

"This advert in the Guernsey Press. Look."

She leaned forward to take the paper from him, and studied it. "I can't believe they can do it for the price! It includes the boat trip and bed, breakfast and evening meal."

"Yes," he said thoughtfully. "Perhaps we could get in on that act. In reverse."

"And from the mainland. Package holidays. That's a rather exciting idea!" She grinned at him. "In fact they are both exciting ideas! But let's us do the Jersey one first and see how it works."

It worked better than they could have hoped. Easter week,

and the reopening of La Rocque Hotel at Port Grat, was still a fortnight away, but fortunately the weather was kind and none of the children were sick on the boat. The hotel bus met their arrival in St Helier and within three hours of leaving home they were installed in their bedrooms.

Roddy, Stephanie and Debbie were all wildly excited, chasing each other from room to room through the connecting doors and bouncing on all the beds.

Sue was anxious to stop them before Jonathan got angry, but he forestalled her.

"Come on, you lot. Let's get down on the sand while the sun is out."

The hotel overlooked St Brelade's Bay and as soon as Sue had helped Jonathan down the slipway onto the sand, he started a serious ball-catching session with Roddy while Sue set to work on a sandcastle for the girls.

"Why haven't we done more of this?" Jonathan said pensively, when all three children ran to the water's edge to paddle. "My fault, I know. I've been too wet to face competing with the fathers with functional legs."

Sue couldn't think of a response, so instead she put a hand on his shoulder and squeezed.

Jonathan covered her hand with his own, looked up and smiled ruefully. "My poor, dear Sue. What have I done to you?"

"Glad you could get away this morning." George stood in the wheelhouse, one hand on the helm, a mug of tea in the other.

"Bert is an excellent foreman and I know I can rely on him." Greg was unravelling the fishing gear out on deck; the friends intended bringing back a good haul by evening. "You know, I've made up my mind about that business with Richard."

"What have you decided?"

"That there's no point forcing him to stay at school. You can lead a horse to water . . ."

"True! So?"

"Do you reckon you could use him if he leaves at the end of the summer term?"

"Of course. In a way, I suppose you must be disappointed he's not going into the greenhouses with you?"

Greg finished tying on a fish hook. "On the contrary. It's darned hard work: eighty hours a week, sometimes. And one is always at the mercy of the markets, and the bugs and diseases."

"But you've done all right out of them."

"So far. And long may it last, but I doubt it will go on forever. One has to spend more and more each year on modernisation, just to be able to compete. The time is going to come when the costs will be so high that producers on the continent will overtake us."

"Great Scott! You amaze me! Yet I suppose you could be right. I mean, look at this dear old tub." He stroked a hand lovingly along the varnished woodwork. "She was built years before the war and she'll still be going strong twenty years from now, if she's well-maintained. But this isn't what people want, today. It's all speed and easy maintenance. They say that soon all the new hulls are going to be made of this new-fangled fibreglass. Terrible shame."

"Nothing stays the same, does it?"

George snorted. "You can say that again. The island is

being ruined with so many cars on the roads now. There must be over twenty thousand."

"Never mind," Greg laughed. "There's still plenty of fish in the sea." He headed for the stern and cast out his line.

"How is Aline nowadays?" John asked.

Sue had driven up to the Val du Douit Hotel to collect some eggs from the farm. "I never see her. I have phoned a couple of times, but Bertrand always answers and says she is out. And she never rings back."

"I saw her driving him along the Forest Road a few days ago and I waved," Edna said over the sponge mixture she was spooning into baking tins. "But of course I wouldn't expect her to acknowledge me."

"I had better try to see her sometime. Thanks very much for the eggs." Driving home Sue vowed to make an effort, soon.

The opportunity arose accidently.

She had to go to the doctor's surgery to collect a prescription for Debbie's cough, and went into the waiting room while it was made up. Aline was sitting there alone. "Hallo, Auntie! I've been trying to get hold of you for ages, but your husband always tells me you're out."

"Oh?" Aline looked up at her favourite niece. "He doesn't like me going off to visit my relatives, you know." She glanced up nervously at the door.

Why ever not? Sue wondered. "Anyway, how are you?"

"I'm all right. I've just brought Bertrand here for his check-up."

Sue knew her aunt was not all right. She had lost weight

and there were dark circles round her eyes. "Well, perhaps I could come round and see you, sometime?"

"Aline!" Bertrand was standing in the doorway. He summoned her with a jerk of his head.

Aline jumped up, muttered a goodbye and followed him out.

Debbie's medicine was ready and Sue followed, just in time to overhear Bertrand saying ". . . even talking to one of them, after the way they have behaved to you."

So! Aline had strung him a hard luck tale about her wicked relatives! And now she was reaping her reward!

"Are you sure you should be going out? You don't look at all well." In fact, Jonathan had been looking quite poorly, recently.

"Come and give me a hug," he said, holding out his arms. "You really are so sweet, Sue. I do love you."

She held his head against her breasts, not in a sexual way, but rather as she would with her children. Well, in a way he was one of her children, wasn't he? She kissed his hair. "Seriously, darling, I do think you should go to the doc for an overhaul. Tomorrow, promise me?"

"I promise I will think about it." He glanced at the clock. "It's nearly nine! If I don't go now it won't be worth going out at all."

"Why don't you give it a miss, tonight?"

He smiled up at her, shaking his head. "I need to do this, darling. It's good for my soul."

"What! Having a drink with the boys?" she laughed. "Okay. Off you go and drive carefully." She had never stopped worrying about him driving, being so disabled. She heard the chair wheels roll along the hall and pause at

Roddy's bedroom door. Moments later when she peeped out of the sitting room, he was leaving the girls' room. She smiled. He did love them so.

Sue had intended to stay awake in case Jonathan needed help when he came in. But it had been an exceptionally busy day. The hotel was full, every bedroom occupied – which was unusual so early in the season, their advertising drive had obviously paid off – so there were far more problems to sort out and queries to answer. Twice she had had to produce the First Aid kit after over-adventurous children's escapades. One lady had contrived to rip the heel off her shoe, which required the alternative repair kit; plus two diabetic menus had to be organised, and arrangements made for an elderly visitor to get to a dentist for his top set to be glued back together! All on top of her regular day's work. So although she propped herself up on pillows with a book, it fell out of her hands in minutes and she was fast asleep.

It was four in the morning when a stiff neck woke her. She was surprised to find the light still on. Managing to turn her head, wincing at the pain, she discovered another surprise. No Jonathan! Wide awake in seconds, she swung her feet out of bed and dashed out of the room to find him. Might he have fallen out of his chair, or had he remained in the sitting room to avoid waking her?

She looked into every room in the bungalow twice before accepting that he had not come home. It was now four-fifteen: there was no way he would still be out with friends at this hour. Oh, dear God! Not another accident?

The police assured her that no accident had been reported, so she rang the hospital. No. No Mr Martel had been admitted since the old man from the Castel, last week. She would have to try Norton, whatever the time.

"Er . . . I don't follow you, Sue," he said sleepily. "We didn't go out together last night."

"Might he have been with any of the others?"

"I doubt it. Most of them were rehearsing for the Eisteddfod last evening. What time did he go out?" He was now thoroughly awake and sounded concerned.

"Quite late: about nine."

"Do you want me to come round?" he offered.

"I can't think what you can do here, at the moment. If he is found, I mean . . . if I have to go out, I might need someone to stay with the children."

"Of course. Just give a call, any time."

Sue was totally confused. It seemed the next priority was to get dressed in case people came. What people? She dragged on a pair of slacks and a jumper. Stephen. She desperately wanted to speak to him. He would know what to do. But supposing his mother answered? So what?

Julia sounded as sleepy as Norton had done. "Sue? Do you know the time?"

Sue explained as coherently as she could.

"Oh my dear! We'll be around to you in five minutes."

It was actually ten minutes, by which time Sue had suddenly thought of the hotel. Perhaps Jonathan had spent the night there! She ran along the cement path through thick drizzle, unlocked the side door and began switching on lights. Tip-toeing past the reception desk she looked down at her feet and realised they were bare.

Her hunt was fruitless: Jonathan was nowhere on the

ground floor, nor was his wheelchair, and he couldn't get up to the first floor.

She was just home, pushing damp feet into her slippers when she heard a car on the gravel. She flew out of the front door but it was only the Martels. All three of them.

They stood around the kitchen while Julia boiled the kettle, going over all the possibilities.

"I think I'll try the police again," Ted decided. "You never know. What's the number of his car?"

At six o'clock Julia asked if Sue would mind if Ted and Stephen went home.

Stephen shook his head. "No. You and Dad go. I'll stay here."

"But you have to get to work tomorrow . . . I mean today."

"Mother, I am not leaving Sue. Nor will I go to work until Jonathan turns up. Right?"

Julia peered at him under lowered lids, wondering. "Very well. It's up to you."

When Ted and Julia had left, Stephen and Sue remained sitting either side of the kitchen table.

"Why don't you go back to bed?" he asked eventually. "I'll man the phone."

"I couldn't possibly sleep."

"No, but at least you will be resting."

"Why is Uncle Stephen here, Mummy?" Roddy asked with his mouth full of Puffed Wheat.

Sue was too befuddled to think of an answer, but Stephen stepped into the breach. "I came round early to bring some things."

"What things?" Debbie asked.

"Er . . . garden tools."

"Where are they?"

"I left them in the garage."

Sue sent him a half smile for his ingenuity.

"Come on, hurry up and I'll drop you off at school on my way home," he added, mouthing to Sue over their heads that he would come straight back.

Sue phoned the hotel with a brief explanation for her absence. "Call me if you have any problems," she added, "I will probably be at home most of the day."

Stephen was walking in through the door when the police telephoned to say they had found Jonathan's car in the Pembroke Bay car park.

"Couldn't you see the wheelchair anywhere?" Sue asked.

"No, Ma'am. But we will keep looking."

Sue was frowning as she put back the receiver, an unpleasant thought building in her mind. "Steve, where's the tide?"

"No idea, but it will be in yesterday's Press. Where is it?"

"Still in the sitting room where Jonathan left it last night."

Stephen fetched it, noting that by coincidence it was folded open at the tide table. "Let's see. Judging by yesterday's times it should be low water in a couple of hours. At around eleven. Why?" He looked up at Sue and saw the anguish in her face. "Oh Lord! No! You don't think . . ."

She shrugged. "I don't know what to think. Except that I think I'm beyond thinking." She picked up the kettle. "I feel like having a really strong coffee."

"Had I better go down and tell Aunt Jessica?"

Sue nodded. "I've been putting off telling her, not wanting to worry her unnecessarily. But now it is time she knew. Bring her back here if she'll come."

The three of them were sitting round the kitchen table finishing another round of coffees, when the police arrived looking solemn. "Mrs Martel?" a plain clothes man asked. "I'm afraid the news is not good. At ten forty-five this morning a wheelchair was found embedded in the sand near the bottom of the tide."

Sue dropped her face into her hands.

Jessica took a long, deep breath, nodding gently.

Stephen stood between the two women looking and feeling helpless. He laid a hand on Sue's shoulder; then removed it. He took his aunt's hand and drew her up into his arms.

She breathed deeply again, and laid her head on his chest.

Three weeks later Jonathan's body was taken from the water by fishermen setting their crab pots off the Platte Fougere lighthouse.

The coroner decided that Jonathan must have been trundling across the beach taking the evening air when the wheels of his chair stuck in the sand, and no one was near enough to hear his cries for help before he was submerged by the tide. Death was obviously from accidental drowning.

Those three weeks had been sheer mental torture. Twenty-one days of asking, "Why?" Everyone was terribly kind but Sue honestly did not want their sympathy. All the family took turns in coming to the bungalow to sit with her and she couldn't wait to get rid of them. Especially Stephen: her guilt was heavy enough without the added reminder every time she saw him. Luckily he soon got the message, understood, and stayed away. It was easier being alone with the children, once she had found a way to explain their father's absence.

The funeral in St Sampson's Church was short and sad. The family and a few close friends accepted Sue's invitation to come back to the bungalow afterwards, and though Roddy remained indoors in solemn silence, the girls ran outside to play, their squeals of laughter carried in on the breeze through the open windows.

The word suicide was never spoken, but it hung in the room like a dark cloud, blotting out the sunshine.

It was during a long silence when no one could think of anything to say, that Jonathan's doctor stood up and cleared his throat. "Sue, would you mind very much if I said a few words about Jonathan?"

"Oh no, please do." Anything to break the embarrassing silence.

"In the past eight or nine months I came to know Jonathan as an extremely brave, thoughtful and caring man. I must admit it was not an opinion I had always held, though, Heaven knows, he had good reason to feel a degree of resentment, being so crippled." Julian Collard's hands were clasped behind his back as he rocked to and fro on heels and toes. "Unfortunately, the visible problems Jonathan had were not the only ones: I had been treating him for kidney and pancreatic malfunctioning for nearly a year."

"But . . ." Sue moved towards him.

"No, I never told you, Sue. He insisted he didn't

want you or anyone else to know. I was bound to secrecy."

"Did he know it was serious?" she asked.

"Not at first. Nor did I, for that matter. No one could have known the extent of the problem without operating. But gradually he became worse and the medication had to be stepped up. By last autumn it was obvious that his condition was terminal."

The mourners, sitting or standing around the room in funereal black dresses and ties, began little pockets of whispered discussion and speculation.

Dr Collard held up his hand. "Jonathan had already realised the fact and demanded the truth. When it was explained to him that the condition might well be eased, though not corrected, with surgery, he refused. He was well aware that this could only mean prolonging his pain and discomfort which, I assure you, was already considerable. All he wanted to know was how long he had left." He paused to finish his drink. "A normal man might have lasted three or four months. It was a credit to his guts and determination to put his affairs in order and leave his family well provided for, that he lived so much longer. His last weeks were agony." He turned slowly, staring each person in the eye. "I am sure you will all agree with me, that tragic as his accident was, three weeks ago, it came as a merciful release. It allowed him to escape the final torturous end."

He sat down.

No one said a word. Even the children playing outside fell silent.

The only sound was of mewling gulls, far out to sea beyond Port Grat.

*   *   *

Everyone was keen to help. Family, friends, hotel staff and guests offered assistance of every kind. Even Major Potter and his wife, who returned year after year despite their endless complaints, felt obliged to lend a hand when they returned to their bedroom one morning after a shopping expedition, to find General Sir Gordon Banks lying under their bed in shirt sleeves replacing a wobbly bed leg.

"I am beginning to feel quite superfluous," Sue told Sybil.

"Great. That is the object of the exercise. Now we can take the children shrimping without having to suffer your nervous twitches every two minutes. Come on, I've filled a big tin with sandwiches."

The intention was to tire the children but they were still tearing in and out of the water squealing and splashing each other when Sue and Sybil collapsed on their beach towels on the sand. "I'd forgotten how exhausting three hours of fish-hooks and shrimping nets could be!" the young widow gasped.

"Are you sleeping any better, now?" Sybil asked through the cloud of yellow hair drifting across her face.

"Yes. I'm beginning to feel more relaxed."

"What about Stephen?"

"*What* about Stephen?" Sue frowned.

Sybil sat up, brushing her hair aside. "You were still having those crazy spasms of guilt when we last spoke."

"Yes. Difficult not to. And no, we haven't seen anything of each other since the day of the funeral."

"Why?"

"It just hasn't happened."

Sybil fully understood. Which didn't lessen her determination to see that it did happen. Soon.

She gave the matter serious thought as she drove Sue and children home, and as they climbed out of the car and collected their rods, nets and piles of sandy wet towels and bathing suits from the boot, she invited her cousin to dinner, sometime. "Whenever it suits you. Let me know and I'll organise it."

Visualising sitting round a dinner table in embarrassed silence, everyone trying not to say the wrong thing, Sue wanted to decline the offer. "I don't think it would be practical before the end of the season," she hedged.

"That's only a month away. Why don't we settle for the first week of October?"

Sue hitched the bag of beach toys onto her shoulder. "Okay. I mean, yes. Thanks. Lovely." Sybil was trying to be helpful and it was difficult to refuse outright. Anyway, surely October was far enough away?

Jessica was only sixty-five but her heart was not strong and Jonathan's death had been a severe shock. Sue was very fond of her and very concerned, visiting her daily or inviting her up to the bungalow or the hotel for meals. One blustery September day they sat in the corner of the hotel dining room, at one of only three occupied tables. Of the remaining guests, most ate out at midday.

"You're not socialising much yet, are you?" Jessica remarked.

"Nor are you!"

"One doesn't expect to at my age. But you have got to start living again. What is holding you back? Some delusion of guilt?" Jonathan's mother had always had the

269

knack of hitting the nail on the head . . . and the nerve to speak her mind.

Sue threw her a half grin. "Yes."

"Why? Because of Stephen?"

"Uh?" Sue gave an audible gasp and peered, frowning into Jessica's face.

"I haven't mentioned it before: obviously it's a pretty sensitive topic. But surely you don't imagine I didn't know?"

"Know? Know what?" What could she know?

"That you and Stephen are in love with each other. Look here," her thin hand, big sapphire and diamond engagement ring swivelling loose round her bony finger, was stretched across the table to take Sue's forearm in a fierce grip, "I am not some mealy-mouthed, narrow-minded idiot. I know damn well what your life has been in the past few years, both mentally and physically. I was only too glad to see you had Stephen's love and support. No . . ." she shook her head as Sue opened her mouth to speak, "I have no idea whether or not that love was consummated; that is immaterial. If you didn't feel the need, fair enough, if you did I couldn't blame you." She released her grip on Sue's arm, sat back and smiled. "I love you, Sue, like the daughter I never had. You have been a wonderful daughter-in-law in the worst imaginable circumstances. But I also love my grandchildren, and seeing you moping around the place with a long face is not helping them get over their own loss. They need a normal home life, full of love, joy and laughter. And one day, in the not too distant future, I hope, they will need to have two parents again."

Sue turned to gaze out across the garden, not seeing the

frothy little cotton wool clouds playing chase against their deep blue backdrop and casting momentary shadows over the sea and rocks. When she turned back to face Jessica she was smiling. "You are right, of course. But one of my worst fears is that Jonathan . . . did this . . . because he knew about Stephen, too."

"Oh, he knew that Stephen had always been very fond of you, and he knew you liked the boy, too. What he didn't know about was the love you shared."

"But you knew, so why shouldn't he?"

"He was far too young. One needs a lot of extra years, years of experience of reading people, interpreting the nuances of their body movements and their conversation." Jessica shook her softly permed grey head, setting the gold pendant earrings swinging. "No. I think that once he learned his illness was terminal he began to face up to all the faults he would be carrying when he came to face his Maker."

Sue looked puzzled. She had had ample evidence of Jonathan's kindness in the months leading up to his death, but the idea of him having had some sort of religious awakening seemed a bit far-fetched.

Jessica read her thoughts. "No, I'm not suggesting he had some holy blinding flash! But when you know you are dying anyway, your priorities can change. His concern was transferred from himself to his family, and to their future."

Sue pondered on Jessica's words, in silence.

"You have already had problems with young Roddy because of his disturbed background," Jessica continued. "And knowing how well you and Stephen seemed to like each other, Jonathan may well have hoped that together you could create a new stabilty for the children."

Sue nodded to the waitress standing at her shoulder, coffee pot poised. When the girl had gone she said, "You have certainly given me some food for thought. Now you will have to give me time."

Two days later, a call from Edna gave Sue something else to think about.

"Have you heard how Aline is?"

"No. Why, is she ill?" Sue was standing at the reception desk, checking out the last of the season's guests.

"So we understand from the grapevine. We hoped you might have more positive news from her or Bertrand."

"I haven't heard a thing. I'll call you back if I learn anything."

Realising that to telephone would be useless, Sue drove into town as soon as she was able, up to Aline and Bertrand's house.

A nurse in starched apron opened the door. "I'm afraid Mr Mitchell is out at present. If you would care to call again later?"

"It's my aunt, Mrs Mitchell, I am hoping to see," Sue smiled sweetly.

"Oh! Well I have instructions to admit only the doctor, I'm afraid . . ."

"That would be because Mr Mitchell wasn't aware I was coming."

The nurse stood aside. "Well, I suppose it will be all right."

Aline was lying upstairs in bed, almost unrecognisable, her yellow skin pulled taut over sunken features, thin hair cut short, colourless lips stretched over teeth browned with drugs. Her alarmed surprise at the sight of Sue was obvious. "Did Bertrand say you could come?" she croaked.

"Your nurse let me in," Sue replied, bending to take her hand, aware of the starched presence behind her.

Aline's breathing was a series of short rasps. "Nurse is very good to me. She understands." She closed her eyes, resting from the effort to talk. Then she gave the woman the semblance of a smile. "You know where those things are."

The nurse nodded.

"Get them, please."

Aline was lying on a divan bed. The nurse quickly knelt, lifted the counterpane and opened a drawer. "Here. Is this all?" She handed the patient two towel-wrapped parcels.

Aline was too weak to hold them, indicating with her eyes that they should be passed to Sue. "Don't open them now. You had better go before he returns."

Recognising Aline's anxiety, Sue didn't argue. "Okay, Auntie. I'll be away. But I will come back." She bent to kiss the dry forehead, then hurried down the stairs ahead of the nurse.

"What is it?" Sue hissed.

"Cancer. Of the pancreas."

"But what is all this about her husband?"

The nurse opened the door and peered out. "You had better go, quickly."

Clutching her weird parcels, Sue ran along the pavement to her car to drive directly to St Saviour's, to John and Edna at Val du Douit.

All three stood round the table while the parcels

were unwrapped, disclosing a small collection of Marie Ozanne's silver; two Queen Anne candlesticks, a covered entrée dish and miscellaneous cutlery – salad and fish servers, gravy spoons and ladles. And a small box. In it were Marie's pearls, her diamond crescent brooch, and Aline's own diamond stud earrings. Stuck in the lid of the box was an envelope.

"You had better open that," Sue said, breaking the silence and handing it to John.

"Why me? She handed it all to you."

"Only as courier."

There were actually two envelopes, one inside the other, the larger one containing a green-ribboned legal document. "It's her Will!" John exclaimed unfolding it. "She leaves the obligatory third of her estate to Bertrand, and the remainder to 'my beloved niece, Suzanne Martel'."

Sue stared at him open-mouthed.

"And what is in there?" Edna indicated the smaller envelope.

Sue slit it open with her little finger and withdrew a single sheet of spiral notepad, torn roughly from the wire. She recognised the thin scrawl immediately: a pathetic reminder of the once boldly written letters she received from Aline throughout the war.

'My dear Sue, I hope this reaches you. I want you to have these things of Grandma's and mine.
   They come with my love.
   Auntie Aline.'

"I need a drink," John announced.

"Make it two."

"Three!"

They sipped Edna's cooking sherry out of kitchen tumblers.

"You do realise I have no intention of keeping all this. It belongs to the family. You in particular, Uncle John, as head of the family." Sue was quite adamant.

"No!" John sounded equally adamant. "Aline and I never got on; she would hate the thought that you, the only person in her life she ever loved, were handing it over to me, of all people."

"I would happily keep her earrings, but Aunt Edna is your wife. She should have Grandma's jewellery. And these other things," she picked up a ladle to examine it, "These should be divided amongst all members of the family: Uncle William's lot in England, and Aunt Ethel's in New Zealand."

John started to argue, but Edna held up a hand. "Half a mo! Aren't we jumping the gun a bit? Aline may be ill but she is still alive, as far as we know."

John and Sue grinned sheepishly.

"And what's more, won't Bertrand challenge that Will? How do we know there isn't a subsequent one? And," she waved her hand over the things on the table, "he will want to know where all this has gone. We can't have him accusing that poor nurse!"

John looked at Sue. "She is right, you know. Tell you what, why don't I take all this to Advocate Mahy and let him sort it out. He was Dad's lawyer before the war."

Aline died three days later.

Much to Bertrand's fury, Advocate Mahy insisted that all the family should be allowed to attend her funeral and, apart from Bertrand, they all went on to Val du Douit after the ceremony, including William and Ethel who had flown over especially. The elderly widower was also furious about Aline's Will, but it was her last, so everything was to be shared out as Sue requested.

They were standing in their old family home, little changed since they had played there as happy, carefree children, when John asked for silence. "I want to propose a toast, folks." He raised his glass. "Here's to happy, united families, free from suspicion, bitterness and jealousy. And here's to Sue, whose generous nature has helped us to attain that freedom."

Jessica had volunteered to sit in while Sue went off to Sybil's dinner party. She was sitting by the fire reading aloud, the three children squatting on the hearth rug in their pyjamas, when car tyres scrunched on the gravel, a door slammed and the bell rang.

"I'm ready. I'll get it," Sue called from her bedroom. Sybil had promised to organise a lift so she wouldn't have to drive herself in evening shoes. But as she hurried down the hall the door swung open . . . and Stephen stepped inside.

"Oh! Are you my lift?" Her face turned scarlet; it was the first time she had seen him for months.

"Do you mind?"

Did she? She hadn't a clue but shook her head, anyway. "No. Of course not," she smiled weakly, mentally cursing Sybil. No doubt she had been planning this all along, but she could have warned her. "I must say goodnight to the children before leaving." She headed for the sitting room.

Stephen followed, appreciating her slim figure encased in a slinky green grosgrain suit, her dark hair swinging in soft waves onto her shoulders.

"Uncle Stephen!" Story forgotten, the children leapt up at him, hugging him and peppering him with questions.

Jessica remained in her chair, smiling, hoping, fingers lying crossed in her lap.

The drive to Bordeaux was brief and the conversation general: enquiries about health, parents and business, conveniently occupying the time.

Sir Gordon opened the door. "Hallo, you two. Good to see you. Let me take your coats. Oh! Thanks very much," he added as Stephen handed him a bottle of claret. They separated immediately, mingling with other guests.

"Rat!" Sue hissed at her hostess at the first opportunity. "And you can take that innocent look off your face. It won't wash!"

Sybil smothered a giggle. "Well, someone had to do it."

The Banks were enthusiastic collectors of antiques, and Sue looked round the dining room with interest at the latest additions. She was seated between Stephen and an old army crony of Gordon's called Quinton.

"You are, admittedly, only the second female in your family whom I have met, so far, but tell me, are you all so devastatingly beautiful?"

Quite a forceful opening gambit, Sue thought, trying to keep her face straight. "Only the legitimate ones," she responded solemnly, "the others are painfully ugly."

Quinton threw back his head and bellowed.

The meal was perfect and the evening continued as brightly as it began.

Sue tried to keep her mind off Stephen, the feel of his arm brushing hers, the deep resonance of his voice. Their conversation was limited to general politenesses, chiefly because Quinton was appropriating most of her attention.

It was not until Stephen was driving her home that he felt able to talk privately. "How have you felt about this evening?" he began.

"You mean getting out into the social whirl?"

"With me."

It was several moments before she spoke. "Difficult to say." In the darkness she blushed with the embarrassment of her non-committal reply.

"Don't you feel there is anything between us any longer?"

"I honestly don't know. My thinking has been so confused since Jonathan died. He was . . . so good and kind, towards the end, and I . . ."

". . . felt so guilty?" he prompted.

"Yes."

"Me too. Until after the funeral when Collard told us about Jonty's illness. He always knew I was keen on you, but he couldn't have minded, otherwise he would never have suggested I should take you out that famous evening."

"He never realised how seriously you felt."

"Or how seriously you felt, too?" He swung the car off the road onto the grass verge overlooking the sea. "Could you ever feel that seriously again?"

After a pause she said, "I would like to. We had something so precious, so wonderful, once."

"We could again." He took her hand. "Want to try?"

"Only if we could start again from the beginning. Not from where we left off. I wasn't free then; I was cheating my crippled husband, committing adultery."

"But . . ."

"Believe me, I know all the buts, better than anyone. So can you understand why I want a fresh start?"

"Yes, my dearest Sue. Of course I can. And I promise I won't rush you. You can have all the time in the world."

She felt the gentle caress of his fingers through her glove. "Dearest Stephen. I don't think I'll need that long."

She leaned across the handbrake to kiss his cheek.

Suddenly she knew she was free.